Mário d

The Great Shadow
(and other stories)

Translated from the Portuguese by
Margaret Jull Costa

Dedalus

Dedalus would like to thank the Calouste Gulbenkian Foundation in London and the Camões Institute in Lisbon for their assistance in producing this book.

Published in the UK by Dedalus Ltd, Langford Lodge, St Judith's Lane, Sawtry, Cambs, PE17 5XE

ISBN 1873982 72 0

Distributed in the USA by Subterranean Company, P.O. Box 160, 265 5th Street, Monroe, Oregon 97456

Distributed in Australia & New Zealand by Peribo Pty Ltd, 58 Beaumont Road, Mount Kuring-gai N.S.W. 2080

Distributed in Canada by Marginal Distribution, Unit 102, 277 George Street North, Peterborough, Ontario, KJ9 3G9

First published in Portugal in 1915 as Céu em fogo
First published by Dedalus in 1996

Translation & Introduction copyright © 1996 Margaret Jull Costa

Printed in Finland by Wsoy

This book is sold etc

A C.I.P. listing for this book is available on request.

The translator would like to thank Ben Sherriff for all his help and advice.

DEDALUS EUROPE 1992–1997

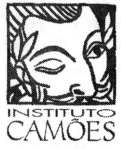

INSTITUTO
CAMÕES

Dedalus, as part of its Europe 1992–97 programme, with the assistance of the Calouste Gulbenkian Foundation in London and the Camões Institute in Lisbon, has embarked on a series of new translations by Margaret Jull Costa of some of the major classics of Portuguese literature.

Titles so far selected are:

Dedalus European Classics

The Mandarin (and other stories) – Eça de Queiroz
The Relic – Eça de Queiroz

Decadence from Dedalus

Lúcio's Confession – Mário de Sá-Carneiro
The Great Shadow – Mário de Sá-Carneiro

Literary Fantasy Anthologies

The Dedalus Book of Portuguese Fantasy – editors Eugénio Lisboa and Helder Macedo

Further titles will be announced shortly.

THE TRANSLATOR

Margaret Jull Costa has translated novels and short stories by Portuguese, Spanish and Latin American writers, amongst them: *Obabakoak* and *The Lone Man* by Bernardo Atxaga; *All Souls*, *A Heart So White* and *Tomorrow in the Battle Think on Me* by Javier Marías; *The Mandarin* by Eça de Queiroz; *Lúcio's Confession* by Mário de Sá-Carneiro; *The Flanders Panel* by Arturo Pérez-Reverte; *The Dedalus Book of Portuguese Fantasy;* and *Variable Cloud* by Carmen Martín Gaite.

She was joint-winner of the Portuguese Translation Prize in 1992 for her translation of *The Book of Disquiet* by Fernando Pessoa and was shortlisted for the 1996 Prize for her translation of *The Relic* by Eça de Queiroz.

Contents

'What if it is a disease?' he decided at last. 'What does it matter that it is an abnormal tension if the result, if the moment of sensation, remembered and analysed in a state of health, turns out to be harmony and beauty brought to their highest point of perfection . . .?'

The Idiot, Fyodor Dostoevsky
(translated by David Magarshack)

Foreword

Mário de Sá-Carneiro was born in Lisbon in 1890 and died in Paris in 1916. He seems to have been travelling swiftly towards death from the moment his mother died when he was two and a half. Subsequently, he was by turns pampered and neglected by a steadfast if over-anxious nanny and a wealthy, globetrotting father. Childhood was a prison for him. Photos taken when he was eight years old show a fat-cheeked, un-utterably world-weary little boy. In an early short story he wrote: 'I genuinely feel as if they had smeared my body with a layer of very thick plaster that inhibits all movement and atro-phies my muscles.' Of another character, a young girl, he wrote: 'The child is given over to the care of strangers, she lives in the kitchen with the servants. She becomes aloof, demoralised before her time, devoid of delicate feelings.'

When Sá-Carneiro was still at school, his best friend (who had also lost his mother at an early age) shot himself in the head. He did this in front of teachers and fellow students. Sá-Carneiro, whilst obviously deeply shocked by his friend's death, was also impressed by the theatricality of his suicide. In a poem he wrote at the time, he praised his friend's courage and rebuked himself for his own cowardice, his 'existing without living'.

The short stories he wrote between eighteen and twenty-one have two themes only – suicide and madness. Marriage is merely an act of folly, sex a peculiarly repellent pastime, and procreation a crime, since, through it, parents condemn their children to life. His friend and literary executor, the poet Fernando Pessoa, excluded these early stories from Sá-Carneiro's complete works as being unworthy and unrepresentative.

Like many other Portuguese artists and writers, Sá-Carneiro considered Paris to be the centre of the cultural world, a place where life could be lived intensely and freely. In

Resurrection he likens Paris to 'a great salon brilliantly lit' and Lisbon to 'a narrow yellow house'. However, when, in 1912, he realised his dream of going to live in Paris, he was only slightly less bored than he was in Lisbon. He described himself sitting in cafés waiting for life, 'which never turns up'. And yet, despite this inertia, this *ennui*, his letters to Fernando Pessoa are full of news about stories and poems he has written or is about to write; they are full of life, plans for the future, a future he cannot really believe he will inhabit.

Sá-Carneiro collapsed into hysteria and incoherence when he saw enforced adulthood looming on the horizon. His father had become involved with a prostitute and ended up marrying her. Having squandered most of his fortune on travel and the good life for the last twenty-four years, his father was obliged to take a job in Mozambique (then still a Portuguese colony) from where it was very difficult to send money to Paris. His second wife apparently wielded considerable influence over him and was clearly impatient with her plump, spoiled stepson's inability to fend for himself. Thus Mário was faced not only with the ignominy of having an ex-prostitute for a stepmother, but also with the prospect of losing his allowance and having to return to provincial Lisbon. Or perhaps he just needed a satisfactory excuse finally to 'disappear' and lack of money was as good a reason as any. Despite the endless rehearsals for death in his short stories, his own suicide was not the golden moment he so often describes; it was a piece of bungled theatre. He took a large quantity of strychnine and died alone and in excruciating pain, the unwitting friend he had invited to keep him company in death having rushed off in search of a doctor.

The stories in this collection were all written during Sá-Carneiro's time in Paris. (The title Sá-Carneiro gave to the collection was *Céu em fogo* [*The Sky Ablaze*] probably a reference to Baudelaire's phrase 'cieux embrasés' in *Le voyage*.) The stories buzz with the same kind of energy – negative and positive – evident in his letters. His protagonists' lives may be brief but they are intense. They share his distaste for the banal and the ordinary, his longing for some supreme experience that will fill the void inside. Achieving one's goal, reaching perfection or finding the ideal lover all culminate in death: the leap into the dark, the golden-winged secret, the great shadow. When reality becomes too pressingly real, there are always the escape routes of madness and suicide. His characters, however, always have fairly grand reasons for their retreats into insanity and self-murder – they have written the perfect poem, they are being pursued by a dark alter ego, they have found a way of travelling through time.

Suicide, madness and death are the key themes in these stories. The world is a tawdry place to be transcended through art and the imagination. He celebrates the glories of great cities like Paris and Venice, but as seen through a beautiful, hallucinatory haze. Venice is the 'sacred city of fantasy, brocaded with waking dreams, with magical penumbras – twilight rainbow, early-morning anemone . . . ' Reality is simply not enough. His characters are constantly struggling to get beyond life – 'beyond' being a word that occurs again and again throughout the book – by building a world of dreams, by fixing certain places and moments in their imaginations, by killing themselves or another, even the person they most love, by stepping back in time, by retreating into madness, or, as in *Mystery*, by becoming so perfectly fused with their lover that they simply die. His characters despise what most people would see as decent, ordinary folk living healthy lives, people 'who never fly into a rage, who never dare to offend anyone, . . . who always speak softly and listen intently to what others say . . . [who] are just, honest, sincere, coherent in all their actions.' They are the true 'scoundrels' not criminals, murderers, drug addicts, who at least have the courage to transgress the limits set by society. Sá-Carneiro sees the artist – and all his heroes are artists – as, by nature, a transgressor who cannot, therefore, expect to feel at home in the world.

Sá-Carneiro blended the Futurists' exclamatory style and love of speed and all things modern with the lavish vocabulary of the decadents, their fusing of sex and death, their search for sensation, but the stories are more than just a combination of literary styles. They are painful, and often exhilarating, explorations of what he sees as the very narrow range of options open to a sensitive soul. Like the fat, sullen child imprisoned in his own flesh, Sá-Carneiro's heroes pace their cells, but always hit against the wall of their guilt or their failure or their self-disgust; death, in whatever guise it comes, is a release.

As with his short novel *Lúcio's Confession* (1914, Dedalus 1993), one is often conscious that this is a young man's work, but any youthful lack of control is more than made up for by the sheer opulence of the writing. Sensations and emotions flicker and scintillate in the contradictory, synaesthetic universe he creates. Light blooms and blossoms or is 'like a torrent of black agate', someone has 'a young crystalline voice that sounds as if it were muffled by black crepes and silks', sounds have smells and colours can be felt, fears are 'silvery', sleep 'jade-green', women are convulsed 'in jasper waves of ecstasy'.

The reverse side of this opulence is the desolation, the 'invincible drowsiness' that afflicts his characters, whose souls are likened to 'a vast house in winter, cluttered with furniture draped in sacking, and with open windows through which the sibilant wind rushed in'. We are left, after reading the stories, with the unsettling sense of someone simultaneously embracing and recoiling from life.

Margaret Jull Costa

THE GREAT SHADOW

For Fernando Pessoa

The Great Shadow

Le Prince d'Aquitaine à la tour abolie
Gérard de Nerval

I

December 1905

Oh, mystery.

This obsession has troubled me since infancy – its charm makes me swoon . . .

In the big bedroom where I used to sleep, I would spend long, fearful hours before finally drifting off in the undulating, hesitant light of the oil lamp they left lit for me on the bedside table. I was afraid that the shadows might suddenly stop being shadows and come to life, and that monsters, shadowy monsters, would leap on me and tug at me, mouths gaping.

Now I recall those remote moments of childhood fear with nostalgia, because then, though I suffered, at least my fever wore bright colours, had a kind of marbled voluptuousness. During the day, I would grow bored playing always with the same toys, and I would be filled with sinuous longings for the night and for my own silvery fears beating inside it.

From my bed, I would imagine great houses plunged in darkness, houses I had never entered and which, nevertheless, I would have found perfectly familiar had I visited them in daylight; I would recreate them in the silence and the gloom, fantastic, terrifying and marvellous. I would think: 'How wonderful to walk through that solitude, to touch the objects they contain!' I would imagine getting up out of my small white cot and setting off to visit them, stealthily, barefoot, so that the servants would not hear; but my terror was always stronger than my desire. I would hide my head under the sheets, even in summer, until I forgot and fell deep asleep.

15

Vast houses plunged in darkness . . .

Even today I cannot enter them without a tremor, and I always avoid having to walk through their rooms.

Intellectually, I know that there is nothing ghostly there, no magical vibrations, no lurking signs of witchcraft, yet I am still afraid. They make me think of ghosts . . . cold triangles . . . naked swords . . . bands of varicoloured fire.

I tremble and hesitate. I draw back . . .

.   .   .   .

.   .   .   .

The peerless opulence of the mystery!

Yes, ever since I was a child I have known that the only way one could make life truly, glitteringly beautiful, with battlements of ivory and gold, would be somehow to link it to the mystery, to include it in that mystery. But how?

By seeking, by going down into the darkness, by imperially piling enigma on enigma. Ah, I have sought in vain for secrets with which to anoint my existence, to immortalise it with Shadow. Everything around me is so certain, more than certain, irremediably real. Only my imagination manages to tremble with mysteries, mysteries that are just so much smoke – obscure, mythical enchantments.

The light always shines above me, the light of rough, material certainty.

That was what it was like in childhood too. Only in my fantasies was I afraid, only in them was I sensitive to the delicious, disquieting charm of trap doors, tunnels (if they spoke to me of some ancient palace), of bridges, domes, great arches, just as I sometimes had a chill, tenuous recollection of black aqueducts which, of course, I had never seen.

There was in our house a strange attic which, during my childhood years, became for me the focus of a whole mysterious world.

That attic – which I had glimpsed but once, and then only vaguely – had no actual floor. It was, I now conclude, merely a void between the upper ceiling of the house and the roof, one part of the building being higher than the other. Very occasionally, the servants would go up there and do a bit of cleaning, I think. They would perhaps have let me go with them, but I never asked, I was afraid, and I realise now that I was actually afraid of it becoming a reality and thereby losing all its charm.

Ah, but the number of times I went up to the door to listen. The wind whirled in through the cracks, now and then the beams creaked, and in my imagination all that became the beating of black wings, the sweep of powerful currents, the sound of bones cracking, who knows. One day, I even got up the courage to half open the door. Inside, all was thick shadow; then a ray of evening sun, slipping in through a crack, lit up the magical palpitations of a halo of multicoloured specks of dust. Astonished, dazzled by the marvel, I immediately shut the door and fled.

After that, at night, before going to sleep, I would spend hours on end thinking about that attic which, more than ever, had become for me a bizarre, unknown, seductive world. And I created in it, truly created, a whole life. I dreamed it, its woods, its rivers and bridges, its mountains, its oceans, its towns, its inhabitants. I saw its polychrome forests made out of cotton wool, like sequins, like Christmas tree decorations; the mountains were made out of water, the rivers out of precious stones and, above them, in moonlit arches, there were great bridges of stars. I imagined the human beings inhabiting my country to be deformed, plump, picaresque dwarves with violet-coloured eyes and I invented a whole fauna of bizarre animals that defied description: birds with no heads, rabbits with wings, fish with lions' manes, butterflies that were flowers born out of the earth. For some obscure reason, I deemed the king of this nation to be a great multicoloured ant surrounded by golden mice with silver wings who were the nobles of his court – and I believed it utterly. Only the people were ridiculous homunculi.

This world of my childish imagination formed a mysterious, proliferating whole – indistinct, diffuse, haphazard, impossible to pin down: there was sea where there was also a city, there were royal palaces where there were forests. The most peculiar thing was that in this world in which everything was of such diverse colours, it was, at the same time, grey! Yes, I saw the cotton-wool trees, some white, some purple, blue, scarlet or orange, and the violet eyes of the dwarves, the golden mouse-vassals, the king – the great multicoloured ant – and the rainbow rivers of jewels and the indigo glass mountains, and yet, even as I imagined that infinity of colours, I could not help but see it also as if it were uniformly grey.

Ah, a child's imagination . . . where else would you find a more beautiful, more disquieting imagination, one that can so easily connect with the impossible? It is, without a doubt, the best suited to transforming fear, to harbouring vague conjectures, for in that fluctuating period of one's life, one is pure, credulous fantasy. Later on come reason, lucidity and distrust and then everything vanishes. We are left only with certainty – a sense of hopeless disillusion.

That is why I had the most extraordinary, most troubling experience of my life when I was just eight years old.

We were at our house in the country.

I had never dared walk alone through the garden at night, along the cool paths lined with box hedges, so pleasant and bucolic, where, by day, I would fearlessly run about and play, my cheeks ablaze. From the great courtyard next to the kitchen, though, I would look at those paths opening out in front of me and dream of discovering them on some marvellous night journey. For the truth is that, by night, the garden must be magical. Gnomes would gambol there, and elves; in the great pools, in the moonlight, fairies would bathe, and on the tiled benches – of this I was sure – a whole court of princes and enchanted queens would sit and daydream. Then, what fear I would experience down there, beneath the ancient walnut tree, next to the well, on the edge of which, perhaps, nymphs would disdainfully lean, bewitched and naked.

I dreamed all this with fixed and fascinated eyes, but trembling too, never daring to stray more than a few steps from the kitchen, where there were gossiping servants and plenty of light. I would sleepily dream of this night-time adventure, with a picture book forgotten on my lap, and my eyes would drift once more to the orange grove I could see nearby, wrapped in a pale penumbra, and in which, by sheer force of imagination, I could make out – could really see – the glittering fruits, miraculously turned into golden apples of enchantment.

I had, in fact, already walked the garden paths at night with the caretaker, but that, of course, meant nothing: having someone with me broke the spell. That magical world would only reveal itself to my solitary child's eyes, I knew that all too well.

In vain I went on dreaming, gripped by an intense desire to escape into the darkness, but I was always fettered by fear.

Until one night, I don't know quite how it came about, I suddenly closed my eyes and ran wildly out into the garden.

I only opened my eyes after having run for a few minutes, to be sure that I would not turn back. And for a long time, in a fever of fear, rife with mystery, I wandered in the shadows.

My God, how can I possibly describe all the beauty, all the marvels I experienced during that time? Fear itself gave me wings, it both destroyed and gratified me.

What a fantastic scene!

At night, amongst the darkness and the distances, familiar places – the orchards, the vineyards, the threshing floors, the gardens – reared up in terrifyingly different shapes. The paths were lined by the monsters of green fog into which the box trees had been transformed – jolly, kindly monsters, with clownish, lopsided grins – and the pillars supporting the vine trellis gleamed whitely like erect soldiers, soldiers wearing busbies, some smoking pipes, of which the fluttering glow-worms were the embers.

Everything was shadow, shifting shadow, subtly and constantly modifying the night landscape.

The trees whispered secrets, their shadows were perhaps witches' sabbaths, so crimped and crackling was the rustling of their branches in the wind.

(Ah, but that night wind blowing through the reeds did not feel the same as the wind does in daylight hours, it was more fluid; its strange, veiled whistling made it sound to me like the ghost of a wind, a fearful, croaking ghost, full of dull echoes.)

The pools reflected only blackness, because the night was

dark, with no moon or stars; they were like hideous pools of pitch, but the coolness emanating from them dissipated that fear, and on the water, if you looked closely, there were a thousand fantastic, indeterminate shapes, carved out of a translucent, barely visible, indigo mist that fluttered, capricious and mysterious.

I kept running.

The roses in the garden provided gentler enchantments, whilst the round, leafy myrtle tree had turned itself into a drooping Chinese bonze venerably crossing his legs, and the lilies had become bells in an ivory tower.

. . . .

Now I was leaning over the well. Amidst the sound of splashing, the long, black wings of unfamiliar creatures brushed my face. My fear, at that point, was an agony.

Looming in the distance, I could still see a great secret shape, possibly tawny in colour.

I have no idea what happened after that. When I came to, I was back sitting openmouthed on the bench in the pantry, next to the kitchen, with the same picture book on my lap. My favourite companion – the large yellow dog that belonged to the caretaker and which I would harness to my dog-carts – was gently licking my hands . . .

. . . .
. . . .

Yes, those still constitute the greatest moments of my life. I never achieved a more intense illusion, that of penetrating the Shadow and including myself in the Secret. Ah, but on the nights that followed, how my fears grew. I often woke up crying, thrashing around hysterically.

That was when I had the dream for the first time – another of my brightest memories.

In fact, one morning, when I awoke, I remembered perfectly clearly – where, I don't know, but it happened that night – how a certain queen decked out in brocades had held me on her lap, had opened to me her coffers of precious stones, had unbraided her long, golden hair for me so that I could run my feverish fingers through it, to cool them.

A princess could not exist in my room, not even at night, and I had not left my room. And yet I had spoken to her, I had seen her quite clearly. But where, where? I could almost remember her features, her mouth filled with pearls, her flower-like gestures. There were walls of mist around my eyes.

Finally, embarrassed, I told all this to the maids, but they, distractedly, said only:

'It was just a dream.'

A dream.

I spent all day – I'll never forget it – trying to relive that lovely mystery, the magical queen, her rings, her necklaces, the rustling gleam of her dress, her unbraided hair. Perhaps I was in love with her, who knows, but I was, above all, proud of having dreamed her for the first time, of being capable of dreaming her, because I could not believe that such a glory could happen to just anyone.

. . . .

I never deceived myself like that again. That is why I remember my childhood with a kind of amazed nostalgia.

Although my whole art is intimately bound up with Mystery, I never manage truly to immerse myself in the Beyond. In my books I may have left some shadow, some diademed shadow, but it is the shadow of artifice, a dead, unchanging shadow that does not excite me, a shadow I create, but which does not touch me, one that I cold-bloodedly devise.

Each night, longingly, humbly, I return to my silent, childhood memories, to my miraculous night-time walk, to my fantasy attic, and to the long hours on sunny mornings spent lying on my bed, staring into my own eyelids – that kaleidoscope of illusion – at the discs, arrows, claws, ribbons, stars, multicoloured crescents set in a red penumbra, spinning and sparkling and dappling.

How remote that rich life seems! How great I was then! Then I had a sombre fear of belfries . . . if there were turrets on a palace, I could only believe in them if there were naked princesses inside, dining on bitter fruits . . . and I was afraid of thick tapestries, I would shudder at the sight of heavy drapes, hot velvets.

Even today I have not lost that fear of what might lie behind a curtain, just as I am still troubled in ancient palaces by Persian carpets, Arras tapestries, huge unlit chandeliers, dead mirrors.

But it is all quite useless, and so uncertain . . .

. . . .

I have an overwhelming desire to plunge myself into the Shadow and actually to experience it, to live it!

II

January 1906

Such a strange enchantment . . . There is something intensely sexual in the attraction I feel for the Mystery. Whenever I dream or think about it, I do so lost in desire, in the grip of a delicate, spasmodic flow of sensuality, just as memories of water, fire and naked bodies, the sensations of Secrecy, whether real or evoked, all fill me with fluid ecstasies, golden and perverse.

Everything that moves me has become sexualised and it is through sex alone that I sense it, desire it, suffer it. That is why I have always consciously and excitedly catalogued splendid, naked bodies, tumultuous European cities, perfumes, shimmering theatres carpeted in purple, moonlit waterscapes, noisy cafés, restaurants at night, long journeys, the contemporary murmur of vast mills and factories, madness and iced drinks, particular flowers such as violets and camellias, certain fruits, such as pineapples . . . and strawberries, with their sharp, naked, capricious acidity.

. . . .

I glance behind me at the silent hours and I evoke all the people in my life . . . the strange, chance bodies I have possessed, *in order to unknow them,* and even those people whom I never knew, but who passed for an instant through my life.

Does not my most beautiful memory, and also the most secret, belong in that category?

One night, in a restaurant in Paris, a girl sat down opposite me, when I was having dessert, and asked me for the French name of the sweet I was eating. Afterwards, we chatted for a few moments. She was Russian, from Moscow, and I from a far-off country in the West that had lost all in vain adventures. We said goodbye without exchanging names. We never saw each other again.

Our lives, however, so distant, so diverse, had touched for a second, had for a moment been shared, perhaps in the fulfilment of some unknowable destiny.

23

Ah, when I remember those tiny moments, I feel proud, because I know how to unlock their disturbing inner meaning, veiled in shadow.

Thus, I constantly relive each embrace, each chance encounter, each person, in fact, with whom one day I happened to speak, yes, even passers–by who simply asked me for directions. I evoke them all and I feel beauty, a beauty entwined with a subtle fear that makes me tremble. For who were they, who were all those strangers who, after all, had a part, a speaking part, in my life?

My God, so much shadow! . . .

What catastrophes must I have fleetingly stumbled upon? Could I have spoken for minutes at a time with great criminals on their way to commit a crime that same night, or with poor wretches in the culminating hours perhaps of a wasted existence?

I even remember the faces of people I barely glimpsed from afar, but which, for some strange reason, I have never forgotten. Like the tawny-haired woman I saw on the Rialto bridge and the pale, solitary man I noticed one night in Monaco, wearing a red bow tie.

Come mirages, grow and multiply within me, come all, however small a role you played in my life, however fantastic the theory! Make me tremble, groan with fear and wonder, until I struggle up and flail my arms about to scatter you!

I could perhaps embroider whole moments around such images, moments I could thrill to.

But, no, they refuse to come to life.

. . . .
. . . .

Besides, I have never been able to keep a secret.

If some friend confides in me the secrets of his life, I feel so proud to know something others do not know that I immediately tell someone else. I have to put an end to the mystery entrusted to me, to prove vaingloriously that I am greater than he, because I can destroy him.

Should I feel affection for some gentle, delicate, piquant young woman, I pour all my desire into lending a little enigma to that banal, insignificant life. That is why I have sent to many a poor young girl whom I have never embraced fanciful letters, flowers, telegrams, a copy of one of my books – if I happened to be abroad.

III

I find the future terribly moving too, because it is so utterly full of secrets.

For nights on end – disquieting, zebrine, polymorphous nights – I immerse myself in daydreaming future episodes and characters in my life, future heroes in novels as yet unplanned.

And it occurs to me that all this exists already, *because it must exist*. That is why I become so confused when I imagine it.

Impossible, impossible!

All I have to do is wait.

. . . .

Oh, how I would love to possess today my future lovers, not engendered by fantasy, with imaginary forms and faces, but merely the idea of them, translucent, subtle . . . carved out of the unknown, out of nebulous possibilities, vibrant with light . . .

. . . .

. . . .

To be able one day to savour – at last! – the purple, macerated taste of the Mystery!

IV

Movement . . . journeys . . .

Yet another voluptuous pleasure, intoxicating, enigmatic. It has always amazed me that I can be here, now, in my own mediocre country, in this city on the far west of southern Europe, and in five days (only a matter of hours) can reach the north and the capital of the sombre, dense Empire of my unquiet longings.

After wandering aimlessly for some time through other countries, I almost forget who I am, I can neither remember the atmosphere nor the landscape, let alone the people around me. I doubt that I am myself, I convince myself that I am not. I have never believed that we are complete in ourselves, the surrounding milieu is surely also part of us. Therefore our souls (and even perhaps our bodies) must vary according to the countries in which we live.

That is why I hate it when someone I admire goes away, leaving me with the fear of their return, and when I wait at the station for a friend who has been absent for some months, a great confusion grips me when I see him, I stutter and stammer, barely able to bring myself to address him as 'tu' as I used to do before.

. . . .

I travel and travel, always randomly. That is my way of changing myself, at least in fantasy – I grow more adept in the Mystery . . .

And, more precisely, in a great café in a European city, I study some charming young woman of pleasure, who, sitting bored in front of her glass of wine, is doubtless waiting – in the evening – for a lover. I look at her. Almost without realising it, I find myself writing her life. I embellish and poeticise it, I dramatise it according to her face, the gleam in her eyes, the curve of her painted lips, the colour of her hair. A life, for me, always springs from someone's profile . . . I can find an appropriate denouement for every type of beauty, events that could only be lived by certain eyes, certain hands, certain smiles.

The plot unfolds from there . . . I compose the subtle tones, her whole life . . . then, at last, her lover arrives, or doesn't arrive, or perhaps he was never even expected.

But the unknown woman gets up, leaves. I follow her with my eyes until she disappears, and I feel so happy, so happy, so satisfyingly happy. I feel happier than if I were her lover, even the lover who did not arrive, because then I would know all about her and I would be unable to create a life according to those eyes, a life in accordance with those gestures.

A subtle triumph! With no hesitation on her part, without first obtaining her permission, I entered, really entered, her existence, because I included her in my inner world, gently imagining her.

These frivolous pastimes furnish me with my soul's deepest pleasures. That is why I travel in a state of ecstasy, I lose myself in the search. There is one particular golden night which I love above all: it happened very late one night in the aristo-cratic quarter of some capital city. I came upon a millionaire's gleaming car waiting outside a palace. I stopped. After a few moments, the door − adorned with a coat of arms − swung open. An extremely tall, elegant man got in and was joined by a sumptuous woman in sables and lace.

And how much greater was my victory then, alone in the wind, than that of the two people in the car, perhaps at that very moment mingling mouths, because I could imagine them, and they, alas, *knew only too exactly who they were.*

. . . .

The great cities . . . the wonder of climbing up the sym-bolic columns in their monumental squares and, from that height, like a statue, letting one's eyes rove over all the houses. Rapt, one's eyes zigzag along streets, along avenues, through parks, they gaze infinitely out over the sea of rooftops. It is an anthill of buildings which, from on high, become a panorama;

they intermingle, intersect, are swallowed up one by the other, dizzyingly, inextricably intertwined.

Moment by moment, the whirlpool whirls faster . . . We soon lose all notion of distance, a vertigo grips us . . . until, ahead of us, the whole horizon shifts and darkens, occupied by the mirage of another composite city.

We tremble . . . our sacred eyes flicker, grow feverish with flight.

And life flows by at our feet, *life*!

V

In my pursuit of what is secret I have struggled to give my senses at least a *different* vibration, disjointed, intense and diverse, thus affording myself glimpses of a strange, disquieting illusion.

Thus, on some evenings, quite suddenly, in certain lights, I manage to feel – automatically, albeit using artifice – a painful nostalgia for a certain dead female companion, gentle and pale, a companion I never knew. That is enough to cast the propitious shadow that caresses me with doubt, fills me with colour.

On other occasions, I get a sense of things ending, of the close of a certain era in life, of the beginnings of another, with new characters, new habits. And all around me, everything is the same, existing on the same planes . . .

There are facts, too, that present me with blank contradictions. For example, one night in an ordinary theatre in Lisbon, a great, lacerating sadness swept over me on seeing a couple of old drunks – a hilarious double act from a famous review. When the two grotesque characters came on stage and sang their clumsy songs, swaying about in time to the harsh, jerky music, what I felt was a final bitterness, pungent, rueful, an ancient sadness, and pity too, a wrenching, pointless pity, tinged with sorrow. They reminded me painfully of the end of a life. And while the whole audience was shouting 'encore' and roaring with laughter, I felt like crying, for myself, mysteriously enough.

On other days, I experience sudden great joyful bursts of enthusiasm and everything around me speaks of glory. If I meet a friend, I take him by the arm and laugh and laugh, like a child. In vain do I seek the reasons for this joy, nothing has happened to provoke it. It is a Mystery, and yet somehow there *is* a motive for this joy, that, at least, is how I experience it, as a diffuse idea, caressing and undulant.

In just the same way I am filled at each step by motiveless

feelings of tenderness and, even more bizarrely, by motiveless feelings of tender modesty.

Only a short while ago, an insidious feeling rose up in me, a tenuous caprice: I felt that I was a sweet, blonde young girl who had just given herself to her lover, and all because a friend of mine had shown me some postcards he had bought and which I had already seen in a shopwindow. They showed a pretty young girl with adorable bare breasts, the girl whom I perhaps blushingly thought I was at that very moment.

At times, I suffer from minor physical aches and pains, but I experience them only on my palate, as if they were unpleasant tastes.

Often, when I turn around in a street, in a room, I suddenly find myself in a scene in some distant, foreign city. I see it all with absolute clarity – a square, a harbour – I feel the pulsating violet penumbra beneath the majestic columns of a particular cathedral. (Here, I know, there is a possible explanation: any dislocation in the atmosphere which actually intersects parallel planes might break the vertices of light and shadow in exactly the same way as those I perhaps chanced to witness in the scene now evoked.)

Sometimes, in the depths of winter, I suddenly feel as if it were autumn or spring and there are times when, without having been ill, I feel as if I were convalescing from a long sickness, as if I had been saved from death only by a miracle.

Bizarre, picaresque, complicated ideas occur to me as I wander through my soul – creating a synthesis of its ruins – possibly the only ideas capable of expressing, by suggestion, the most intimate particularities of my inner world.

So when I am hopelessly weighed down by sadness or desolating tedium, I remember that my torment derives only from this: a hollow sheath of tin wrapped around my flesh, and something else as well, my soul I suppose. (And I fear then that my soul might be merely a green liquid – sickly, oily, turbid – contained inside that receptacle.)

I imagine the utter devastation of my life as a series of zinc lozenges, bruised and twisted, spattered with various colours, in particular, by a shade of dirty red.

And many a night, in bed, reviewing the stagnant nausea of my existence, a ridiculous longing arises in me to make of my body a triangle and to have the vertices honed into sharp steel blades. Ah, if only I could shape my body into a thread, then – I think confidently – my desolation would end.

. . . .

But, I do not want to create a false impression, I feel all these things sincerely and naturally. I did not train my emotions to tremble in this confused manner. They grew disjointed of their own accord, a result of all that vain vacillation, all that useless twisting and turning.

Then, if I put something of myself in the protagonists who inhabit my works of art – idle, sumptuously detailed mirages – the eunuch-public immediately claim it is all a joke or simply incomprehensible. Incomprehensible. There is so little to comprehend in what I write, in all this. I say: 'My life seems to me like a series of zinc lozenges.' And that is that. Don't look for a meaning, there's nothing to understand. That's all it is! I can't even express it any other way, any more clearly, because that is the way it is – just that.

And because I know how to feel these things, a certain uncertainty filters through, which is why my extravagances are a source of pride to me; I love them with a tawny, leonine love.

. . . .

(On the hillside of the olive grove in our garden, when I was little, why was there a paper saint set beneath a pane of glass embedded in the earth?)

. . . .

Meanwhile, despite everything, taking everything into consideration, there is only light, insipid light, around me. In vain do I attempt to plumb the mystery, to dig shadowy tunnels.

Impossible! Impossible!

Ah, how I envy those great criminals who escape justice and who pass or, rather, disappear bloodily into murders and violations.

At least they left a little mist behind them.

Enclosed in their secret, they must live glorious lives with no regrets, gorged on marvels.

I, of course, feel only self-disgust!

VI

If I were a millionaire and a Prince, how would I build my domain of Mystery?

In the north, amongst magnificent gardens, my lofty castle, cloaked in shadows, would raise its taciturn towers, spread its broad, heavy bulk, utterly absorbed.

Inside, there would be long, windowless ballrooms designed by great architects and decorated with frescos by wonderful painters; the marvellous domes would be inlaid with silver and gold, the wood panelling with exotic encrustations, mother-of-pearl and jade.

The rustle and rich gleam of floor-length velvet curtains; deep, majestic carpets that muffle footsteps; candelabra, three-branched candlesticks and chandeliers emblazoned with coats of arms, chandeliers that are never lit.

I might never even see those theatrical rooms in the light. I would walk through them in the half-darkness, feeling their richness with my fingers; I would merely guess at their appearance in dubious mirrors, in the shadow of their lushness, guided by the distant, faintly flickering light that managed to filter in through the cracks in the doors.

My God, but that would be wonderful! What ornate enchantments, what diffuse, latent vertices would dazzle me as I crossed these ballrooms where no one would ever dance, rooms that I barely knew, even though on special nights I might hear from their sofas – still in the half-dark – solemn concerts played by Asiatic orchestras hidden in other galleries.

If I allow myself these swooning thoughts, I lose myself in dreaming my whole domain of Error.

Tangled gardens surround the palace and there are parks too. Further off lie dense, tumultuous woods, impenetrable to the sun, with sudden clearings where I would order monuments to be erected to heroes, navigators and warriors who never lived.

At the far end of unexpected rose gardens, lost amongst the

forest, there would be temples to divinities that required no rituals, false divinities that I alone had created, raising them up there on altars of fantasy. Inscriptions would be carved on ancient, Gothic tombs, beneath the domes of the temples, on stone slabs covering non-existent graves, and farther off, next to the swamps, at the edge of the woods, amongst the cypress trees, there would be mausoleums, again false, empty of bones.

I would complete this ludicrous world by building ruins next to a great dried-up lake, ruins with crumbling lancet arches, columns and vaults. Along the paths of my garden, I would hide treasures, at random, deep down, as in olden times; I would bury toys there. I would build high, bristling walls and broad iron gateways enclosing nothing at all; lastly, I would order caves to be created and have blind subterranean passages built throughout my lands, just as in my palace there would be absurd trap doors, sudden false entrances, stairways one could not go down, strange secret mechanisms.

All of this, all of this, would be *learned* uncertainly, walking only at night through my domain, never crossing certain avenues, never walking along the shores of certain lakes whose existence I could only surmise from the ashen murmur of their light, lapping waters. Yes, everything would be only half-seen in distraction and in doubt, hesitantly, the better to embroider it with magic.

And from the monumental windows of my golden room, I would gaze out at twilight on my fading empire spilling out into the distance, imagining it, foreseeing it in undulating shadows, in the whisper of the leaves, in aquatic murmurings, beneath the scintillating stars.

But my whole principality is nothing but a dream.

. . . .

And what if I were a dream too?

VII

April 1908

The days pass and I bend more and more to the curve of my obsession.

In my brain, agate-barbed rhythms have started up.

Ah, the impossible struggle against reality!

If only madness would finally overtake me.

That, at least, would plunge me into a great shadow . . .

But no, no. Everything is real in life, even death.

And yet some people have found a way to disappear!

I remember two friends I used to know: one of them, pale, blond and freckled, used to talk to me about his grandparents in France. Whether alive or dead, he vanished without trace. Only later did I learn, through his parents, that he had never had any foreign relatives, that there had never been any large estates in the north, where he had invited me to spend that summer.

I feel shocked now, remembering him. I detested his company. He was such an uninteresting fellow, yet I often spent time with him, not knowing how to avoid him, perhaps out of gratitude – for he was the one who so insistently sought me – out of a kind of idle sympathy. In the end, his brusque manners and his vulgar habits – the mean, contemptible actions or foolish extravagances of a *parvenu* – had made me almost come to hate him.

Only now do I discover that I was completely wrong. His was such a remarkable spirit! He too doubtless had that amber longing for the Mystery – coarse perhaps, but deep. That is why he would only speak to me of unrealities – of his gardens, cars and guns – and commit acts of wilful folly; he was, by turns, miserly and profligate, but never fair.

Then one night, driven by a more noble impetus, he resolved to disappear, thus creating an even greater lie. And he did so with absolute success. No one ever wore mourning for him. If he died, no one ever found his body. If he is still alive, he must today be someone else.

Not a trace did he leave behind him.

A marvellous Artist!

.   .   .   .

The fate of my second friend was perhaps more beautiful still. One evening, he came into my house and announced to me his imminent suicide. I was tidying the books on my shelves and I dismissed the remark with a shrug. I was all too familiar with his love of drama, his ingenuous tendency to romanticise himself. That same night, we went for a lovely, carefree walk together . . .

Some weeks later, he again declared his plan to me. I politely demanded explanations. He refused to give them, merely alluding, in a roundabout way, to vague impossibilities.

The next day, I questioned him again, this time with rather more conviction. He made a tremendous scene. He threw himself down on a sofa and ran his slender, manicured hands through his long hair. He was wearing a flower in his buttonhole. He pulled it out and flung it to the floor. Standing at a window, with my back to him, I could barely suppress my laughter.

He crumpled a few more silken cushions, wiped away tears he had not shed and, with gestures redolent of feminine artifice, he told me what had brought him to that resolve.

My God, such an unexpected motive, so trivial, almost crazy in its absurdity, ridiculous, the last thing one could possibly imagine.

Taking my role now entirely seriously, I put my arms around him and forced him to see how insignificant and inadmissible his reasons were. He agreed with me. He swore he would repent. We went out to the bookshop to buy the latest novels.

I saw him again that night at the theatre, smiling and impeccable; he was in evening dress, a fresh flower in his lapel, a large red rose.

We met the following day too. He told me the plot of yet another play he was about to write and which he had thought up that very morning. He spoke to me of his plans for the following summer, he went to see his shirtmaker to place a very complicated order. He asked me for the address of a French publisher in order to send off for a book he had borrowed from me, so as to have it in his own library.

Two days later he shot himself through the heart.

That was when I learned that he had announced his plans to kill himself to other friends too, always adding, in absolute confidence, the reasons that drove him to such depths of despair: but to each of us he had told a different story.

. . . .

Whatever else they are, such creatures at least manage to clothe themselves in a little mystery; they fade and fly away, anoint themselves with lies.

True, they are greater than I, always talking about my Yearnings and yet stuck eternally in everyday clarity, unbesmirched by secrets.

Out of incoherence, a fear of sacrilege, perhaps, faced by the work I should be doing, I am all hopeless scepticism, weary disillusion, a marasmus of resignation.

And if anyone finds my uneven life peculiar, empty but somehow different, I cannot help but shout out the truth: that the reason behind my sudden departure one night was a desire to go to bed early – my silvery envelopes contain no love letters; if I disappear for long periods at a time it is only in order to be at home or, at most, in some café in another quarter, reading and writing.

Out of a vain mysticism, a furious desire for harmony, I am the first to discount any false mystery that might easily exist in the eyes of others, as if mysteries were not always falsehoods.

. . . .

. . . .

Yes, my forgotten friends of yesteryear, you, tall and pale with your French grandparents and you with your dishevelled hair and painted nails, I am so much your inferior, so much more soulless, nerveless; I sicken myself, I am a mockery of myself, a cardboard sphinx.

And how I miss you then, you and your pride, oh mad kings who died in the moonlight, in order to plunge into blue lakes, perhaps . . . into uncertain intrigues . . .

VIII

My God, my God, how can I bear this endless light, inevitable, obsessive.

I have outdone myself in tedium. Everything has emptied out around me.

My nerves have been hung out on an iron hook, tied to a dry plait of straw.

I am afraid of myself, of my sadness.

I walk alone along the streets and my gaze, my own gaze, bothers me.

In vain do I seek the company of ghosts.

Everything around me is living *this life*.

If at least other lives existed . . . I don't know, unstable lives, perfume-lives, fluid organisms that could condense, solidify and evaporate again.

22 November

I know I am right. Lately there has been a change in my soul. I no longer feel it in the same way. It has become a spiral and my senses spin like coloured wheels – feverish fairground tombolas.

.   .   .   .

Daydreams, daydreams . . .

Always ahead of me, cruel reality, the white sheet on which I write, the conscious will that makes me write.

.   .   .   .
.   .   .   .
.   .   .   .

IX

At last at last! The triumph, the golden triumph!

How wrong I was to despair!

Today I am alive with apotheoses; everything prostrates itself before the miracle!

Whirlwinds of wings, precious stones and stars closed about my eyes.

There were fireworks of perfumes.

What does anything else matter if the magic has made me perfect, mistily unfathomable?

I do not know what will happen next, what will become of me, but whatever my destiny, I will have experienced beauty, beauty deeply intertwined with shadow. I experienced the Mystery. I slipped through into a rainbow of colours. I won!

Do I see any blood?

. . . .

That was my triumph. I want to set it down now, only a few hours after my return, the better to be able to go over it all later.

Longing for light and distraction after all my expectant wanderings – immersed in wan bitternesses, vain struggles – I inevitably ended up spending this harsh winter on the Côte d'Azur.

And somehow one night, during carnival in Nice, I found myself at the Casino ball.

The atmosphere suited me. Amidst a cacophony of sounds, a thousand colours whirled about me, the usual party glitter to which, oddly enough, I felt my spirit warm.

Pushing my way through that motley crowd, I remembered the mercurial words of a dear friend of mine, one night in a café in Paris:

'I adore masked balls! An Imperial masked ball at the Opéra . . . But if I were there, my friend, if I were there, every woman

40

present would be my lover, *because they would all be wearing masks.*'

My eyes then looked with more interest at the Secret encircling me – a banal enough secret, it's true, but an entrancing one nevertheless.

It was indeed both troubling and beautiful.

So much silk!

And I abandoned myself to the tumult, to the confetti and the streamers.

'How very odd,' I thought to myself, 'I have drunk no alcohol, taken no drugs, yet my senses feel confused, scattered: a bitter swooning, only subtler, sweeter, more delicious, a kind of weary transparency.'

Disconcerted, I walked on; then, suddenly, the lights flickered and span before my throbbing eyes.

At the same time, someone took my arm, murmuring something that woke me from my torpor:

'I am perhaps the veiled Princess . . .'

I do not know quite what happened next, only that, after a few moments, I could finally *see* the splendid woman who had taken my arm. Tall, statuesque, peerless, she was wearing a strange disguise: the sort of uniform a page might wear in a fairy tale set in some distant, blue country.

Her body was sheathed in a bodice of gold brocade, out of which peeked, with pernicious boldness, the insolent nipple of one brown breast.

Her otherwise bare legs were clad in skin-tight breeches in a subtle shade of violet.

On her torrential hair she wore a scarlet satin cap adorned with a strange feather from some magical bird – dazzling and multicoloured.

Around her waist she wore a mysterious black belt of worked leather, with a narrow dagger in a sheath.

A green silk mask covered her face.

. . . .

As I said, I do not know quite what happened in those first few minutes. My torpor gradually evaporated, but as it drained away, I felt my skin creep and my feelings grow more clouded than ever.

My lucidity only returned – and it was a very relative lucidity – when the two of us were drinking champagne at the bar.

With a feeling of intermittent disquiet, my eyes had fixed now on the dagger, but the woman, following the direction of my gaze, immediately removed it from its silver sheath and held it out to me, to reassure me.

I took it in trembling hands, with a heavy sense of symbolism.

It was both a terrible weapon and a solemn jewel.

The hilt was encrusted with secret, glittering stones full of bewildering reflections – the remote gleam of sombre pageantry, infinite colours. The cruel steel blade, whilst short and narrow, was extremely sharp, and engraved on it were intriguing characters from some lost alphabet.

Dumbstruck, I examined the bejewelled knife. A shadow crossed my face. My fingers grew cold. Smiling, the woman said: 'It's a family heirloom, precious, emblematic, terribly old. It has a fearful, obscure legend attached to it, an eternal curse. Perhaps one day I'll tell you about it . . . '

It was as if someone had smashed my fingers with a hammer of ice. I dropped the dagger. She picked it up at once, fearlessly, laughing loudly. Then she ordered me to fill her glass again, while, still laughing, she calmly sheathed the piercing blade.

We left the bar. She leaned amorously against me, in fact, her body twined about mine. Our fingers interlaced and, for a moment, as she adjusted her golden bodice, she revealed the painted nipple of her other breast.

As never before, a strange, dark shudder ran through me.

Half-mad, savouring the glory of having that magnificent dream-woman's arms about me, all I feared was the inevitably banal outcome of the affair. Meanwhile, our sumptuous kisses were far from banal. Drunk on happiness, I walked, without thinking, without saying a word, out of the room.

My companion, however, had clearly come to a decision.

Still holding my arm, she went to the cloakroom to ask for her coat, a cloak of rich furs.

I was trembling with fear now, lacking the courage to make the inevitable comment about our night together.

She was not in the least surprised by my silence, though, and I still wonder how it is that I suddenly found myself getting into the limousine that was doubtless waiting for her.

The car drew away, it drove very fast. Only then did I regain a little of my sangfroid.

My feeling of triumph grew, the enigma continued. My fear dissented: 'Was it really an enigma, or merely an interesting, strange, unexpected adventure, but perfectly normal for all that?' If only I were at last in possession of a Secret!

Then suddenly, with new resolve, even if it meant plunging myself into disillusion, I indirectly provoked her into an explanation.

My blithe companion laughed and laced her fingers in mine; she told me not to be afraid, that there was no danger, not even of masked highwaymen, that she was merely taking me to her house, her mansion, adding:

'There no one knows that I am perhaps the veiled Princess. I didn't give them my name. I gave a false name or, rather, I didn't give any name. They have never even seen me.'

Then I really did feel as if many-coloured planes of light were shifting about me: the Mystery was continuing and I was not the one creating it. On the contrary, I had even tried to clarify it. Triumph was certain and golden.

Thus I forgot about the time, determined to surrender blindly to the magic, half-closing my eyes so that I would see even less.

Simultaneously, effortlessly, without even thinking to suggest it, I experienced a return – anaesthetising and tenuous, more delicious than ever, this time in shades of violet – of that feeling of disparateness and dispersion to which I referred a while before and which had flowed through me before I had met her.

(One curious thing, which I only noticed afterwards, was that from the depths of that paralysing diffuseness oozed a hidden fear tinged with magenta.)

I noticed that the car was heading with vertiginous speed away from the Casino and along the Boulevard MacMahon, then down the Boulevard du Pont-Vieux as far as the Place

Garibaldi. However, after reaching that square, where we stopped for a moment for the driver to light a lamp that had gone out, I could not say with any certainty whether we took the rue Cassini, the rue de la République, or some other street.

From then on, in fact, I transmigrated into a world of dreams. Reality became relative, all my thoughts and all my gestures were mere projections of subtle movements executed on other planes. I fell into a jade-green sleep. Something was eclipsed in me, possibly the moon of my inner world. I was sensitive only to the Mystery accompanying me.

I could not say how much time had passed when the car drew up outside an iron door. We got out. The strange woman opened the door with a tiny key that glinted in the night.

We entered a murmurous garden. She gave an order to the driver who then drove off. The night was very dark. At the far end of the garden, however, I sensed the shadow of a great building.

The enchantress again took my arm and we went along a path that emerged opposite an isolated pavilion, on the left-hand side of the garden.

Then she pulled out a shining key. She opened a door. We went up a few steps.

The interior of the house was a delight, it was a sort of luxuriously decorated studio.

The blue-grey atmosphere was lit at strange angles by opaque electric lamps; it was soft with perfume, silken.

It was furnished with rustling draperies, deep carpets patterned with purple moons, fragile oriental furniture and, in the middle, a low bed covered in velvet − unfathomable, secret. Yet what most impressed me about that narcotic atmosphere was the light, which was never still, it undulated in the air, changing constantly, a perpetual blossoming of light in crescent-shaped bands that danced across tenuous planes to an iridescent rhythm.

As soon as we arrived, my unknown hostess threw her cloak down on to a heavy armchair and, standing before a large mirror, she immediately took off her costume. She stood there completely naked, apart from the green mask.

It was an extraordinary moment when her body emerged free and splendid, still as a statue, in the middle of the room; the light changed. The bands of light arced and bloomed round about, ever faster, ever subtler, doubtless the influence of the platinum nimbus dimly surrounding her softening body . . .

My pride then was a deep violet dappled with emeralds! All that secret flesh would be mine! And all my fears vanished when I saw that she had kept the mask on, thus preserving the golden enigma intact.

We rolled wildly about the great bed. Beneath my body her flesh – all Apotheosis and soul – groaned in delirium.

But suddenly my eyes fixed on something brighter shining near at hand, on the pink marble mantelpiece above the fireplace: the dagger which she had carelessly left there when she had got undressed.

I continued kissing and biting her lips, but, as if obsessed, I could not take my eyes off that other marvel!

In that atmosphere of silken, mutable shadows, the glitter of that legendary weapon was like some infernal spell, magical, sparkling, fearsome.

The dazzling effect of those discarded jewels could not just have been caused by the multicoloured light, and I can only describe it in fantastic terms: first, a luminous scintillation, like lightning, emanated from the fiery stones, then, suddenly, in mid-trajectory, that scintillating light condensed in the blue shadows into a crystalline nucleus out of which, in turn, there emerged a halo of rainbow-coloured reverberations that left actual traces on the air. That was the most bizarre and inexplicable thing: the light was both fluid and substantial, its brilliance and its colours produced clear, capricious, palpable effects.

In short, my whole life was focused on that dagger. I do not know why, but I was filled by a strident certainty that this was none other than the Mystery I had so dreamed of meeting.

I had the hallucinatory, slithering sense of being bound about, minute by minute, by occult powers . . .

My ears were assaulted by engulfing planes, aromas whistled past, transforming themselves into dissonant music, until, with each ever more fantastic coruscation, it seemed to me secretly that my whole inner world was being landscaped. The crepitations of the dazzling lights were actually invading my soul, pouring burning sun on my desires, drenching with rain my tedium that lay spreading uselessly out over a plain, shedding moonlight on the graveyards of my nostalgias, and, even more extraordinarily, constructing around my enthusiasms a vast square built on a monumental scale (although in the middle there was no heroic statue, just a large well). And I foresaw in that moment, with utter certainty, that the future life of my soul would be in that square, closed off and possibly drowned for ever in that great central well.

Intermingled with all these magical ideas – so real, at least at the time – were the kisses I bestowed on the madwoman's painted breasts, on every inch of her wanton flesh, convulsed in vaporous, jasper waves of ecstasy.

There was a moment when I managed to drag my eyes away from the dagger and I was transfixed by the idea that everything around me was falling endlessly into space – I was the only thing not falling. It seemed to me that even the enchanted body vibrating beneath mine was being drawn dizzyingly down. Or rather, she grew more substantial, and even while she was falling and I remained fixed, I could still feel her beneath me.

But then my eyes glanced back at the dagger. Even more intensely than before, my whole world was focused on it. An opiate haze hovered about everything.

Then, at last, a spasm shook me – starry, intricate . . . and as I came, it was not that lush, opulent flesh that I possessed, it was the light glinting imperially on that cursèd dagger!

. . . .
. . . .
. . . .

Suddenly, I lost control . . . I hurled myself on the dagger. It was time! The Mystery was about to crumble . . . She had already sat up . . . She was bound to remove her mask . . . and I would see her . . . know who she was . . . I would see her eyes. I could not allow her to do that, no, it was impossible.

Once the ecstasy was over, I would be forced to see the room for what it was. Only in orgasm would I still perhaps manage, imperially, to imagine it.

I was about to wake up . . . I was waking up from the gold . . . I was about to lose the whole Miracle.

I was afraid. I feared for my pride. What would become of me if I was not genius enough to fix – nobly – that sculptural Secret, to curl up inside it for ever, to perfect it in myself and savour it for all eternity?

I was seized by a ghastly anxiety, but I won through! I grabbed the dagger, then, swaying, my head in a whirl, I buried it in her heart.

Not a moan. Her breasts merely trembled.

What a magnificent moment!

It seemed to me that I had collided head-on with fate and that only my arm had stopped it in its tracks.

.   .   .   .

.   .   .   .

Yes, yes, I had triumphed! I had successfully completed my work – I had created fog, called down mists, built vaults of shadow . . . and all around me reality was crumbling into raucous, black buds.

Ivory thrones caprioled about me . . . cavalcades of stars filed by . . . diadems roared past in cataracts . . .

Ah, the infinite moment!

That was not all though. One thing was missing to make the work complete. On an impulse, I closed my eyes and slashed the face beneath the green silk mask – the face of that woman I had never seen – so that no one else would see her, not even I!

I looked at the dagger. Miraculously, there was not a drop of blood on it, only the letters of that enigmatic inscription were tinged with red, for ever. And the stones encrusting the hilt had grown calm, the light glancing from them quiet at last.

I flung the knife away. I fled . . .

I found my way back along the paths in the garden, like a sleepwalker. I went out of the heavy iron door, the key of which was doubtless still in the lock. I wandered for what seemed like hours along unfamiliar streets.

When lucidity returned and I regained some notion of time and space, I found that I was back in the Place Garibaldi, though how I do not know.

.   .   .   .

That same morning I caught an express train at Ville-Franche station. No one stopped me.

I have no idea what I left behind me . . . a corpse, at least. I have no idea what will happen now . . . if I will be pursued.

But what does all that matter in the face of the diamond-and-marble work I created?

I have made myself subtle as the stars . . . I am full of sorceries . . . I am rooted for all time in Nostalgia and Beauty . . .

I myself am Mystery. I tremble and swoon with terror, with a delicate translucence!

Everything about me is shadow – Shadow!

The supreme triumph: *the* Triumph!

.   .   .   .
.   .   .   .
.   .   .   .

X

So much time has passed. I take up my notes in order to savour my glory.

Yes, my triumph was complete!

I am so different now – hesitant, abstracted, insensitive to everything I gaze upon. (I no longer look at things, though probably they look at me . . .)

I have adapted myself to Exile. I have ceased to be Myself in relation to what surrounds me. The Mystery built for me long aqueducts and, out of kindness, the echoes amongst those lancet arches keep from me the noise of life. Nothing exists around me now but I – an unequivocal victory!

For me there is only 'before' and 'after' the Marvel. I remember nothing about 'before'. No one can remember a life before birth. On that tigerish night, at the moment when I plunged the dagger into her, I awoke (it is true) into another world, I was born into another life: a slender life where it is always the same season, where moments remain fixed in time, a different time, inexpressible, directionless, which is neither space nor movement, but something like a fluid rhythm held constant by a pulsating transparency.

To my senses everything seems diluted, as if surrounded by a nimbus of subtlety. I merely guess at things now. That is how I manage to maintain my state of forgetting, fastened by shadowy threads to my enchantment.

I cannot hear my footsteps; I can barely see my gestures.

I have made of myself a twilight zone, I have dimmed all the lights.

I walk now as if through ruins.

I dream of towers and fanaticisms in flickering Levants.

I seem to myself a discoverer of worlds that never existed.

If I speak out loud, alone, my voice sounds as if it were filtered through damask and plush; at other times, it sounds more distant, as if heard through pink marble.

Beauty and Mystery have dissolved in my blood.

I have the clear impression that, at the moment of the crime, I cast off anything in myself that would make a noise at the feet of the corpse, and thus I freed myself and donned a sphinx-like individuality.

. . . .

10 February

What pomp surrounds me!
I am Byzantine hierarchies . . .
The Secret hovers inside me.
Who was she? *Who was her face?*
That woman had a life, her own existence. Many people saw her . . .
And she disappeared – she vanished through a stage trap door.
Doubtless, her lovers wept for her, and her family perhaps mourned her death.
Her death exists – but only I can swear to it!

. . . .
. . . .

They would have made a thorough search after the crime. In vain . . . I had left no traces behind me. It all happened as if in a legend.
I felt strangely confident; I never felt afraid that they might find me. Nor could I ever feel any fear that my crime would one day be punished. It was as if I had never committed it.
I did, however, stop reading the newspapers.
Once, though, in some city or other, my eye suddenly fell on the unfurled pages of a foreign newspaper that a passer-by was reading. I happened to see in large letters:

'The Mystery of the Villa of . . .'

At that moment, the stranger turned the page.
Could that be my Secret?
Yet the letters did not flicker and zig-zag in flames.

20 February

On certain astral mornings, I feel surrounded by a camellia-

50

like tenderness, a buoyant nostalgia for the flesh I only ever kissed on that one night, and for the frenetic tremblings of those aggressive breasts.

.   .   .   .

My mad love, how beautiful you must have been — an entirely new beauty, delicate in an utterly new way.

I killed you. I renounced you without even knowing you. That, you see, was the greatest proof of love.

28 February

I walk . . .

Diffuse oscillations of gentle, watery colours whirl around me, refreshing the air; multicoloured messages founder and are lost; vanishing blue sounds curl about me leaving a grey echo; filigree sensations circle me, scattering ivory harmonies.

Such is the landscape of subtlety that encloses me today, a landscape filled with a nostalgia for other worlds!

Everything darkens and flickers. Everything in me has become imponderable.

I know, I know. The fact is that since that Imperial Hour my life has become sensitive to other dimensions, and it is in those dimensions that my static life proceeds.

Moonlight celebrations!

XI

December 1912

For the first time since the miracle, I can see something of the reality about me. I am in Venice – a sensibility suited to my present state of soul.

The triumph did not paralyse me. On the contrary, ever since I found myself in the Shadow, I am more of a wanderer than ever, my uncertainty more intractable, more flexible and undulating.

I feel today, however, that it would be best if I stayed here, for ever, in this waterscape of a city, touched by Mystery.

However fluctuating my own agitation might be, nothing could be less uncertain than living in this blue city, set in Time like marble – constant, a place of stopped clocks, water clocks.

. . . .

Venice!

Oh, sacred city of fantasy, city brocaded with waking dreams, with magical penumbras – twilight rainbow, early-morning anemone . . .

The dull gold and bronze light ebbing from the evening squares, the salons of royal palaces, like mosaics, you might say, and the buildings round about like walls of sculptures, the shadows, swaying draperies.

I always saw Venice, as a whole, as if through a great polished window, in perspective, like an artificial panorama, theatrically lit.

I am quite different when I walk through its ancient atmosphere of crumpled lace – architectural, stubborn and forgotten.

And along the quays outside the palaces, on the city quays – like the mad son of the Doge perhaps – I lead processions of dead emigrants in splendid disguises.

Everything echoes, everything echoes around me. Smiles from other ages remain caught in the mirrors; in this room, the air still laughs: the murmurs of voluble parties held in other eras.

Colourful dances are etched into the wood panelling.

Ashen masks grow darker.

On the canals, the black gondolas glide by as they have always done. I cannot believe that they are propelled along by oars, but instead by the funeral marches played on the Cathedral organ.

In the distance, bell towers and cupolas look like mirages.

Everything inspires enchantment. Even the horizon is a filter . . .

Venice! Oh fairy-tale sleeping-Princess-city – hesitant lily, nostalgic mirage, fleeting as the new moon . . .

.   .   .   .

I must mingle myself with you for ever.

Today you seem even more tenuous, more pulsating.

My secret made you more so, increased your sense of Hiddenness . . .

I walk around your squares, I enter your palaces, I kneel in your basilica, and I realise that I am part of your architecture.

I go down splendid staircases, I lose myself in galleries . . .

I become fused with your monuments, your marble, your gilding, your secret rooms, your sinister bridges.

We conceal the same suggestions.

Who knows, perhaps once I was your soul!

XII

Yesterday, in the Florian, I had an unavoidable encounter.

Every so often, inoffensive but enervating reality does still ooze about me.

It was one of my rare acquaintances, an insignificant friend from Paris.

I did not even try to hide my contempt when he introduced me to his companion, an Englishman, Lord Ronald Nevile.

(Now why should I remember that name?)

28 January

It's odd. I begin, fearfully, to notice a change in my spirit. There is more clarity in me. I have once more begun to hear my own footsteps. Can I have deceived myself?

2 February

Every day, without fail, I meet my friend and Lord Ronald.

I must calm myself. It is merely these hours too redolent of truth that trouble my spirit.

I try to flee, but cannot. It is a small city.

And wherever I go, I always meet them. At least, I always meet Lord Ronald.

3 February

The Englishman's appearance is both interesting and bizarre.

In profile he seems very erect; he has a concise, aristocratic distinction about him.

He is tall and thin. His skin is very pale, almost golden on his long hands, but on his face it takes on a somnambulous pallor. His eyes are of an intense, cruel blue; they shine out with such a profound brilliance that they seem not to exist in the eyes themselves, but behind them, peeping out through his pupils as if through lenses.

His ambiguous mouth is just a thin gash with a feminine curve to it; the corners of his mouth form triangles that cast harsh shadows. His blond hair has a coppery sheen.

His arid face is completely cleanshaven and — a sinister detail this — his broad cheeks are etched with mysterious green lines.

The most singular thing about him, however, are his gestures, which are all very brittle, hard and cold, by that I mean, physically cold. Whenever Lord Ronald makes a gesture or alters his pose, I feel an actual sensation of cold — a withering, acid, silent cold.

His voice is no less extraordinary. He has a young, crystalline voice that sounds as if it were muffled by black crepes and silks.

His footsteps are of mother-of-pearl.

. . . .

5 February

The brightness has grown around me.

With every day that passes I feel the Miracle move farther off.

Gradually, the backdrop of artifice that hung me with Empires and Ambiguity is disappearing.

The shifting planes no longer roar about me, transposing Certainty.

My life seems to return to its former dimensions.

But I must be strong and not allow the magic to disappear.

All this stems from my contact with the ubiquitous foreigners. That must be the reason.

I must put an end to our meetings.

8 February

A waste of effort!

I determine to stay at home, I swear that I will not go out, then suddenly, why, I don't know, I am walking down streets, at random, yawning.

I know what awaits me. I always meet *him*.

But is it light, real light that surrounds me today? Isn't it, rather, something more dangerous that I cannot yet express — some dazzling thing, dense and remote?

12 February

Whatever I do, I cannot forget Lord Ronald.

What I find most disquieting is this ridiculous fact: whenever I think of his face, I always imagine him with that sleepy pallor and his skin etched with those strange, inexplicable green lines. *Those lines do not exist.* Whenever I am with him, I look in vain for them on his cheeks. I never actually saw them *and yet I cannot call his face to mind without those fantastic green lines.*

. . . .
. . . .

16 February

At last!

I can again enclose myself in the Mystery, return to the Marvel.

My friend and Lord Ronald left today.

I went with them to the station!

XIII

A purple enchantment has twined about me. Sullen macerations in golden, vacillating tones flow forth from me and bewitch both soul and body. I inhabit only half of my self; the incredible, brazen hand of a giant has me by the scruff of the neck. Stunned, I proceed in terrifying, complex, viscous directions.

A strange inverted force has fixed itself in my spirit and, subconsciously, that is what leads me. Nearby, a black thread unravels, guides me – imponderable but fatal.

How else can I explain this disconcerting error?

I had decided, with absolute conviction, to stay in Venice for some considerable time, to immerse myself in indecision and adornment and thus make my inward journey back to my jealous ecstasy-Statue.

I had, in fact, uttered a cry of relief, like a madman, when I saw the train disappear, carrying that stranger far away, a banal incident, but one which my senses, nonetheless, secretly understood.

Free, alone, I would doubtless become whole again, absolute in my tenuousness, glorious in my pride.

However, one morning, a few days later, without thinking, without noticing (*without noticing*, that is exactly how it was), I packed my bags, I think, and ran to the station where I jumped on board an express train . . . without even knowing my destination, although I myself had bought the ticket.

The most ridiculous, most terrifying thing was that, despite all this, I did know – ah, deep down, how well I knew – exactly where I was going, why I was going there and what lay behind my sudden departure.

I got out at the station in Nice. On the platform someone was waiting for me: Lord Ronald. He ran to meet me and casually took my arm, as if he had known that I was going to arrive on that train. He took me to his hotel.

I had written to no one about my plans to leave Italy.

XIV

27 February

More than ever I feel as if I were slipping through a series of grey veils. The spell continues, but it is different now, rebellious, more sphinxlike perhaps, yet aggressive, never soothing.

The days pass and I have the bizarre impression that they are I and I am the time in which they live.

Picaresque, yellow, triangular lights glitter before my eyes which are focused implacably on the distance, on two irritating points of light, dirty red in colour.

At other times, especially in the tremulous hours before falling asleep, I see picture frames dancing before me, just the frames, ovals with no portraits in them.

Sleep has become for me a physical illness. I am not tormented by remorseful nightmares, on the contrary, I sleep deeply, densely, and it is the very weight of my sleep that afflicts and crushes me. It takes me until late afternoon to recover from my waking.

1 March

Thanks to my extraordinary companion, I find that within a matter of a few short days, I have become part of a great circle of acquaintances.

Lord Ronald is received everywhere and is treated with the greatest respect, although for some reason that respect seems grudging.

He spends money like water. Everyone adores him, everyone knows him. Or rather, when he passes, everyone looks at him; people point him out and mutter.

Yet he seems to know no one, even the people he introduces to me.

I often accompany him. I am staying at the same hotel. First thing in the morning, he comes to my room. We eat at the same table. We spend the days together. So much so that I have not a moment to myself. Sometimes his continual presence irritates me.

On the other hand, he could not be kinder. He seems to have great respect for me. He asks about my work. He talks all the time, but there are sudden gaps in his sentences.

He refuses to let me pay for anything. Sometimes his attentiveness vexes me.

. . . .

The centre of our social life is the Marchesa de Santo-Stefano who lives in a luxurious villa in Cimiez. She entertains there every night, in the most lavish fashion. I have made many acquaintances there. Oddly enough, it is always Lord Ronald who introduces me to people.

The Marchesa de Santo-Stefano is an extraordinarily beautiful woman. I have heard it said that her husband is paralysed and never leaves his castle in the Abruzzi. I do not know if that is true, but I have never seen her husband. Her salon is frequented by the cream of society.

2 March

There are no pavilions in the gardens of the Marchesa's villa.

4th March

I am standing in the gilded rooms. The couples whirl by in a thousand colours. The waltzes are like roses. And yet I am increasingly shaken by shudders of fear. I tremble all over. My teeth chatter. I make every effort to hide my disquiet from others.

I walk through different rooms. I have an impression of golden bridges opening up as I pass. There is a sound like the rapid beating of strips of glass; I feel as if that glass were about to break . . .

My brain zigzags. I keep close to the walls so as not to fall over.

Lord Ronald has not yet arrived. He had arranged to meet me that night at the Marchesa's villa.

What is it that I fear? His arrival? That is a possibility. It seems to me, though, that it is his absence that makes me tremble.

59

Where is he now? What will he be doing now?

And that thought torments me as if, far from my side, he could do me harm, or worse.

At last he arrives. I calm down a little. He seems paler than usual. His hair is a different colour. His footsteps have a different sheen to them . . .

6 March

How is it possible to suffer so much?

And why, my God, why?

What has my life to do with that of this stranger?

Nothing binds me to him. *No one binds me to him.* I am free, perfectly free. If I wanted to leave tomorrow, even today, I could. No one stops me doing so. That is perhaps the reason why I stay.

I really do not know what attracts me to this man. It is terrible. I cannot forget him for a moment. I cannot forget that I am with him even in his presence. When you are with another person, you forget their presence, *their presence is natural*, but that does not happen when I am with Lord Ronald, as if only by virtue of some miracle was it possible for the two of us to be there together, face to face.

I have less and less idea where I am going.

I have a sense of something ending, of ancient, purple-tinged silver.

8 March

Who is this man? Who is he?

I know virtually nothing about him.

I want to find out at all costs.

But I dare not ask him any direct questions, even though, given our close friendship, that would seem only natural.

Up until now, I have only dared ask the friend from Paris who originally introduced us. I stood there petrified. He said lightly that he had met him by chance, on the train journey from Rome to Venice, during which they had shared the same compartment.

Sometimes, I still try to persuade myself that everything is perfectly simple, perfectly real, that there is no mystery about this person, however sinister he may seem.

The illusion is short-lived.

I have started to notice that his frequently broken sentences are interspersed now and then with incoherent, disconnected words, words that are rigid and dead, words that stand out in mid-sentence like so much dross: they grate and crackle like fallen leaves.

What I saw tonight only increased my fear and horror, my terrible doubts.

We were dining at the house of the Marchesa de Santo-Stefano. She introduced us to some guests that we did not know.

And I heard, I distinctly heard the Marchesa introduce him as 'Lord *Roland* Nevile'.

He did not even protest.

True, in English it is easy to confuse *Roland* and *Ronald*. Even so, it seemed an unnatural mistake for her to make.

It would seem easy enough to ask my friend and thus clear up the matter. I even tried to do so, but I couldn't. When I prepared to ask him about the mistake, I started trembling all over and a seal of fire closed my lips.

So now, I am not even certain of his name. Where am I going, my God, where am I going?

Yesterday, after lunch, we were alone on the hotel terrace.

He suddenly started talking to me about feelings of mystery and fear, asking me about my own experiences.

The conversation drifted on quite plausibly, then, suddenly, he gave a loud laugh and cried out almost crazily:

'So my friend . . . have you by any chance . . . my friend . . . ever experienced such a moment of glory? . . . Have you ever slept in a great deserted palace . . . in the dark . . . and before sleeping, by sheer force of concentration . . . by pure will-power . . . have you peopled empty houses with figures . . . in the darkness . . . terrifying figures . . . *kesskrsss* . . . mutilated . . . guttural . . . rustling . . . It's beautiful, beautiful! . . . Never do it! . . . There is a danger that, if they become too real, the chrysalids will hurl themselves upon you . . . and crush you . . . slime-green and twisted . . . twisted . . . *rrrr* . . .'

I looked at him, astonished. A sticky nimbus surrounded him.

I do not know how many hours we remained there after that – in silence, face to face . . .

. . . .

XV

With every night, the sense I have that something is about to end grows stronger – it has taken on reddish inflections now. I even believe, extravagantly, that I am no longer I, but merely an embalmed version of myself.

I spin and turn amongst polychrome fluids.

I am merely a series of shipwrecks adorned with black flags. Yet, in the midst of this sorcery and of my increasingly electric fear, the shimmering caprice that colours my being is fading painfully, albeit transparently, sourly, coolly.

Ah, I heard it today; it does not just trouble me, it torments me too, for his voice is beginning to have the same effect on my nerves as a rasp on metal, a bony shiver like that produced by strong acids or ice on our teeth.

There is another strange thing, we conduct all our conversations in French, but then I barely know his language. It is clear, though, that he is not French, yet he does not have an English accent. Not a trace of one. Nor does he have any other recognisable foreign accent: Spanish, Italian, Russian, German, Oriental. He does not have an accent. You can tell that he is a foreigner, but not by his accent, by something else, something more obscure, lost.

I have only ever heard him speak French – *even with his compatriots.*

His voice reminds me of a shadow.

In fact, everything about that man reminds me of a shadow . . .

· · · · · · · · · · · · · · · · · ·

XVI

Oh, sepulchral fear!

I am lost. I can have no illusions now, I am hopelessly lost.

It happened last night when, suddenly, a flash of light illuminated his face; for the first time, mad with fear, unable to suppress a scream, I realised that the subtle, gentle, unmistakable curve of his chin is exactly like that of the dead woman *. . . all that I saw of the masked woman's face.*

My God, what is going to happen to me, forever in this man's company, now that any hopes I had of escaping him lie shattered?

It occurred to me today – rather confusedly – that *he, not I,* might have committed my crime.

It is true, absolutely true: something horrible, something incomprehensible chains me to this man. I do not yet know what it is . . .

I live in constant torment. I am my own anxiety. I find my own terror even in the faces of the people who talk to me, in the eyes of passers-by.

· But what a victory too! My pain has become intertwined with Mystery, it sculpts me into something unknown, spreads chaos in me.

Great viscous cables, capillary filaments made out of a purplish substance twist and twine picaresquely before my eyes. And in my moments of greatest fear I feel, physically feel, as if tiny trains were travelling through my soul, pulled along on a string, and that my guts had become a complex system of glass and ivory wheels, tiny multicoloured discs, rusty clock hands – everything spins madly, like some aimless clockwork mechanism.

From time to time, from amongst the toothed wheels, the

sharp tones of electric bells ring out, minuscule lightbulbs come on, circuits open and close, and, even more ridiculous, spouts of coloured alcohol appear, unexpectedly, from where I do not know.

I walk the streets, feeling empty, astonished, driving this ridiculous mechanism around inside me, a trifle, a child's toy, a toy that fills me with fear, a fear shot through with sarcastic laughter.

My nerves grate like bones.

. . . .
. . . .

Why should I be sorry though? My triumph, however wretched, is assured.

I have what I wanted: the Shadow.

27 March

Every day I grow closer to Lord Ronald. For it is with him – imprisoned by his eyes – that my torment diminishes slightly.

Yesterday he spoke to me about his estate in Scotland, about an immense castle set amongst woods.

He spoke in very sombre tones when he talked about his lands. His throat seemed to be veiled in shadow, perhaps the shadow cast by the ancient trees in his forests.

Listening to him, a visual memory came to me of the Principality I had imagined once before.

29 March

The fog closes in on me, a fog of storms, presaging thunder.

In the distance, I can vaguely make out a shadow advancing on me – a great shadow, sharp, triangular, with sudden vertices.

30 March

My obsession with picture frames has returned, tarnished gold frames which now, however, contain only canvases, canvases with no portraits painted on them.

I make a final attempt to disengage myself, not so much in order to flee from madness – though, who knows – as to be able to assess the strength of my Mystery.

I try in vain to throw some light on it. In all of this there are tiny certainties – real, artless – that merely confirm to me what is doubtful, lend it greater significance.

I am right! Both the Error and the Shadow exist in me.

At the same time, I foresee that the most extraordinary, the greatest, the most sombre part, has not yet been revealed to me.

We will wait and see.

As for me, I am finished. I am living through my final days. The only thing I do not know is how long those final days will last.

2 April

There are traces of green on the empty canvases in their golden frames.

4 April

Tender memories of childhood rise up in me, tinging my inner world with pink. My sleep is less troubled; I sleep as children do, with the sheets pulled up over my head.

But a new fear assails me: the fear of moonlight. I curse it without knowing why I do so.

6 April

The shudders overwhelming me all came together in a single sharp point.

8 April

For two nights now I have dreamed of great fires amongst ruined buildings.

9 April

Portraits of complete strangers have appeared in the gilt frames.

. . . .
. . . .
. . . .
. . . .

16 April

At last, I know everything!

So that is why I cursed the moonlight . . .

The truth was revealed to me yesterday, when the two of us were talking and we paused beneath a shaft of moonlight.

I do not know how I guessed it, but, suddenly, the mystery revealed itself to me in scarlet certainty, illuminated in torrents of light – fatal, irreducible.

It could not be otherwise. He was bound to be linked in some way to my secret.

LORD RONALD IS THE MASKED WOMAN'S DEATH.

XVII

The 'end', then, has come – in black velvets and crepes.
I no longer tremble.
I have slipped out of my inner world.
The wheels and clock hands have stopped moving inside me, the bells have fallen silent, the lights have all gone out.
I know where I am going now.
Why should I try to flee from him?
From now on, my footsteps can only be his footsteps.
I have plunged in and there is no return.
I have reached the great Shadow.
But where will we go, where?
That will be the final Enigma.
Because we have to leave, we have to.

. . . .

. . . .

In the secret frames, still at last (before, they were always trembling), the portraits of strangers have become *his* portrait – uniform, green. That too was fated to happen.

18 April

Yet, what nameless terror!

19 April

Yesterday we were supposed to dine at the Marchesa de Santo-Stefano's villa.
At the last moment, though, *he* decided that we should stay at the hotel and, today, on the Promenade des Anglais, every one of our acquaintances ignored us, amongst them, the friend from Paris who had introduced us.
Lord Ronald seems not to have noticed.
I continue to progress from abyss to abyss.

20 April

He went out at dawn.

I was alone in my room when the maître-d'hotel called me.

He told me that a foreign woman, in a state of great agitation, was looking for the PRINCE; she had to speak to him urgently . . . it was a matter of life or death. If he wasn't in, she begged that his friend might hear what she had to say instead.

We hurried to the reception room.

The stranger had gone.

. . . .

The Prince!

21 April

Yesterday, the Marchesa de Santo-Stefano committed suicide. Lord Ronald warned me at lunch that we would be leaving today. We will take the train from the station in Villefranche.

It is a different force now that drags me along.

. . . .

. . . .

Her death, *her* death, *her* death!

XVIII

We did not cross the sea. The journey was all by train. I cannot say how many days it lasted.

The express train hurtled along, stopping at only very few stations, stations I could not see when I peered out through the window.

Feverish with enchantments, distracted by omens, I was troubled by the feeling that the train was travelling not horizontally, but vertically, crumbling into clouds that sifted it — and my body — through narrow pores.

Stripped of any inner world, exiled from it for ever, I felt things only very distantly (and very vaguely), still less can I describe now what I felt then. My life, my feelings, my memories were enacted only in *his* eyes.

We sat face to face all the time.

In the depths of night, we arrived at a huge station, this time real and visible. Yet it was a most peculiar station, deserted, with not even a station master. At least I saw no station master, no soldiers, no porters.

A large, sleek, grey car was waiting for us. We got in. The car travelled for some hours, even faster than the express train. During the journey, we exchanged not a word. I think we never again exchanged a word.

The night was deep and dense, so densely dark that it resisted the passage of the car itself.

At last, the car stopped. Everything around us was still plunged in darkness. Meanwhile, nearby, you could feel the shadow of a great turreted building — you could not see it, you could just sense something emanating from on high.

We got out. We walked along the paths of what I imagine was a garden. At the top of some stairs, very long stairs made out of black marble, a lackey in a white uniform was holding an ancient candlestick, the candle seemed barely alight.

We went in to a room with an immensely high ceiling, where a long table was set for many guests. Here too the lights were very dim.

We sat down, but no one came.

We drank sherry. I bit into a fruit.

He had disappeared.

The same erect, silent lackey guided me along endless stairways and long corridors to the great vaulted room where I am writing these pages, by the flickering light of a fat wax candle . . .

.   .   .   .

.   .   .   .

My God, where am I, where am I? Where have they brought me . . . what are they going to do to me . . . what do they want of me . . . what will they make me do?

My soul still retains some vestiges of fear, so drear is the night, so complete the enigma.

My scalp prickles in anticipation.

The moments become iron statues.

.   .   .   .

.   .   .   .

I look around. I peer into the darkness.

Shadows dance about the room: slow, heavy, solid shadows that flutter winglessly, shadows that the sad flame of the candle fails to banish.

The bed waits for me at the far side of the room – silent, unknowable – beneath purple damask curtains, linen sheets, Indian quilts.

To the right stands a large wardrobe with a mirror. I tremble, I shake with foreboding. The mirror is broken, cracked from top to bottom.

There are doors, doubtless opening on to attics, doors I am too frightened to open, just as I am afraid to lift the massive bar keeping the great window at the other end of the room firmly shut.

A cathedral-like silence fills the corridors outside, fills the whole palace.

The room has a damp atmosphere, thick with the smell of treachery, aggression.

I make a sudden decision.

I lift the heavy bar . . . I open the window.

A gust of wind, of wind and of something less fluid, beats against my face, blows out the candle.

I lean out. There is nothing but darkness. I can sense, though, that there is a steep drop below me.

I must be in a tower.

Far off, the sea roars . . . perhaps . . . the sea, or else the murmur of forests. It is a sombre, opaque clamour which, at a distance, could as easily be the sound of birches as the sea.

What lies before me, below me?

Not a single star shines . . . a forgotten light . . .

But it is clear that there is only immense space plunging down and all about me.

It is as if I were suspended in the blue, as though I were in the basket of a hot air balloon.

I spend long minutes at the window.

Always the same darkness, the same murmuring . . .

. . . .

. . . .

I make one last effort at lucidity.

No one ever experienced more thrilling moments.

A solemn secret.

Where am I? What exists around me? *What does not exist?* What happened yesterday? What will happen tomorrow?

I have embraced my astral work. What more can I hope for?

I fall on to the bed.

And only now, in the darkness, do I realise that on the walls around me there are frescos, great sombre frescos, masterworks of chiaroscuro. I feel their figures projected on to my body – in damp relief.

. . . .

. . . .

Will he be sleeping too?

. . . .

. . . .

In order to write, I relight the candle.

Damnation! Let us dream no more!

We must wake up and save ourselves.

No matter how, no matter what, no matter who, everything else will disappear and I will be forced to recognise myself, for I am alive, I am still alive.

I feel my body . . . it is all there. My heart is beating.

It is time to save myself. Illusion, illusion!

Let us not dream, then, let us assure ourselves of Victory. Only a wretch would let such a triumph slip by out of mere doubt.

Soon, day will dawn. And I will know, I will know, I will know!

Anything but this.

Even if I could be certain that he is the Prince.

What, waste all this dead gold, let all this Shadow crumble into ruins? No, no! On the contrary. Plunge into it once and for all, mingle with it, be it, be it, whatever the cost!

What ermine-white ecstasies! Crucified moonlight . . . sphinxes of the deep . . .

. . . .

. . . .

Then everything fades before this Marvel. So it is this that I must fix in silver intrigues. Fix it, yes, set it in jade – slithering opium . . . prophetic opulence . . .

. . . .

. . . .

With me are these pages from my red notebook, also secret, entrusted to the Heights . . .

. . . .

. . . .

The lancet wind blew the casement wide open.

The shadows grew, and now they parade in triumph, a docile, rustling funeral procession.

In the solitary corridors, images of violet mist progress inevitably towards this apotheosis . . . just as brocades sway in the rooms next door, gilding clinks in the air, tapestries fall, draperies draw back . . .

. . . .

. . . .

Cortèges pass by . . .

I am a funeral ceremony in Memphis . . .

. . . .

. . . .

   . . . Ample and unfathomable, the window stands open to
the night – a velvet lake, the veiled orchid of my Desire . . .

. . . .

. . . .

. . . .

   Go, like a lion – in one leap!
   The great leap . . . into the Secret . . . into the Shadow . . .
for ever . . . and ah, into the Gold . . . Gold . . . Gold!

Lisbon and Paris, April–September 1914

RESURRECTION

For Vitoriano Braga

Resurrection

I

Inácio de Gouveia was certainly not unhappy any more. We grow used to everything, we grow tired of everything, and the fact is that whilst the novelist had not exactly adapted himself to his misfortune, he had at least grown sick of it. It no longer interested him. He had plumbed its depths, he had explored it thoroughly, he had embraced it with admirable intensity in his works. He had ridden his pain through flailing gold, he had whistled it up through distant, magical clouds, across the broad expanses of other worlds, other colours, other sounds . . . But the abundant spring had at last run dry. Not a drop of that wealth had escaped his sacred hands. Why peer any more into his own soul when he knew and had probed every inch? He had never re-read a book, however sublime; he would never re-read his own soul either. Weary of his pain, he had spurned it, put it behind him, bored and perhaps saddened too, for his torment had, after all, been so beautiful, so proud . . .

He had overstepped the bounds, the great boundary. He had disentangled himself almost effortlessly, and now there was no doubt about it, he was happy, for did not a path of silver stretch out before him? Assured of his own genius, his imagination stuffed with marvellous longings, confident that he would be able to immortalise them in gold and fire, his share of life's riches was growing. It was also a source of great bitterness. However, there is a price for every victory and, given the clarity of that victory, it was a small price to pay . . .

That was why the artist was now taking a cold, hard look at himself, bored with his misfortunes, accustomed to them. His former flounderings had been nothing more in the end than a soul's struggle against an infinite number of golden things, the struggle of an egotistical soul trying to drive out all that richness because only inferior beings live contented lives . . . Ultimately, though, determined and courageous, he had surrendered to his glorious fate.

Looking back, Inácio could not even remember his past life very clearly. It rose up from amongst his pains and his pleasures as if it had been lived by someone else. In his memories there were inevitably lacunae and errors too, no doubt. Certain episodes, which he still occasionally evoked, had certainly not evolved as he remembered them now – no, he himself, his present-day self, could not, in fact, have been the protagonist of those events. It even occurred to him that perhaps he was confused and that the events he recalled had, in fact, happened to someone else, a close friend, perhaps, who had told him about them one night, in confidence.

He experienced a most singular split in himself. Not that he had ever come face to face with his double. What afflicted him was more complex than that. Inácio only encountered this split in the past. When he recollected certain times, certain episodes he had lived through, he was immediately gripped by that troubling, mysterious feeling: that it was not he who had experienced them, but projections of himself – projections that would still exist in Time, in stylised form. He had a real sense that the red car which, one night, had carried him and a certain painted young woman through Paris' monumental streets was still driving through that same festive city, zigzagging down the same streets, carrying the same passengers, still kissing each other hard on the mouth, their fingers entwined, the same caresses . . . It seemed to him impossible that it should be otherwise – he could even hear the carriage slipping by . . . in distant, sombre, richly transparent tones.

In the same way, he could not believe that the self he was in another instant, some fifteen years before, had not remained in his father's spacious room on the night that his grandmother died, surrounded by all his family, eating cakes, in winter, muffled up in a white, woollen shawl . . .

Whenever he recalled the most painful scenes from his past life – or the sweetest and saddest, or the happiest – he was always seized by a piercing sense of longing and nostalgia, but not a nostalgia for the scene he had evoked or for the people with whom he had experienced it, rather – in one last flash of egotism – merely a nostalgia for the person he was at that moment, fixed for ever in time, and which the artist would never feel or see again, because one cannot go back.

Other bizarre sensations occasionally shook him, which provided further proof that his past life had not, in effect, been lived by him.

Thus, a few days ago, he and a group of friends had visited a park on the outskirts of the city – traditional, redolent of romanticism – a place he had not been to for a long time . . . The paths were broad and shaded by huge trees. There were flowerbeds thick with flowers, there were lakes and the occasional gentle hillock scattered with rustic, stone benches. At the far end stood a great palace, a long, weighty structure, the windows closed, the glass cut into small panes in the old style. An atmosphere of antiquity, a sad, grey poetry, wrapped about everything – a vague melancholy that slipped past one clothed in velvets, in silks embroidered with multicoloured flowers, splendid, albeit faded by time. And a soft murmur of the dances of yesteryear whirled tenuously by like light husks: kisses snatched in corners, hoop skirts bobbing pinkly in the air; low-cut satin bodices in which round, pearly breasts rested as if in nests, unfastened ribbons, blushes, locks of dead hair, lost letters, nosegays, elegies, forgotten perfumes . . . Werther, Antony, *la Dame aux camélias* . . .

Finding himself once more in this melancholy setting, the artist thought back nostalgically to the last time he had walked along those romantic paths . . . Halfway across a hill he was assailed by a memory: he had sat for a long time there on one of the stone benches . . . And a painful, golden, evanescent sadness had penetrated him then; he could remember it perfectly – doubtless the sadness of some love affair, tender, affectionate, that had ended a few days before. He had been all rapture, white nostalgia, resignation . . . And it was that melodious hour that he sweetly evoked today. Although he knew exactly what his state of mind had been at the time, he could not remember the events that had provoked it. He sought in vain through his memory for that sad love affair. He was sure, absolutely sure, that he had never experienced it. How then could he remember those unreal feelings of longing? Probably because it had not been him who, one April evening, years before, had sat sorrowfully in that garden, but *another* who would possess some of the same qualities, another *self* whom the artist had fleetingly inhabited, feeling his current state of mind (the same state of mind he was remembering today), but not knowing what had provoked it, because he had only been that other self for an instant, and thus could not know what his past had been.

At a different time in his life, long past, when a certain woman had unexpectedly become his lover, he would often walk in glory by her side along the city streets and, since their relationship was not an established one, he would be gripped by a violent desire to possess her that very night, in order to feel certain that he had already possessed her . . . and only the following day would he walk beside that splendid woman – at whose passing other men would stop and stare – confident of his triumph.

. . . .

Yes, Inácio de Gouveia really had no reason to complain about his life. His lot was the best possible one, the most golden of fates. His life might lack tenderness, but what did that matter if, in its place, there was such opulence? There were no fingers to entwine, no lips to kiss, no affection or love – a multitude of violet, smiling, tender, insignificant acts. In compensation there were great bundles of newspapers, the sacred volumes filling his library and, above all, his work, his elusive work, rustling with chimaera, ecstatic with gold, anointed with uncertainty, tigerish with pride, leonine with longing . . .

. . . .

His books . . . the bundles of newspapers . . .

Sitting alone there at his table in the large restaurant, on that luminous Christmas Day, both books and newspapers were his best companions. His lot in life could well be summed up in those foreign newspapers, some of which spoke of his latest novel, and in the book with yellow covers that he had received from Paris that morning, from a French friend and fellow novelist.

The next table was occupied by a bourgeois family, modest and quiet, doubtless unused to dining in restaurants: a father, a mother and a daughter. The parents were already old, the daughter was about twenty, slender, delicate, pale and pure. The writer drifted into following their banal conversation: references to their delightful stroll in the countryside that day, plans for the next Sunday, vague allusions to other members of the family, ingenuous comments about each new dish brought by the waiter, household items that they needed to buy . . . The parents were doubtless extremely attached to that one daughter, belated proof of their sincere albeit common-place love.

Listening to them, looking at them, the artist increasingly felt something verging on regret. At least it was warm inside their lives, and it was always so cold out in the street . . .

But then he reacted indignantly, a wave of pride washed over him. He belonged to quite another Race, another World – he was so much greater than they were!

And, in the end, he was left sitting opposite the poor creatures, his tenderness in ashes. He had for a moment focused his regal thoughts on them, and for that moment had even dreamed of bringing himself down to their level; he had anointed them with himself. One day he might perhaps touchingly immortalise them on one of his admirable pages.

At other times, however, Inácio de Gouveia would draw back from that position and think quite differently about his unhappiness. He was deceiving himself; the fact that it no longer existed might mean that his pain was even greater. He no longer suffered, but then he would worry that perhaps this was merely the beginning of the 'end' – the limit, complete saturation, irremediable sterility. Before, in effect, he had still enjoyed moments of superb, tawny, tremulous joy when he looked into himself, growing drunk on his own inspired pain, and then leaping to his feet, aflame. Now, knowing himself through and through, sick of his misfortune, he had grown indifferent to it; that is, he had grown indifferent to himself, and he felt a remote fear that this would be followed by the drying up of his inspiration.

Now, the artist knew himself by heart, like a book. Even if he had wanted to re-read himself, he could not. When he concentrated his thoughts, he could no longer follow the thread of his own reflections on himself. When we are dead tired, we cannot speak coherently, our tongue grows thick, we fumble for words. The same thing happened to him as regards his own thoughts about himself: *it was as if he were tired of those thoughts*.

Then another wave would carry him back to his original idea: that his satiety with his torment was a price worth paying for his soul's freedom, since he was definitely no longer unhappy. And his fears about the imminent death of his genius? Pure madness. On the contrary, putting his pain behind him, his genius could only grow – distinct, hovering sublimely above life, finding freedom in that greater victory.

For the rest, whatever happened, even if he were still bleeding from those wounds, the fact was that his longings, his torments would merely be further motives for glory. Being able to suffer, to feel intensely, to roar, to burn – could there be a more certain victory?

For example, one great motive for pride was his ability still to feel his love for Paris, attenuated by nostalgia and distance, whilst not knowing whether he would ever experience it again . . .

'Paris!'

The great avenues, the tumultuous boulevards, and, at night, the Seine, flowing beneath its heraldic bridges, shimmering with a thousand lights.

La Cité . . . Notre Dame de Paris . . . the tragic cathedral launching itself on the air, fearsome, pale with exorcisms, shivering with icy shadows, brooding on mysteries; the fantastic church – its stone outline, the skeleton of a soul – marvellously tracing a slender, sonorous movement, damp, translucent, a rhythmic flow, rising fleetingly up into the sky only to disappear into the ash–grey heights.

Inside were the vaults and astonishing naves – a mixture of marvel and awe at the light filtering in through the images in the stained-glass windows.

'Avenue de l'Opéra!'

That European street, the street of all races, broad, crammed with traffic, resonant with life, huge with colour, brilliant with activity!

The Place Vendôme at five o'clock, rue de la Paix all satins and emeralds – princesses with gleaming red nails – gold, veils, laces, feathers, sables – courtesans and actresses, the painted idols of our time, fragile, sharp, spirited . . .

The Montmartre of narcotics and nocturnal celebrations – sequins and filigree amongst the rabble – dances from Andalusia, songs from Italy – the elusive intoxication of champagne, insomnia silvered with scarlet kisses . . .

Romantic gardens redolent with love and tradition . . .

Royal palaces, stairways, arches . . .

Plinths, columns and obelisks . . .

The setting sun burning on misty horizons . . .

Distances of steel towers, tall factory chimneys – bridges, scaffolding, cranes, gears – titanic mills, the whistle of trains – the vibrations of Progress, the murmurs of Tomorrow . . .

'Aristocratic Paris!'

'The Paris of the *bas-fonds*!'

'The Paris of La Ruche!'

Paris, Paris! Orgiastic and solemn, monumental and frivolous . . .

.   .   .   .

.   .   .   .

For Inácio, living alone in that great city with no one to kiss was the same as living with an elegant, tender, boldly physical companion. Whereas now, in Lisbon, even if he had the best of lovers, he would feel just as lonely, removed from all kisses, all kindness.

Paris evoked for him a great salon brilliantly lit – subtle perfumes, zebrine moons, intense, whirling colours . . .

Lisbon was a narrow, yellow house, old parents who refuse to let their daughters out in the streets, oil lamps, harsh voices, the smell of lavender . . .

And it was his great love of Paris so lucidly felt that had saved his life more than a year before.

For no particular reason, he was going through an extreme crisis, desolate with anguish. He felt powerless, dead to all enthusiasms, his brain turned to water, his soul shattered – so much so that he had resolved to put a bullet through his heart . . . But he had been in Paris at the time and he remembered so well the circular wave of triumphal pride that escaped him one afternoon, sweeping away that black idea.

It had happened in the Place Blanche. He was with a friend, a young Cubist painter wearing a fur cap. They were standing opposite the Moulin Rouge, talking.

The painter was chattering on about some banal event, he, barely listening, was absorbed by the atmosphere surrounding them.

All about him was the joy of a fairground. The red lights on the windmill of the famous music hall were gently starting to turn, hawkers were calling out the names of the evening papers, there was a merry-go-round nearby, operating to the hoarse sound of a barrel organ, heavily made-up young girls were strolling in the twilight, their faces flirtatiously averted. It was the concentrated essence of Paris in festive mood, traditional Paris, the Paris that all we foreigners, in our various lands, have dreamed of ever since we were children.

And before that futile, rather cheap scene, Inácio had suddenly felt, as if in a hallucination, that Paris was inside him: piercing him, washing his soul, illuminating him with a thousand lights, spewing out breasts, overturning champagne, spilling forth gold . . .

. . . .

. . . .

A parallel vanity flowed through him today, far from him, painfully nostalgic – and why? Because his sadness had but one source: in mundane Lisbon there were no sumptuously dressed women wearing audaciously revealing clothes out of the latest fashion journals, nor were there honking cars cramming the avenues; there were no museums or vast libraries, no nude bodies in the finales at the theatre, and the cafés were empty; lovers did not walk along holding hands or stop to kiss in the middle of the street; one was not surrounded by magnificent buildings, great palaces, huge department stores, towers, churches, heraldic columns!

Feeling all this, aware of all this, he was filled by a child-like pride, he was almost happy . . . he could see himself hovering high up above the inferior, anonymous crowd elbowing their way past him.

He had always loathed that throng of normality, ordinary people, contented people, who do not have a state of mind and who, no sooner have they entered this life, have adapted to society's uses and customs, to its preconceived ideas.

'The golden mean?'

How lazy!

Is the alternative then madness?

Of course, madness – only sensible people are bad and stupid!

Madness had always seemed to him a consecration. 'To be mad,' he declared, 'is to have a little of God in your soul.'

Besides, his heart did not go out only to madmen, to those who had genius enough to burn, to make the great leap, to plunge into the abyss; no, it went out, with a kind of desperate violence, to all criminals – murderers, thieves, arsonists – to anyone capable of subterfuge, revolt, longing, those who never bowed the knee, who kicked against the pricks . . . His love for these was as great as the scorn he spat out at the others, the castrati, worthy, commonsensical people, who never flew into a rage, who never dared to offend anyone, those who always speak softly and listen intently to what others say and who never thrill to childish enthusiasms, frivolous affections, but are just, honest, sincere, coherent in all their actions!

Scoundrels! Scoundrels!

II

Unhappiness . . .

It was true that, in moments of melancholy, Inácio de Gouveia still felt a faint, intoxicating pain because he lacked certain tenuous things of which, at times, he dimly dreamed. And it hurt him not to have them. But then, looking deeper into himself, he saw how unjustified his bitter feelings were. Those small things that he lacked did not really exist for him, rather, if you touched them, they would dissolve into infinite disillusion, utter disenchantment, because they were not at all what he was seeking through them . . .

By nature excitable, violently sexual, he had, since childhood, imagined naked bodies, red-gold embraces, iridescent ecstasies, a thousand magical, sensual pleasures that mingled water and sun . . . Later, when he could at last move convulsively above those bodies so often evoked on sleepless nights, how disillusioned those embraces had left him . . .

'Possession?'

A great nausea, the bile that succeeded the golden orgasm. Damp, sticky things, evil-smelling, repugnant. What beauty was there to be found in such sexual contacts? Beauty . . . could there be anything more ridiculous, more vile? Ah, the horror of sex – hideous cartilages, wrinkled, hilarious . . . And the sighs of copulating couples, the sweaty, picaresque contractions . . . How shameful! How could a sensitive soul bear such things?

He often thought: 'What an incomparable triumph it must be for those who, without the ignominy of sex, enjoy a different kind of orgasm, unreal, undulating and translucent, indescribably golden, just pressing lips to lips, or not even that, an astral meeting of two distant bodies, purified, formless and free!'

. . . .

It was not only the physical side of love that disgusted Inácio, he found the emotional side equally repellent. He had put this to the test only a short time before.

It had happened in Paris. One night, by chance, he found

86

himself in a small theatre near Montmartre, yawning with tedium. Then suddenly, amongst the performers in that idiotic review, his eyes fell upon a half-naked dancer, a splendid figure, strikingly beautiful: a wild, muscular body, small, tremulous breasts, dark red lips, wide eyes, black hair – and her flesh, her luminous flesh, golden brown, born to be covered in emeralds. It could well have been – oh, excelsior! – the triumphal body of Salomé.

And caught in the dark rapture of that marvel, watching her, open-mouthed, his imaginative brain immediately thought to write a novel about her – a rather cheap novel, alas.

A sudden yearning for tenderness came over him, for one of those sweet, blond episodes which, at least, unlace the soul and hang out pink veils about our life.

Yes, across café tables, how often had he envied men waiting for some gentle female companion, who would arrive, light, modest, affable, whilst he stayed there, always obstinately alone. So many contradictions. Despite his feelings of repugnance, he had still not managed definitively to renounce the things that other men had, and which must, in truth, be tinged with such soft colours . . .

He did not seek out his first lover; she came to him. Nor had he possessed her, she alone possessed him. The others had been so few, so distant . . .

Confronted by that aurora of a body, remembering his jealousies, his disappointments, he began, instead, to weave a plot . . .

He himself blushed to remember that wretched story, he could not even believe it had happened.

It was like this:

The following day he sent the dancer a splendid copy of his latest work, accompanied by a letter written, in deliberately romantic fashion, in the Pavillon d'Armenonville, a foolish letter which he justified thus: the dancer had provoked in him such a sense of beauty – of beauty alone, he did not want her to think he was in love – that he, the artist, the divinity who sought everywhere only glorious emotions, had felt impelled to thank her for the sublime, aesthetic vision that her body had given him, to express a desire to approach a little closer to the marvel – he did not at any time mention her. He sent her the book – which the enchantress would not, anyway, be able to read, written as it was in a foreign tongue – so that her slender, painted, troubling fingers would at least touch something of his (his name, his words, that letter), and one day, much later, after long years had passed, her withered hands might find it, who knows, amongst some old papers. And then, she would distantly recall him, that is, whatever happened, he would become a character in her existence.

There was more, for – sweet glory! – from then on, from that evening when he had written to her, he, the stranger, having admired her as she danced naked at the theatre, would actually know something of her past, that she had once received a letter from him, a book from a foreigner . . .

The fact was that, without ever having met, they would miraculously cease to be two strangers, one tiny thing would link them from that moment on: they would, in effect, exist in relation one to the other.

The young girl – who was, perhaps, romantic or simply egotistical – had replied with a barely literate letter, acknowledging receipt of the book, saying how much she had enjoyed *his* letter, and asking him to write again. And there was in her clumsy phrases such a desire to reciprocate his delicate thoughts, to be gracious, that Inácio felt overwhelmed by a wave of tenderness.

That same afternoon, he ran eagerly to a large florist's in rue Scribe and ordered fifty francs of carnations to be sent to the dancer, along with a simple visiting card and a promise to write again.

He wrote to her the next day. Then, treacherously, he set the plot in motion, boldly singing the praises of her splendid, intoxicating flesh, but making it clear that he was not rich, and only twenty years old – in order to prevent any disappointments.

He ended by saying, slyly, that his role as mysterious stranger was delightful, but he wondered if he would have the courage to play it to the end.

By return of post he received a reply and again he felt that wave of emotion. Her writing was better, she had taken more care over her spelling and her grammar. It showed an evident desire to show her gratitude. And with adorable simplicity, the young girl asked why they could not meet. She would like that so much.

A feeling of infinite, splendid joy ran through him. He kissed the letter again and again.

At last, a little sun had touched his life. What a triumph to walk along the streets of Paris with that golden woman, to possess her, to lie imperiously upon her auroral flesh, to surrender himself entirely to love and fluid desire. He would bite and wound her — yes, wound her — with his dark kisses.

And she seemed to him so humble, so pathetic, so insignificant . . . He would take her to the best restaurants, the most elegant tea rooms. He could not cover her in jewels, but he could teach her that the best perfumiers are Delettrez, Houbigant, Lenthéric, and that the best chocolates come from Boissier, Marquis . . .

How happy he would be, how beautiful. The following morning he was expecting to receive 3,000 francs from Lisbon.

He went out. After lunch, he went into the Napolitano in order to write her a letter arranging a first rendez-vous in two days' time. He ordered a coffee, paper, envelopes, then, suddenly, he found himself thinking:

'Why? Where am I going? What is the point of dragging this out any longer? I will meet her, kiss her perhaps and what then? What will she and I have in common? Poor frivolous, banal, insensitive creature . . . And if I possess her? I know well enough what awaits me there! It will be followed by a thousand tiny vexations, a thousand tiny disappointments, meetings at certain times, a thousand pointless complications. For what? Why? No, it really isn't worth it . . . not at all.'

And he took a sudden decision, he merely wrote her a brief note in which he said that their distant affair was so enchanting, so pure, that it would be best to put an end to it, to remain subtle to the last, to stop now, in order not to break the spell.

He went out. He stamped the letter in the post office in Boulevard des Italiens and put it in the letter-box, with not a flicker of pain or regret.

.   .   .   .

.   .   .   .

Of course, he thought about the sad episode for some days, but always lightly, tenderly.

The girl never wrote to him again and he thought about the cruel disappointment his last letter might have been for her. He imagined her too dreaming of love, with him, at certain hours, and of advancing towards a mundane, shoddy, but in her eyes, possibly ideal affair.

He felt a vague, perverse pity for the naked dancer, only because she had once, perhaps, suffered greatly because of him.

He kept her letters in a large envelope; they were precious because they would help him palpably to fix those few moments of that period of his life, a few moments in the Paris of his twenties.

He realized now how right he had been to put an end to the affair. Once embarked upon, nothing would have held him back, and for what? The fact was that however many kisses he bestowed on that splendid body, he would never attain what one night he had longed for. Indeed, the artist could never sate his desires convulsed above a magnificent, naked body, that was something he could only do by possessing the dancer's steps as she crossed the tiny stage of a Montmartre theatre, along with her gestures, her smiles, the red of her lips, her veils, her sequins, her fake jewels, the lights that lit her, all the rhythms of colour and sound that foundered and whirled about her flesh, rarefying her and surrounding her indistinct body with madness and apotheosis!

.   .   .   .

★

★   ★

Besides, despite his complexities and his evasions, his feelings of repugnance, Inácio de Gouveia had already experienced every kind of ecstasy, every caress, every perversion. He had experienced and fled from them all. He had not even found refuge in onanism, doubtless the greatest, most complete, most humiliating and vaguest of perversions, and therefore also the most impassioned.

For during his clean, sharp, solitary caresses, even when everything about him was still golden, lost amongst the pale nimbus of the unreal flesh of other sexes, other horrors, he had never been able to concentrate wholly on those visions, to make them endlessly orgasmic. The memory of the real world, sexualized and vile, would always surface to pervert those glittering images, to besmirch with crude laughter his most expansive ecstasies: dead breasts, gangrenous thighs, memories of damp rags and guttural cries, the smell of old wood, muddy ponds, squalid pleasures, vinous breath, the hairy chest of a porter, the genitals of children and animals . . .

Only once did he achieve a pure, golden orgasm – fantastic, infinite, sumptuous, ultimate, incomparable.

One night, suddenly, half-asleep and half-awake, he had called up in his mind an immense, tumultuous European city that spread out before him – noisy, excessive, full of light. And he had victoriously possessed that whole astonishing capital, possessed all its movement, confusion, brilliance . . . he had felt it beat in his blood, he had been that city for an instant . . . exhausted it in one huge orgasm – crystalline, arching, tangled, multicoloured and subtle . . .

· · · · · · · · · · · · · · · · · ·

★

★   ★

But that was all in the past.

However things had been then, Inácio now lived an almost tranquil life. It was not a matter of being resigned – great souls never resign themselves to anything – but it was as if he had resigned himself to his life.

His future would no longer hold many surprises for him, it was pointless to fantasise about it because, daydreams apart, it rolled away self-evidently before him.

He had reached port, that much was certain. His work was easier than ever, his imagination brilliant and fertile. Certain worrying material circumstances would doubtless improve shortly. His life looked set to be most pleasant; he would live free and solitary of soul, living only for his art.

And if, from time to time, certain bitter feelings stirred vaguely in his memory, he no longer knew how to suffer them, even if he had wanted to.

Now, he merely observed with interest when – for no reason, inexplicably – singular, incoherent, troubling ideas occurred to him; they never disturbed him, however; on the contrary, they provided him with new imaginative impulses.

One evening, for example, walking up a steep street in Lisbon, a wild desire rose up in him – like a circling flash of lightning – to be able to focus everyone, the whole world inside himself, to make the whole universe whirl towards a magnetic centre that was himself.

On another occasion, he came to the conclusion that the greatest triumph would be to exist without existing . . . And he soon found a way of achieving such a victory.

Imagine a man who managed to forget himself entirely, entirely but successively, living only in the present moment. This man would see himself in a mirror, but would immediately forget what he looked like. He would speak, make gestures, but each gesture made, each word spoken would be wiped at once from his memory. Forgetting every moment in this way would be equivalent to forgetting oneself, since he would lack any point of reference by which he could prove his reality. Thus, having no notion of his own reality, it would be as if he did not exist.

However, even though he did not exist for himself, he would, of course, exist for the other people who saw him and spoke to him.

When we were little, we may have fallen gravely ill with a painful illness that brought us to death's door – this had actually happened to the novelist, who had contracted typhoid fever when he was two years old. That illness existed for the other people who witnessed our pain, who saw us suffering, crying out, delirious. The fact is, though, that despite our cries, they did not exist for us; with the passing of the years, no memory of those pains, however excruciating, remains. If other people had not told us about them, we would never even have guessed that we once suffered them.

The case of the man who managed to forget each successive minute of his life would be like that.

. . . .

. . . .

Certain hours, then, were filled merely by grotesque, disjointed ideas that rolled about in his mind.

For example, one afternoon, he happened to glance at a woman. The woman was not beautiful and yet a desire arose in him to possess her. Why? He realised why at once: because that woman was at the outer limit of women with whom he would be capable of having sex. Yes, he would still be capable of possessing that woman, but not another woman only slightly uglier.

And in that same moment he conceived of a person who, in all things in life, was only attracted to limits, a lover of limits.

. . . .

Also, before certain objects, he would feel a violent, impossible desire to be them – he especially wanted to be the large blue cupboard in the dining room in his villa: that cupboard full of wine bottles, tins and fat jars of sugar.

These extravagant ideas did not worry him in the least, however, they merely made him laugh. They were just the aberrations of his admirably imaginative and restless spirit.

He had never been afraid of going mad precisely because madness already existed inside him. Just as an organism can sometimes adapt to certain pernicious microbes – living unharmed by them, invulnerable to the illness which those same microbes would provoke in other organisms – so his spirit had grown invulnerable to madness, adapted to it, immunized against it by madness itself.

For a similar reason, alcohol merely made him sleepy and tobacco bored him; drugs – apart from the repellently greasy feeling they gave him – only depressed him and never excited him or made him dream or swoon.

93

He was, in fact, his own alcohol, his own ether, his own cocaine.

After all, a vice is nothing more than a bad habit, and Inácio had never been capable of having a habit.

. . . .

. . . .

Yes, he was finally safe from himself – entirely adapted to himself. All his former sorrows were mere literature; now, only very occasionally, he felt a vague regret that he could no longer control his pleasures, that he would never one day experience a ghost-ecstasy in which, without touching the body he was possessing, he managed nevertheless to make it triumphantly tremble and thrill – to suck it dry of all its splendour, its magic, its golden beauty distilled into Soul!

III

Some months passed. He found himself back in Paris, free of all his shadows now and with no financial worries; a free spirit.

His life continued in the normal, exclusively literary fashion he had foreseen.

Every morning he would work for a few hours and then surrender himself voluptuously to the bustle of Paris. He would walk along the broad boulevards, sit down in the large cafés and read the newspapers, write letters or even a few pages of his own. At night, he would lose himself in the artificial atmosphere of the music halls that had always given him such pleasure. Driven away from the theatre by the inept bourgeois productions they insisted on staging, he would entirely forget about himself and spend rapt hours feasting his eyes on the lavish scenery, the wonderful spectacle, the women in low-cut dresses, the flocks of naked dancers. The busy rustle of these places clothed him in a propitious atmosphere of paint and artifice, tinkling with life, anointing him with all things cosmopolitan. He had always, despite everything, been a lover of the world, mad about Europe, just as he had always felt a jaundiced loathing, utter scorn and nausea, for the provinces, with its smell of sweat and manure, its hypocrisy, its rude health, its white houses, its red roofs, its belfries, its Manuels and Marias. He had never been able to understand how certain artists – even genuine artists sometimes – could sing the praises of their village, declaring themselves proud to have been born there. For his part, he prided himself on at least being a native of a European capital.

In the afternoons, at about five o'clock, he would often walk up the Boulevard de Montparnasse to take tea at the studio of his friend Manuel Lopes.

Manuel Lopes was a fairly stupid chap, both as an artist and a man. Yet he was also a true friend and a delightful fellow: plump, thickset, dark and glossy, with a blue-black beard and curly hair. He was a jovial man, always in a good mood.

Besides, as to his imbecility, Inácio sometimes felt that he was being unfair, indeed, he was sure he was.

For the painter's 'lucid moments' were not infrequent, in fact, every day he would recount new scenes, imaginary adventures of which he was the protagonist: amorous triumphs, acts of courage, duels, brilliant ripostes . . . he was the very devil . . . grandiose plans, grandiose ideas – a complete chaos . . . In short, a man of constant imaginings. His was an imagination of a lower order, of course, but it was at least proof that he had some blood in his soul.

Although he hated 'gatherings' of any kind, Inácio still went to his friend's studio because there too he found the atmosphere propitious.

Lopes was the son of a great, barely literate, Alentejo landowner, and whilst in Paris, he spent money like water – about that he was very clear. His studio was magnificent – spacious, luxurious, modern and with every comfort imaginable. He had recently provided further proof that he was not an inferior spirit, that he was in no way a mediocrity, for he had become interested in Cubism. Whether he would ever be able to find his his way around that tangled, brilliant school of painting was unclear, but the fact that he was both its defender and follower, waxing lyrical about the works of Picasso, Léger, Gris, Matisse and Derain, about Archipenko's tormented sculptures, was at least an indication of a certain intensity, curiosity and boldness. A rather dull boldness, perhaps, but it certainly placed him above a couple of vague acquaintances of Inácio's – daubers, insignificant provincials, ex-prizewinning pupils of the Largo da Biblioteca in Lisbon – two idiots who, even in Paris, prudently continued to turn out pretty little pictures using the best of techniques . . . paintings later droolingly exhibited, amidst great jubilation, at the pretentious Salons in Lisbon held by their teachers who were nothing but senile botchers.

But Lopes' studio attracted him in particular because, on the one hand, the people he met there (failed foreign artists, actresses, students) provided him with a cross-section of Paris in all its dubious colours, and on the other, the hours spent in that milieu were like baths of banality which, like the reviews at the Olympia, the Folies Bergère, the Moulin Rouge, provided a respite for his genius.

That was why, having visited the studio only the night before, he was heading there again that rainy February evening.

There weren't many people there: Robert Lagrange, the playwright, one of the painter's best friends, barely recovered from the death of Yvette Dolcey whom he had loved deeply and who had been a sweet, tender, sincere companion to him. As always, of course, there was Jean Lamy, now a 'soiriste' at the Comédie, writer of light reviews and operettas, but, above all, in debt to Lopes. Inácio had a soft spot for the journalist because he had known Ricardo de Loureiro and had unwittingly played a part in the poet's affair with Marta de Valadares, since, at the time, he was working as secretary to her husband, the Comte de la Barre. Such was Inácio's veneration for the work of the Master that anything that touched, however tangentially, on the sublime, unfortunate author of Diadem, held a special significance for the novelist.

Then there was Horácio de Viveiros, the Portuguese musician, now a failed Comédie Royale pianist, Etienne Dalembert, whom he barely knew, a sometime writer of comedies and an even more occasional actor, and, for the rest, half a dozen foreigners: Russians, Balkans, Scandinavians, male and female.

Conversation faltered – it was a rather uninteresting group of people that evening. Inácio was beginning to regret having come and was just preparing to say his goodbyes when there was a sudden peal of laughter.

It was Maroussia – Jean Lamy's lover and the star of his reviews, as well as Inácio's former model – who appeared arm-in-arm with two elegant young women, her new colleagues, the Doré sisters, Rose and Paulette. 'Absolute sweethearts,' she declared.

With his exit cut off, he felt slightly constrained . . .

But, after the actresses' clamorous entrance, the tedium of the evening dissipated and tea was ostentatiously served.

. . . .

★

★   ★

Inácio was currently working on a novel which – he felt quite sure of this – would be his best yet. As an artist, he had evolved considerably of late – he had grown in terms of soul, had plunged more emphatically into the Beyond. He thought only of the glorious moment when he would complete his work.

It was towards the end of March and he was determined to have the book finished by mid-April. Little remained to be done, he had only to put the finishing touches to the two final chapters.

Given over entirely to concluding the work, he wasted few hours. He often spent whole days at home, polishing and perfecting his writing. His visits to Manuel Lopes had thus become most infrequent.

Besides, he was growing bored with seeing the same old faces, finding no repose in that banality tainted by mediocrity. He intended gradually to distance himself from Lopes and his circle.

Today, however, having made unexpected progress in his work – and since he had not seen Lopes for nearly two weeks – he had decided to go up to Montparnasse.

The painter's studio was packed that afternoon. There were some new faces there, some very fair and one Portuguese-speaking Indian, small, dark and bright-eyed, adding a foreign, colonial note, contributing to the gathering's exotic atmosphere.

As soon as he went in, someone rushed up to him, smiling broadly and saying:

'Where have you been all this time? I've asked after you so often!'

It was Paulette Doré.

He said:

'I haven't been out much lately.'

'You haven't been ill, have you?'

'No, not at all. I'm just finishing a novel . . .'

She pulled a childish face and said:

'It's such a shame I can't read it.'

Lopes, spotting him from afar, hurried over to him and embraced him, reproaching him for his prolonged absence.

'You tormented artists always have to take things to such extremes!' he blustered.

. . . .

. . . .

When he left the studio at seven o'clock, Inácio was in a strange mood. He felt infinitely sad – a sublimated, melancholy, an undulating sadness which, nevertheless, had a certain sweetness.

He searched in vain for the cause of this feverish state. Everything was going wonderfully well and in less than a week he would have finished his novel!

He had decided to work on a few pages that night, but he changed his mind now in view of his inexplicable state of agitation, that enigmatic 'discontented contentment'.

He dined hurriedly at Duval's and then, briefly, because he wanted to go to bed early, went into the Café Riche. He took advantage of his sojourn there to reply to a letter he had received from a friend in Lisbon. He asked for paper and an envelope and began scribbling that insignificant note . . . Suddenly, he glanced up from the sheet of paper and found himself staring at a nearby table where a heavily made-up young girl was drinking hot chocolate.

He continued writing his letter. But now, frequent distractions made him write the wrong word or mispell a word. In the end, he became so irritated that he crumpled up the piece of paper he was writing on and abandoned his task – it wasn't urgent, it could be left for a later date.

He called the waiter over so as to pay his bill and leave. Instead, he ordered another coffee.

His eyes returned again and again to the girl, who was now talking brightly to a male companion who had just joined her.

It was odd. He was sure he did not know that woman, that

he had never seen her before and yet he had the feeling that he had spoken to her on more than one occasion. Even more bizarrely, when he looked at her, it seemed to him that by some kind of strange aberration, it was not she herself that he saw.

Aided by her companion, the girl was putting on her furs. The two of them left.

Only then was Inácio de Gouveia able to get up from his table and leave too.

He got home at about ten o'clock and went straight to bed. The strange feeling that had been troubling him had disappeared.

However, as he was about to fall asleep, that magical profile reappeared in his memory.

. . . .

In an urge to finish his novel, he spent the whole of the next day writing.

He did not know why, but he felt a terrible fear that if he did not finish it now, he would have great difficulty in doing so, doubtless for some unforeseen reason.

. . . .

The following afternoon, having decided not to go out (he even had lunch in his rooms, something he rarely did), he was gripped by a sudden tedium, an unusually urgent need to be with other people – he felt he had to visit Lopes.

Besides, he only had another half a dozen pages to edit. It would only take him a few hours to finish it the next day. He was, to all effects, free, that was the truth of the matter.

His feelings of disquiet still lingered, though, indeed a great shudder ran through him as he walked up to Montparnasse.

. . . .

There were only a few people at the studio, almost all of them men. Of the women, only Maroussia and Paulette were there.

The men were standing around in groups at the far end of the room, doubtless discussing art. Maroussia was laughing with Horácio de Viveiros. Sitting exhausted at a table, Manuel Lopes was chatting to Paulette who was standing up.

The novelist went over to his friend, greeting Paulette in passing.

The first thing Lopes said to him, yawning, was: 'It's terribly boring here today, old chap, and I'm the worst culprit. I've had awful stomach pains all day. I ate too much dessert last night.'

Paulette was resting her hands on the edge of the table. Inácio was beside her and took up the same position. Suddenly, he felt the girl's fingers close to his, next to his, touching his fingers and lightly squeezing them . . .

Then some of the others came over to join their group. He and Paulette unclasped hands, so as not to be surprised like that. But secretly, at a propitious moment, he again felt for Paulette's fingers along the edge of the table; this time they slipped away, elusive. Then, as if regretful, she smilingly rested her bare, brown arm on his hand, while still talking brightly to the others.

.   .   .   .

.   .   .   .

Ah, what blond sweetness filled the artist then! How that spontaneous, audacious, kindly gesture touched him. It was an act of singular tenderness, full of compassion and pain – ineffable, but regretful.

Rifling his memory, he came across old events that he had never thought about, that he had barely noticed, and which, nonetheless, had been the origin of that gesture.

It was true . . . Moments when Paulette's sad eyes had fixed admiringly on his face . . . her abrupt questions . . . her special smiles . . . the way, only the other day, she had rushed joyfully to meet him wanting to know the reason for his long absence.

On the afternoon when they had first met – he remembered this too – she had come to sit in one corner of the studio, very close to him, opposite him, and spotting a black thread on his jacket, she had picked it off. Then, distractedly, she had wound the thread about one of his fingers. When she realised what she was doing, she had blushed and pushed his hand away.

Yes, he really ought to have guessed at the feelings impelling her towards him, and yet he had never even noticed.

It was while he was absorbed in these amorous thoughts that the image of the young girl in the Café Riche rose clearly before him again.

Only then did he realise that her face bore a real resemblance to Paulette's face, especially the slender, sad shadow cast by her eyes.

. . . .

. . . .

The following morning, not even wanting to think about that slight, romantic episode, he sat down at his desk in order to finish the manuscript once and for all. He did so quickly and easily, for there were few corrections to be made.

Free from his principal preoccupation, the tender feelings aroused in him on the previous evening surfaced once more, feelings – as he realised for the first time – of infinite gratitude, a gratitude born of egotism.

For what touched him most was that this poor young girl, so humble of soul, so ordinary, had been intelligent enough to pick him out from amongst all the other men, all far more alluring than him: handsome young men with long hair, sensuous lips, slender bodies, gallants who always had a flattering word for the ladies. Boldly, she had been the first to approach him, to squeeze his fingers.

'My love, my love,' he heard himself murmuring.

But he did not desire her . . . not at all. Nothing about Paulette attracted him, apart, perhaps, from her sharp teeth, an elusive quality about her face, her sombre, tapering fingers. Otherwise, she had all the affected habits, the conventional vices, all the defects of any other young girl.

'Why chase after her then?'

It seemed so ungrateful not to.

In short, whatever his feelings, he wanted to see her again, even if only to be absolutely sure that she had, in fact, squeezed his fingers.

That afternoon, however, there was a dress rehearsal at the

theatre. He did not go to the studio and so he only saw her the following day.

Again the same silent, tenuous caresses – in secret, under the noses of everyone.

. . . .

No, it would be impossible not to pursue her. He knew perfectly well what awaited him and yet he did not have the strength to give her up. It seemed a terrible act of cruelty. It would be like beating off a dog that came to lick your hand.

And wanting to forget, wanting to hide these feelings from himself, he went into the large florist's on the rue Scribe, where he had once bought flowers for a dancer in Montmartre, and ordered a large bouquet to be sent to Paulette.

That night, he went to the Comédie Royale, to see the review . . .

During the performance, the actress' eyes never left his. At the end of the show, he waited for her in the street, by the stage door. The moment he saw her, though, he started walking away, suddenly ashamed to have waited for her or, rather, ashamed that she should see him waiting.

Paulette spotted him in the distance and called to him. Inácio came back.

She introduced him to her mother and they walked along, her mother and Rose behind them and the two of them a long way in front, hand-in-hand, without uttering a single word of love.

He walked her home.

The following night, the same thing happened, except, during their walk, their fingers were even more tightly laced.

. . . .

He had launched himself along a mistaken path, there was no doubt about it. Ah, but how sweet and rose-tint-perfumed that path was!

Yes, he needed to step down a little from the pedestal of pride upon which he had erected a marble statue of himself – solitary, golden.

He did, after all, inhabit life. It was a terrible shame not to live it a little.

And even if he stepped off that pedestal entirely, he would feel a magenta pride that he had actually had the courage to step so resolutely down.

. . . .

That afternoon, as usual, he talked to her at the painter's studio. She did not stay long and left with no show of tenderness. There were too many people around her.

. . . .

The next day he could not go to the studio; he had a supper engagement with a friend recently arrived from Lisbon. After supper, though, he persuaded his friend to go to the show at the Comédie Royale.

However, not for one moment during the whole review did Paulette's eyes meet his, or so it seemed to him. He must have been mistaken. He must have made a mistake.

. . . .

That morning, Horácio de Viveiros turned up to ask him out to lunch.

And suddenly he said:

'My dear boy, I know everything!'

'Everything . . . about what?' asked Inácio, trembling.

And Horácio said:

'About your flirtation with Paulette. She was at the rehearsal yesterday, confiding in someone. I heard her mention your name and, since I'm one of your best friends, I forced her to confess to me as well. She said how much she liked you.'

. . . .

That same day, in a cheap jeweller's in Boulevard Raspail, he spent 125 francs on a platinum brooch set with a small emerald.

He waited for her after the rehearsal. He showed her the brooch. She was overwhelmed and squeezed his hands hard.

The following afternoon, however, when they met at the

studio, it seemed to Inácio that she spoke to him rather coldly. There was no doubt about it, she ostentatiously avoided him.

That night, when he went to wait for her after the show, in the Boulevard on the corner of rue Caumartin, he had clear proof that he was right.

When Paulette saw him in the distance, she abruptly took her sister's arm and the two of them headed off in the opposite direction.

. . . .
. . . .

When Inácio arrived at Lopes' studio at about seven the next evening, nearly all the visitors had left.

Grave-faced, the painter greeted him, saying:

'I wasn't expecting you. But it's just as well you came. I need to talk to you alone.'

And when they were at last alone, after a long speech in which Lopes assured him of his affection, his loyalty and his admiration, he said:

'In short, I'm warning you because I'm your friend. Everyone knows that you gave her an emerald brooch. I was furious. I pointed out to her the kind of man you were, that your soul is large and complex, that she should be aware of what she was getting herself into. Then she told me that you were the one who wouldn't leave her alone . . . that she didn't know how to get rid of you . . . that she didn't even dare take her usual route home any more . . .'

. . . .
. . . .

IV

Inácio de Gouveia did not suffer, at least not during the first few days. So bitter, so abrupt had his disappointment been that he had made a deliberate effort to forget all about it, to erase those days from his existence. His pride should not even acknowledge that low deceit.

Apart from that, on the same evening on which Manuel Lopes had spoken to him, he had gone as usual to wait for the actress, before the show, when the artistes were due to arrive, in rue Caumartin, opposite the theatre, so that he would not miss her. And then, coldly, brutally, in front of Rose and Maroussia, he told her that there was no longer any need for her to avoid him, for he never asked anything of anyone. He had pursued her – he pointed out – because Paulette had made the first move, squeezing his fingers, offering him her bare arm.

Then, he had shaken her hand, doffed his hat and said goodbye, just like that.

That scene afforded him considerable relief; it left him numb and thus he managed to get through the first weeks without even thinking much about the affair.

He spent many afternoons at Lopes' studio; he became an even more assiduous visitor and stayed longer; he didn't want anyone to think he was afraid of meeting Paulette. Besides, the Doré sisters had stopped going, Maroussia having abruptly broken with Jean Lamy.

Free from his ill-fated romance, Inácio had decided, in short, to return for a few months to a life of frivolity, deliberately wasting time: long walks, nights spent at the music hall, idle afternoons at the café, often in the company of Horácio de Viveiros.

In his present state of mind, Horácio was indeed the best of company, being intelligent and expansive, of a cheerful, straightforward disposition, with no great anxieties or ambitions, satisfied with what he had, simply living his life . . .

Inácio felt very at ease with him and engaged in pleasant,

aimless chatter which temporarily anaesthetised him against his painful thoughts.

Horácio told him about the banal adventures in Paris in which he was an enthusiastic participant, and about his modest plans, tasteful and, doubtless, feasible.

He often turned up with friends of his from the world of theatre, most often with Etienne Dalembert who currently had a verse play in rehearsal at the Comédie Royale. He felt very drawn to this friend of Horácio's, although he could not have said why.

. . . .

★

★   ★

Thus several weeks went by.

Unconsciously, vague memories of what he had managed at first to forget began to leak out. For sacred souls, as time dilutes reality, instead of wrapping around it and ushering in oblivion – as happens with most people – it makes it doubly subtle, incorporeal and spectral and, therefore, more sensitive, more alive, more stubbornly embedded in those slender souls.

Besides, certain concrete things obliged Inácio to remember. Horácio one day congratulated him for cutting short his relationship with the little actress.

'Frankly,' he said, 'she was not the woman for you. I had even said as much to Lopes and suggested that we should intervene. That wasn't necessary, though. You came to your senses in time. I never thought you had it in you. Given your character, to have continued would have been asking for trouble, you can be sure of that . . .'

On other occasions, it was natural references to Paulette that he heard in Viveiros' conversations with his theatre friends. That was how he learned, for example, that the two sisters had been contracted by a company to take part in the summer season at the Folies Bergéres in a spectacular new review.

However, what really forced Inácio back to his memories was his feeling of horror that he had, in fact, been embroiled in such a tale; he, cured of all base desires, so mindful of his fate, knowing all too well that the glory of being himself should be enough – exultant, proud of his renunciation and his exile.

With hindsight, he said to himself:

'My God . . . my God . . . deep down, I'm the same as all the other poor wretches. I have the same longings, the same desires, identical feelings of bitterness. One day I decided that I would not be like that, because I had lost interest in my own pain, because I was sick of being unhappy. I always decided my opinions, my affections, my states of mind, just as I always determined the states of mind of other people. That is where my mistake began, my illusions and my disgrace . . .'

But then, rejecting such ideas, he rose up, clasped his adamantine pride to him, and recovered his former calm state of mind.

. . . .

To forget, to abolish certain hours of one's life . . . that would be the greatest of triumphs.

Impossible! Impossible!

That is why, despite everything and to his own shame, Inácio found that, after only a few more days, he was recalling – though differently this time, almost nostalgically – certain moments of that pathetic story: those dark fingers approaching his, that voice, those smiles, that wild profile . . .

A feeling of penetrating tenderness divided him then, a melancholy magic, a sharp sweetness, so narcotic and transparent that the artist did not even feel disgusted enough to drive them out . . .

Then one afternoon, in the Boulevard St-Michel, in the midst of one of these trance-like crises, he started following a girl who was not Paulette, but who, for a moment, reminded him of her, which is why he followed her – to see where she was going – *as if she were, in fact, Paulette.*

The least significant thing could spark off memories. Waiting for a friend, he would immediately think sadly of the two or three times he had waited for Paulette in the same street. And one night in a café, his eyes had filled with tears merely because – in an act of utter puerility – he had drunk his coffee without sugar having given his sugar lumps to a dog who begged them from him. In fact, at that moment, he felt that he had suddenly ceased being himself and was instead a petite young girl from Paris, adorable, sweet, kind – Paulette perhaps – who graciously gave her sugar to a white dog and planted him with kisses, and whose kindness impressed him because she seemed so fragile. And it was that imagined fragility that made his eyes fill with tears of self-pity, the pity he would feel for himself if he too were so insignificant.

And he pitied her too . . . so much . . .

Poor thing. She had not dared take things to the limit, she had recoiled like a nervous greyhound. What she had lost . . . what she had lost . . . How extraordinary she would have felt when she emerged from his embraces . . . golden, golden.

The truth of the matter was – a truth that Inácio had not yet perceived – that it was not yesterday that he had been prepared to love and desire the girl, it was today . . . or, at the very least, tomorrow.

None of this troubled Inácio's spirit, given over as he was to his enthusiasm for his completed novel. It was, without a doubt, his greatest work – *the* work – a passionate book in which he had finally managed to distil all his torments, his subtlest emotions, his disgust and his revulsion, his hatreds and his loves, the golden essence of his sexual mysticism, that indigo blue fascination stamped with Mystery, redolent of shadow and the Beyond.

In two months' time, at the beginning of August, he would leave for Lisbon to supervise its publication. The book would be launched in November. He would use the dead summer months to have it printed. And since this gave him great joy – even his trip to Lisbon where he still had two or three true friends – his nostalgia did not make him suffer deeply or feel great bitterness, except that with each hour that passed, he distanced himself further from that nostalgia and – regarding himself from the perspective of the present moment – from ever having lived through such an obscure affair. It occurred to him that if ever he wanted to write about all that in a novel, opening with a description of his own soul, everyone would say that the narrative was psychologically flawed, that a character with such a soul would never have got himself embroiled in such an affair in the first place . . .

. . . and besides, very soon, not a trace would remain in his life of such a minor event.

. . . .

But one afternoon, Horácio de Viveiros said quite naturally, between sips of his aperitif:

'Do you know who's after Paulette now? Etienne Dalembert.'

Inácio did his best to ignore this news, responding merely with an indifferent 'Really?' and then changing the subject.

However, he was filled by a terrible sadness that only proved to him that nothing anyone told him about Paulette could be a matter of indifference. He had not really forgotten anything.

From now on, though, he must forget everything. It would be sinking too low, it would be degrading and shameful to think of her with her new admirer . . . who knows, perhaps her new lover . . . yes, her new lover. Other people were not like him . . . they did not give up at the first rebuff . . . no one did. He must forget everything . . . wipe it from his memory . . . he must not remember, not a trace must remain.

. . . .

The following day, Horácio turned up accompanied by Etienne.

How to define the bizarre sensation that Inácio felt when face to face with him? It was not hatred or repugnance, quite the opposite . . . he was astonished. He felt a kind of wounded joy, an even greater wave of sympathy . . . my God, he even felt stirrings of tenderness, real tenderness, albeit shot through with lilac tones of anger, because at least Etienne would understand his feelings . . . doubtless she had squeezed *his* fingers too . . . as she had his fingers . . . one afternoon . . . surreptitiously . . . in front of everyone.

And if the thought of sharing his affections with someone else – and thus, in some way, being forced into an involvement with a stranger – caused a faint pain to rise up in him, it was that same fleeting pain that filled him with such a disquieting, mystical tenderness; being confronted by that man, who had persisted where he had not, provoked in him a subtle desire – doubtless purely literary – to kiss him on the mouth.

.   .   .   .

At any rate, how Inácio would suffer when he learned that Etienne had achieved what he had never even attempted: to bite her humble lips, to kiss her sombre eyes . . .

If only it had been someone he did not know . . .

A shudder of horror ran through him and, for a moment, he was gripped by a desire for Etienne to possess the girl right then, that instant, before his very eyes.

Several days passed.

From various small hints – Viveiros' tactless, though good-humoured remarks, the questions he asked Etienne – Inácio learned that Dalembert was not at all a happy admirer.

Inácio spent that month of June in a permanent state of nervous excitement.

Every afternoon he met up with his two friends on the terrace of the Café Américain and his one desire was to provoke some word that might tell him of the other's love affair. He watched Etienne's face intently, scrutinised his every gesture, fearful of seeing a smile, a carefree expression, some sunny alteration to his customary melancholy.

.   .   .   .

Once, the actor asked if he could borrow Inácio's pen to write a letter.

When he had finished, Inácio glimpsed the name 'Paulette' on the envelope.

He felt so moved. The girl would receive new words penned by the gold nib with which, one night, he had written the note accompanying the flowers he had sent to the theatre – along with his magnificent novel.

Ah, a pathetic desire to kiss himself welled up in him then, simply because he was capable of experiencing such a futile, child-like tenderness!

. . . .
. . . .

In short, his liking for Etienne grew hour by hour, a liking always tempered by the wild fear that he might see him triumph.

In fact — in a mood of hesitant incoherence — it was precisely that fear that most attracted him. Yes, it was true. Although it was a great relief to know that the other had failed, at the same time, with a strange feeling that was the opposite of pride — a desire for revenge on himself — deep down, deep down, he admired Etienne for persevering.

. . . .

Until one day, on the eve of his departure for Lisbon, Horácio told him that the affair had ended, in the way that these things so often end, by themselves.

Etienne even had a new lover — a very beautiful lover, in fact . . . a dancer at the Opéra Comique.

V

During the first weeks that he spent in Lisbon, Inácio scarcely gave a thought to reality; he was swept along on a wave of enthusiasm, a childish enthusiasm for his plans to publish his latest novel, spending sincere, happy, proudly lucid hours with his few friends and, more especially, with Fernando Passos.

What a golden glory it had been for him, a year ago, to meet that genius, to feel that he was appreciated and understood, yes, understood, by him. His friendship with the poet had had an immensely beneficial effect on his development as a writer or, rather, his letters had, since that friendship had been carried out principally by correspondence during his stay in Paris.

Fernando Passos had awoken his soul. To him Inácio owed the golden unfolding of his undoubted genius, the heraldic rise of his spirit and the touches of Modernity that now marked his work, dappling it with light, diademing it with shadow.

In the long conversations that filled their long walks together, they never managed to exhaust all the many topics that had not been covered in their letters – new literary projects, transcendental longings, their latest shared artistic ideas.

Only rarely did their words descend to banal, intimate details. They felt too large-souled to return to life.

When he went back home after one of those intense nights of serpentine swordplay, of stellar upheavals, Inácio felt celestially happy.

What did anything matter as long as he freed himself for the heights, as long as, alone in himself, he lived sublimely, a royal eagle amongst cliffs of light, heading for the dark red beyond?

He belonged to the same race as Fernando Passos, a race comprising perhaps another two or three people in the whole world, plus another twenty or thirty in the whole of time.

Any occasional nostalgia he felt for the plains, any desire to descend to those plains and mingle with the dwarves below, was madness. In mystical terms, though, that would be shameful. He was his own god. To go down there, therefore, would mean committing a sacrilege against himself.

And during these virtuous apotheoses, glittering with pride, his body really did become rarefied; at dawn he would walk for hours along the broad avenues, like a somnambulist – as if he were pure soul.

. . . .

But his addiction to glory was nothing more than another state of mind, another poor illusion. One night, in fact, he experienced a sudden regression to his former self and all those tiny nostalgias bloomed in him again.

He remembered that he had completely forgotten about that episode in Paris, but remembering that we have forgotten something is the same as still remembering it.

And from that moment on – gradually, but with growing intensity – all his sadnesses, all his nostalgia returned.

Now, he had only to look at his own hands for a shudder of spiralling tenderness to shake him, prostrate him, and all because, one afternoon, Paulette, in front of everyone, had complimented him out loud on his long, slender hands: 'so white . . . always so white'.

Killing time in a café, it occurred to him that, in the great cafés in Paris, he had also whiled away the hours before going to see Paulette at Lopes' gatherings.

He paused to gaze at jeweller's windows, because once he had bought her a brooch.

A letter slipped into a letter box reminded him that he had never sent her a letter by post.

And if anyone mentioned flowers, he would be moved to pity because once, in a famous florist's in Paris, he had chosen a bunch of superb red roses to send to her.

. . . .
. . . .

Meanwhile, Inácio managed if not to avoid these tender feelings, at least not to pay them too much attention. One day, though, he resolved that he must find the strength to drive

114

them out as being feelings unworthy of him. That, of course, was his perdition: minute by minute, they continued to harry him, they glistened and shimmered.

It seemed to him that he had seen the girl only today and knew her every gesture, the nimble shadow of her lips, her long tresses, the tenuous tremor of her breasts, those fingers, dark, elegant, skilful, sensuous.

'My God, my God, why had he let her escape him?'

Then, as he walked aimlessly along, he would abstractly reconstruct the reasons for her flight.

'Poor love, of course, that was the reason . . . she had approached him knowing what a great man he was and never dreaming that he would take her up . . . She had squeezed his fingers and smilingly brushed his hand with her bare arm out of a desire to suffer . . . a religious longing for humiliation . . . in order to anoint herself with yearning . . . to gild herself with renunciation . . .

And he . . . he had risen to the bait . . . he had been like all the others. He had lied to her, disillusioned her . . . he had been a glass idol that lay shattered at her feet.'

. . . .

At other times, he thought: 'Illusion, pure illusion. That wasn't how it was at all. The girl had no idea what she was doing. She had barely noticed him, how could such a small soul see him for what he was? She never suspected even for a moment how great he was, how brilliant . . . She had squeezed his fingers, fleetingly, unwittingly, her mind on something else . . . a ribbon . . . a thimble . . . Just as she had called out to him in the street one night, just as she had fled from him . . . without knowing why.

In fact, had she ever really looked at him, squeezed his fingers, called out his name?'

She had, although now he found that hard to believe.

A parallel memory surfaced of a tiny, fleeting episode in Paris.

At about three o'clock one morning, he and Manuel Lopes had gone into an all-night patisserie in Boulevard St-Michel. It had been Lopes' idea to go in there – he was feeling peckish

– Inácio had merely slumped wearily at a table, bored and sleepy.

They occupied a table at the rear of the shop and sat there chatting.

Shortly afterwards, a pretty young girl came in, very Parisian-looking, a typical denizen of the Latin Quarter – a minor courtesan, no doubt, a model.

The lady who owned the shop obviously knew her well and greeted her warmly. The girl bit into a cake and her small, hesitant eyes immediately fixed on the two foreigners sitting at the other end of the shop talking in a mysterious language. Suddenly, with a roguish gesture, she doffed her hat to them – a straw boater worth a hundred *sous*, no hatpins – greeting them in masculine fashion.

The odd thing was that Inácio felt that she made that gesture without feeling it, as if that were not the movement she thought she was making. He gained exactly the same dubious impression when he studied her more closely, her uncertain steps, her glancing eyes, the smile curving her fugitive lips.

Then, studying her silhouette from afar, Inácio – his gaze perhaps diffuse with tiredness – saw her wrapped in a halo of vagueness, a pulsating transparency, he saw her through a brittle humility, lit by a dim light . . .

Finally, the girl came over to them and asked if they would buy her some more cakes.

Inácio got up and gave her the money, enough for two more.

The girl thanked him, smiling, and gave a pirouette. While Manuel Lopes went off to buy another brioche, she turned to Inácio and, with those same vague, equivocal movements, she said:

'Embrasse-moi sur la joue.'

Inácio kissed her on the corner of her mouth and then left with his friend, thinking no more about it. He had not even felt her kiss: it was as if he had made just one more indistinct gesture out of so many others that were never made.

That whole insignificant episode seemed to have been played out in a fog, far off, miles away, on another plane, so that he remembered it from much the same perspective as his imagination sometimes troublingly foresaw future scenarios, distant, lost in Time: a perspective comparable to the vacillating distillation, the dim light and transparent humidity of cities shading into darkness on days when there is a solar eclipse – all vague outlines and latent, vibrant undulations.

But why did he remember that now, when he was thinking about Paulette?

Obviously, because her attitude had been identical to that of the girl from the Latin Quarter. With him, the actress had never paid any particular attention to her gestures, they could have been any gesture. All her gestures had the same shimmering transparency, the same glassy, stagnant dampness.

And it was because it took place far off, on shifting, haphazardly intersecting planes, that their story had gone so wrong.

For the first time, Inácio understood the singular direction taken by his evocative thoughts – flecked with folly, every line broken, every curve a picaresque inflection.

Whatever the case – without his having any truly lucid understanding of the process – hour by hour the subtle poison was impregnating him with magic: blond at first, then golden-red, then tawny, then eagerly ablaze.

. . . .
★
★   ★

That night he looked in vain for Fernando Passos at his usual haunts.

Just when he had decided to go back to his hotel, while he was walking up the Chiado, he bumped into Vitorino Bragança, the playwright, someone in whom, exceptionally, Inácio took a great interest and for whom he felt a genuine sympathy, the sympathy we feel for those who understand a little about what excites us. Indeed, amongst the hordes of provincials in our literary scene, amongst the hordes of artistic boors, Vitorino Bragança was someone with *psychology*, refined, civilized, aristocratic, intensely European.

They immediately fell to talking about Paris and, still following that thread, they slipped into a discussion of their sexual peculiarities. Like Inácio, the playwright had strange, tangled feelings about the subject.

'I do not find the naked body in itself exciting,' he explained, 'not even simple contact with that body, not even if an exquisite, pulsating breast were pressed into my hand.'

'Absolutely,' Inácio took up the theme, 'in order to feel passion for the naked body and for the mere touch of a breast to pierce us through with delicate longings, we need, first of all, to enlarge our most golden sensualities – each of them created by our spirit – through our deepest fantasies. The flesh is all very well, but what use is it to us if we do not build upon it, ourselves, our kisses, our impulses, our scarlet yearnings? Nature is for healthy people, for the normal sub-classes. People like us, the golden elite, have freed ourselves from it. No, I'm wrong, on the contrary, we have augmented it, we have given it a soul, and only its spirit – the spirit we created for it – can provoke our desire. We are people with soul and we project that soul on to anything that we admire or desire . . . So we can only feel the firmest, most provocative breast if, by dint of our imperial imaginations, we transform it into something other, something transcendently voluptuous, if we make it purely sexual, if we perceive in it alternative contours, macerations, tremors, golden rhythms . . .'

'Admirable, admirable!' cried Vitorino. 'Even as a child, lying in bed alone, I would dream of new ecstasies . . . I would theorise about nude dancers whom I – also naked, but seated on a royal throne – would command to leap into the fire. Obedient, in an act of dark humiliation, they would rush into the flames, rubbing their own genitals. Enraptured, I would hear their painted bodies burning . . . creaking . . . creaking . . . But even under torture, my slaves uttered not a cry, not a complaint. Ah, and with every melted breast, I would be shaken by a cold, dissatisfied, painful spasm.'

Inácio had known such magical deliriums in his own childhood too, though he had never felt the excitement of the fire. He had imagined watery kisses, foam caresses, jasper breasts rising to the surface of the sea, naked bodies on des-

118

erted beaches, elusive princesses, unveiled, bathing in crystal lakes.

Pain had only ever provoked in him horror and repugnance. His was a healthy morbidity.

Fernando Passos had once defined him as 'a sane madman'.

But how Vitorino's other undulant desires drew Inácio to him.

Thus, speaking of a certain actress who, for the first time in Lisbon, had dared to appear on stage bare-legged, Vitorino told him that what he had always vainly desired in these young actresses was their make-up and their ribbons, their sequins, their multicoloured costumes.

'All this, my friend,' he had said at last, 'all these complications, these strange morbidities can be summed up in one word: onanism. That is what we both are: pure, admirable onanists. Indeed, even when we have normal sex with a woman, we are practising an act of onanism, since we possess not her flesh exactly, but something more beautiful, less defined, more sexualised, that we superimpose on her body. Our orgasms are ruled always by our fantasies. For my part, I come only at the moment of my choosing.'

'Just like me!' Inácio cried. 'How extraordinary! We become two and in the other bodies of other sexes, it is ourselves that we possess!'

'And yet,' Vitorino had said after a pause, 'I fear that sometimes I may feel a certain distant nostalgia for what is healthy.'

Inácio protested:

'But isn't health just the absence of beauty, vacuous novelty? For my part, I confess that I cling on to my pride. Other people, those eternal other people, may say that our art (mine and that of Fernando Passos) is ultimately "a masturbatory art"! Poor things, poor things. They would never guess that the phrase for me is a motive for celebration. For, setting aside all preconceived ideas, is not masturbation the soul's most voluptuous act, the most imponderable and visionary of acts, subtly marked by the Beyond? Of course it is. Therefore, what they perceive as an insult, is, for me, simply an indication that my art rises more freely, sharply and completely above mere matter, that it is the greater art. Poor fools, they cannot comprehend that we are so utterly different from them that what might wound their vulgar, workaday sensibility – the sensibility of the greasy turban, scrubby beard, large cravat and pipe – can only favour our sensibility, which is narcotic, vibrant, crystalline? They do not understand that even if they are correct in pointing out our excesses, our supposed madness, we actually love excess and madness for their own sakes, that we glory in their words. I am proud of my proclivities, that is why I put up with them. If I found them repulsive, they would not exist for me.'

There was a brief silence which Vitorino abruptly broke, saying:

'The most insignificant thing can make me weep . . . Shall I give you some foolish examples? The playing of a national anthem, a regiment marching by, a flag being unfurled . . . But if someone I care about deeply should die – even my father – I would shed not a tear . . . I would feel no grief at all in the first instance. Only after a few days, looking bitterly, tenderly nostalgic, at his empty place at the table at supper, his walking stick in the hall, his books, the drawers in his desk . . . My sincerity is itself imagination. That's what I mean when I say that everything is onanism.'

Inácio remarked:

'It's odd how similar we are . . . Once, a certain hesitant girl passed tenuously through my life. I gave her no importance at the time, I didn't even glance at her. I squeezed her fingers without really feeling them, I saw her lips and felt no excitement. And later, when she had long ago disappeared, I suddenly began to desire her, yes, to desire her keenly, to yearn for her.'

But it was only when he had finished his sentence that – in a moment of inner horror – Inácio realised what he had said.

. . . .
. . . .

'So,' he thought on the following morning, remembering

his words of the night before, 'so that was the truth of the matter, that and no other.' He tried in vain to forget it all, to pay no attention to the evolution of such tiny matters, but, little by little, they had dragged him towards the end – towards love or, rather, tormented desire.

Consciously seeing that reality for the first time – a sweet, ever more penetrating tenderness – he began to trace it back: a sky-blue nostalgia, so slender, so tenuous . . .

Only now, with absolute clarity, was he beginning, oddly, to feel – by a process of evocation – all the successive states of mind he had experienced since that episode.

It had not happened when he was talking to her, when he went to wait for her at the stage door, when she used to squeeze his fingers . . . No, it had arrived much later – once it was all over. Only today did he feel it, only today did he evoke all that with any pleasure . . . Sad love . . . sad love.

He had hardly known her and yet she had been good for him. She had grown inside him. Paulette now lived in his inner world. And far off, in the streets of a capital city lost in the south, in a country of failed adventures, one sacred person was softly murmuring her frail, Parisian name . . . Her irrelevant profile – willowy, flexible – faded into distant horizons, above epic cupolas.

She had become part of his life, part of the artist's life – thus would she enjoy a brilliant perpetuity.

It was good that he had never kissed her. That faint regret had grown translucent, intoxicatingly fragile, more sensitive, more susceptible, because more delicate.

.   .   .   .

Then he went back to remembering, hesitantly, how the actress had escaped him . . . and again reconstructed the psychological reasons for that flight. Now he consciously deluded himself, picking only those details that best suited the chosen interpretation. At the same time, by concentrating his thoughts, he tried to transmit his hypnotic will back into the past, pretending that, even though things had not happened as he had wanted, they were now beginning to turn out as he had intended.

121

. . . .

During the days that followed, his state of mind remained unchanged. His feelings of nostalgia were by no means a sterile source of suffering. For in the course of his melancholy rememberings, his flickering desires aroused in him unexpectedly marvellous literary ideas.

Paulette had done him a good turn by fleeing from him, for he had learned to suffer for a shadow, subtly salvaging from that elusive hurt a new impulse for his genius. Like the character in a certain remarkable novel, his spirit was transformed when diluted in literature, all his sorrows brought him masterpieces.

And thus, that night, wandering the streets alone and pondering his anxieties, his mind was once again diverted into the construction of a fearful story:

He would be a bizarre artist, wild and sublime, a religious visionary for whom the mystical adoration of Christ gradually became transformed into a violent passion, a sexual passion, tempestuous and boundless. He would do his best to flee it, first by attempts at lucidity, then, through exorcism, sackcloth, abstinence.

Until that terrible passion, which would be his ruin, became for him an infernal torment; he could no longer suppress it, all that remained for him was the blood-red impossibility of carnal satisfaction.

In the end, in order to douse the flames, the artist — a sculptor — would erect an extraordinary, gigantic statue of Christ. He would build it spasm by spasm, out of ashen longings, purple fury, out of an intermittent, barbarous madness. And once his immortal work was completed, in one final agony of lust — shameless, naked — he would hurl himself upon the sacred block of marble, crushing himself, his lips, his erect penis furiously against it, in order to die on the statue — panting, mutilated, cursed . . .

. . . .

Then Inácio thought how odd that he should have such an idea — splendid, scarlet, constellated with red-gold and amethyst – at a moment in which he had merely evoked with a kind of diffuse sadness the simple figure of Paulette, on the rosy afternoon when she had innocently squeezed his fingers.

He would make of that plot one of his greatest novellas – convulsive, spitting fire . . .

At the same time, through some oblique, transparent process, in an arcing leap of memory, he recalled someone about whom he had completely forgotten until then: yes, suddenly, without knowing why, he saw emphatically imprinted on the statue of the profaned Christ the sharp profile of Etienne Dalembert.

VI

The following day he still remembered that strange association which was, in fact, more absurd than disturbing. Indeed, if he went over in his imagination all the details of the affair, he had not thought about Etienne once since he had found out that he had been rejected, he had not even thought about the tender friendship that had grown up between him and the actor, since, once Inácio felt quite calm about his own fate, Etienne had no longer been of any interest to him. He had ceased to exist in relation to Paulette, therefore he had ceased to exist for Inácio too.

. . . .

His novel had just gone on sale and in the enthusiasm he always felt at the launch of a new book, his anxiety faded into nothing.

What is more, his imperiously original book – a notable phenomenon in that artistic den of fools – had been almost well received!

Indeed, even the imbecilic newspaper reviews recognised his stellar quality, even those least capable of understanding or symphathising with his European pages – naked, tigerish and brocaded, sumptuous with mystery, bronze-green and magenta.

There were the inevitable dark mutterings – the verminous bile of the ineffectual – amongst the literati of the rabble and the café, for example, Epifânio Góis and Eduardo Borba. If, on the next table to him, Inácio and the painter Jorge Pacheco (another vibrant child of Europe, as civilised in his conversation as he was in his art and his life) began, with childish brilliance, to intone extravagant hymns to Paris, evoking mirages of the grand life to be lived in those exotic settings, dreaming of inheriting sudden, magical fortunes that would help them to savour that astonishing city all the more magnificently, Góis – a pampered impressionist who had never shown his work – never missed an opportunity to wound the writer (though, to do him justice, he did so in mordant asides). Borba, on the other hand – a minor poet (and now an assiduous student of Law) who was merely mildly odious – was niceness itself to Inácio's face, the niceness of a hypocritical, illiterate whore, with his reedy voice and his seraphic air. Behind Inácio's back, however, he would take feeble revenge, dubbing him:

'That fool Inácio de Gouveia.'

. . . .

Meanwhile December was upon him once again and, since nothing now demanded his presence in Lisbon, Inácio prepared himself to return to Paris.

Movement, excitement, change – that was what his spirit needed. These had always proved the best balms for his sorrows. Waiting for the moment of departure, he was in the same carefree, distracted mood he had been in during the first weeks of his stay in Lisbon and during the run-up to the launch of his new book, a state of mind that would doubtless continue when he arrived back in Paris and saw its boulevards, its aristocratic squares, its great cafés, even the vague friends he had there, in particular, Horácio de Viveiros.

Nevertheless, he only returned to Paris in the New Year.

Ah, how he had once dreamed of being able to leave Paris freely, certain that he would never lose it, that his return would depend entirely on his will alone. And with what feelings of tenderness did he find himself once more in his banal little room in a modest hotel; even that vulgar detail was interesting, for it was the characteristic, traditional Paris hotel room, as depicted in the engravings of the popular novels we read as children, the waxed parquet floor and flower-patterned, creton curtains at the window, then a fireplace and, above it, a mantelpiece with two candlesticks and a clock beneath a glass dome.

In the days that followed, he would sometimes go to Manuel Lopes' studio – at five o'clock in accordance with his old habit – but only a few people gathered there now and almost all of them were new to him.

Horácio de Viveiros had found himself a splendid job –

quite how no one knew. He was now general secretary of the new Folies Bergère company. He had more or less abandoned music, although that was of little consequence, since his post was in a theatre and a Paris theatre to boot. Music had always been merely a pretext for him to live at the theatre. That was why he was so radiantly happy. He had triumphed.

A couple of nights after his return, Inácio went to the music hall – in honour of his friend and, thanks to him, with a free ticket – to see the final performance of an insipid, Viennese-style operetta, which would be succeeded by the big winter review.

Paulette had a small part in the show. The two sisters had a contract for the whole season at the rue Richer establishment, and Paulette was living for the first time with a lover, the comic actor Daniel Simond, her colleague from the Comédie-Royale.

He learned all this from Viveiros and would not have dared to go to the Folies so soon, had it not been at the invitation of his friend.

He took his seat and, the moment the curtain went up, a shudder ran through him. Oblivious to what was being said on stage, he scrutinised every actress' face in his desire to spot Paulette, perversely fearful lest he should not recognise her, even though he remembered her face perfectly well. In fact, he seemed to see her in each new figure that appeared. When her sister came on, he blushed as if *she* were Paulette. Paulette herself only appeared at the end of the act, amongst a group of bathers. They nearly all had bare legs. She was wearing a bathing suit.

In the interval, he went backstage to talk to Viveiros, who casually introduced Inácio to Daniel Simond.

When the actor left them, Viveiros said:

'Paulette has doubtless been given orders not to speak to you, or to Dalembert who is also in tonight. Poor thing, he knows that you both had a mild flirtation with her at one time. He'll have a terrible night tonight. His luck goes from bad to worse. He's a poor wretch, really. Women always cheat on him.'

In the second interval, he met Etienne in the bar. It was the first time that he had seen him since his return. They shook each other warmly by the hand and talked for a few moments, then said good night.

. . . .

How extraordinary, how truly extraordinary, thought Inácio as he walked back home alone, how he had suffered, how he still suffered in a way, for that obscure creature, so small, so insignificant. A banal dancer in reviews, she wasn't even pretty. Her sister, for example, was really beautiful and a great success, she was well on her way to becoming a music hall star. And she was the younger of the two. The elder sister owed all her contracts to her. Poor thing . . . she had watched her sister's meteoric rise and she had always remained unnoticed. She was all right now though. She had found a lover who suited her . . . a vulgar stage performer.

And yet, it was her very smallness that had made him suffer so much. Even so, poor love, poor love.

. . . .

Yes, there was no doubt about it, no doubt at all, he had clearly meant something in that girl's life . . . (Perhaps she had wept for him, when she had regretfully let him go.) He had been something – the proof of that was Simond's prohibition on her speaking to him . . . to him or to Etienne, yes, that was true, not to Etienne either. He had forgotten about Etienne already and yet he had met him that very night at the Folies.

Inácio had bumped into Paulette's sister. She had recognised him with an exclamation of surprise . . . and had spoken to him, smiling broadly. And suddenly, without knowing why, the writer wondered if that exclamation, those smiles, had not previously been Paulette's.

But he did not see Paulette. Her lover had probably locked her in her dressing room, because of him and because of the other man too, ah yes, because of him too.

. . . .

He reached his hotel. He lay down. He slept fitfully until morning.

127

It was odd. Paulette's eyes had changed a lot, they were larger . . . or, rather, they cast more of a shadow.

And gradually, all those feelings of tenderness and melancholy returned in the form of pure mysticism.

. . . .
. . . .

He was strolling down the boulevards that afternoon when someone called to him from the terrace of the Café Américain. It was Dalembert. He sat down next to him and ordered an aperitif. They talked for a long time, until seven o'clock, then went their separate ways.

Inácio felt painfully jubilant, a kind of strange, inexplicable sweetness.

. . . .

Large posters appeared announcing that in two nights' time the new review at the Folies Bergère would open. The names of Rose Doré and Daniel Simond appeared in large letters. Paulette's name came at the bottom – the last to be mentioned, in small print.

. . . .
. . . .

Inácio and Etienne began meeting every afternoon at the Américain. Inácio felt most put out if Etienne did not appear, although this rarely happened. Sometimes, however, Viveiros would come too, and then, Inácio felt oddly constrained by his presence.

. . . .

Inácio always avoided letting Etienne pay for the drinks, fearing that he might be short of money. With tender compassion he noted Etienne's thin overcoat in that harsh winter weather, and noticed that he always wore the same tie.

. . . .

That night, Inácio went to the new show at the Folies. Paulette appeared in the first scene, bare-legged.

When he went backstage to look for Viveiros, he found him with Dalembert.

. . . .

One morning, when he had just woken up, it suddenly occurred to him how oddly he and Etienne behaved when they were together. They never looked each other in the eye . . . they just kept talking. It was as if they were afraid of the silence.

.   .   .   .

.   .   .   .

That afternoon, Viveiros turned up at the Américain and invited them out to supper. He was so insistent that they accepted.

In the café, he said abruptly:

'There's something I've never really talked about to you two . . . you were rivals or, rather, successors. Now, though, you're the best of friends. Anyway, it's all water under the bridge now, so tell me your impressions. After all, she got rid of you both in the end . . . '

Etienne started to reply. Inácio couldn't understand what he said. Although he was strong enough not to give any outward sign of his agitation, he felt a violent shudder run through his veins.

Only minutes later was he able to hear or, rather, dimly make out, the words that Etienne had just nostalgically spoken:

' . . . because I was very fond of her, I thought about her a lot, I still do, perhaps. Her sister is the pretty one, but she wasn't the one I liked. These are things you feel, but cannot explain. I mean, if you try hard, you can always find a reason. I have such good memories of her, the best. If she wanted, even now, I would take her back.'

'And what about you,' Viveiros asked after a moment.

Unable to help himself, Inácio blushed, then said:

'It will all be in my next novel.'

'An excellent answer,' remarked Dalembert. 'There are some things it is easier to write down than to talk about.'

.   .   .   .

.   .   .   .

'Ah, so that was the truth of the matter, the truth at last! That was why they were always together. The girl had passed into Etienne's life just as she had into his, and she had lodged there. He too still thought about her . . . still, perhaps, suffered for her. Of course. If she chose, he was still ready to take her back. He too, he too!'

Then, more consciously than ever, Inácio was aware of his great tenderness for Etienne – a singular and intoxicating tenderness, tense and subtle.

He could understand him better than anyone else – he had had the same experience, he shared the same sensitivity . . . He too, for example, felt that her sister was the pretty one . . .

.   .   .   .

A few days passed.

Inácio plunged deeper and deeper into the spell, pondering what Etienne had said for hours at a time: 'These are things you feel, but cannot explain. I mean, if you try hard, you can always find a reason.'

Exactly, exactly.

In his case, his reasons had been such insignificant ones: one afternoon, Paulette had squeezed his fingers, boldly at first, and then she had fled him . . . her hands were elegant, golden and somehow mordant . . . the shadow cast by her eyes was charming . . . her distracted footsteps tiny . . . the bobbing of her small breasts gentle, tenuous . . . and so humble . . .

And that was doubtless exactly what had touched Etienne. It is always the same: a smile, a look, a voice, a lock of hair.

.   .   .   .

Now, when they sat face to face, there were long silences between them. Etienne's melancholy was obvious.

Whilst never alluding to the story that they shared, it seemed to Inácio that they had more than once spoken of Paulette.

Although they said nothing, they both knew only too well what was going on in the soul of the other. Which is why they would both now keep silent, with no further attempts to hide their feelings.

One afternoon, a girl stopped opposite them; in silhouette, she looked vaguely like Paulette, her dark face bore a resemblance to Paulette's face. Inácio saw her first and his eyes fixed on her as she stood at the window of a jeweller's.

Etienne spotted her moments later and said:

'She's interesting that girl, don't you think?'

This communion of feelings – whether partially real or totally imaginary – only increased their mutual affection. For Dalembert must have felt equal affection for his friend. It could not be otherwise. He never missed a meeting. They met not only in the afternoons, as at the beginning, now they often spent whole nights together.

In short, Inácio never had a thought about Paulette without immediately attributing it equally to Etienne. He even put down Etienne's wounded expressions, his sighs and many of his vague utterances, to their common sadness.

Besides, their banal conversations showed how often they shared the same feelings about so many things.

Occasionally, Inácio felt uncertain and wondered vaguely if this was all quite unreal, but at those moments, he felt only a great wave of sweet pity for himself. And he thought then that he had always been a child . . . that he would never be anything else in life but a child.

Then, he transferred all the tender feelings he felt for Etienne to himself, experiencing an infinite desire to kiss himself on the lips, in mirrors.

'Oh, by the way, did you know that Paulette has left Simond?' Viveiros announced to them one night. 'She's moved on to a Mexican dancer, a homosexual and a pimp. With brains like hers, she'll go far. She loves everyone.'

And some weeks later, again referring to Paulette:

'Didn't I tell you? The poor girl's a lost cause. The drugs have done for her. Ether, cocaine, not to mention sex. Haven't you noticed her eyes lately?'

To Inácio's torments was added this sexual frisson:

'Poor thing, poor thing. Though small, she had the courage to burn, to surrender boldly to the flame . . . naked . . . And she loved everyone.'

However, Inácio was unable to distinguish his excitement from his tender feelings for Etienne. Those two feelings intermingled in him, they were of the same order, he realised reluctantly. So much so that when he thought about Paulette, he immediately thought about Etienne too.

. . . .

Now, in a new sketch at the theatre, Paulette showed her nipples and deliberately, in all her roles, wore stockings that only reached her knees, exposing her bare thighs.

★

★   ★

Two months passed.

Inácio's feelings grew and burned in golden intensity during those two months. Day by day, he grew closer to Etienne, who had recently moved into his hotel. Now they addressed each other as 'tu'; they had supper together each night in the same restaurant.

. . . .

. . . .

One day, over lunch, Horácio de Viveiros suddenly announced that Paulette was extremely ill. 'The drugs, of course . . . and the high life.' She had missed two performances already.

Three weeks later, the girl was dying.

. . . .

How to express the strange pain that ran through Inácio when he learned of her death. It was not grief or longing, it was this: a mysterious envy, a sensual fury, jealousy, real jealousy! Indeed, when they told him the news of Paulette's death, he felt gripped by a brief, dark spasm.

'So she had genius enough to burn until the end – she is dead!'

And this idea excited him as much as if someone had come and told him that she would be dancing tonight, utterly naked, in a vast red theatre.

The death of a twenty-year-old girl had always struck him as the ultimate audacious act, the ultimate in refinement – a glittering, capricious act of debauchery.

That was why Inácio spent the ensuing days in a prolonged state of vague sexual excitement; as never before, he was filled by tenderness for Etienne, by a strong desire to kiss him, all the better to express his affection for him.

Etienne's behaviour at this time was not at all natural either. His face radiated a great sadness, but, at the same time, he was flushed and feverishly agitated; he twitched nervously. His voice shook and he dared not look his friend in the face.

. . . .

However, after some weeks had passed, they both calmed down and were left only with a feeling of dense melancholy, of useless pity for all that had happened . . . fleetingly, swiftly.

Only then did Inácio really feel Paulette's death, and he felt so sorry for the little actress. She was so insignificant, even in her death. The pathetic death of a Paris girl who had shown her legs on the stage of a music hall, indistinguishable amongst the crowd.

He himself scarcely felt her absence.

How small that absence was.

. . . .

Small absences . . .

Etienne referred to them too, comparing it to the pain he had felt at the death of a dog – a lovely, bright, playful creature.

. . . .

And that was how the tense spell grew moment by moment – unloosening and contorting itself – irresistibly intoxicating.

At first, they had been united by a community of charming things that had grown up about someone who had existed, who was a reality. That remorseful charm fluttered now about a nostalgia – more subtly though, more penetratingly, more delicately torpid.

. . . .

They hardly spoke a word to each other; they spent hours on end gazing into each other's eyes.

They often went for long walks along remote boulevards, walking in silence, slowly, mechanically.

Inácio watched every one of Etienne's gestures, relating them at once to a common state of mind.

. . . .

One afternoon, after just such a meandering walk, they found themselves suddenly, how they didn't know, in Montparnasse cemetery.

Why had they gone there, when they both had such a dread of cemeteries?

They had done so, doubtless, in order more keenly to re-member the dead girl, the elusive girl who, one sunny after-noon, had also entered a cemetery in Paris.

. . . .

. . . .

A shadow, a silence, the colour of a sky, a perfume wafted on the breeze, a shaft of moonlight, the gurgling laughter of a child, certain timbres, certain lights – a multitude of tiny, in-coherent things – all reminded Inácio of her. And if Inácio looked at Etienne at such a moment, he saw in his face the same dreamy expression of painful grief, yearning melancholy.

. . . .

Until one day, without knowing quite how it happened, their naked, masculine bodies entwined.

And that was the moment of Victory, that clean, unisexual embrace, the impossible triumph that one of them had glimpsed in a dream only once before . . . the ghost-ecstasy ineffably vanquished, absolute.

Beyond-Resurrection! An ultra-Reality for the soul alone! The artist felt that it was as if in the mutual psychic splitting of their common yearning, the sexual force of both of them had managed miraculously, astrally, simultaneously, to resuscitate between their bodies – in order to expel her – Paulette herself, naked and subtle, exhaling moonlight.

In the face of that marvellous, lofty vision – bespattered with gold – the very grandeur of it brought it crashing down, the ghost was purged.

Yes, the Artist had not only triumphed in monumentalising their yearning in a tangle of red-gold. He had created a mightier crown. In one moment, for the first time ever, he had possessed someone, at last, exclusively, iridescently free of being, in an aurora-bright ecstasy . . . far off . . . in space . . . far, far off . . . like a star, like a lion . . .

. . . .

. . . .

Lisbon, January–March 1914

MYSELF THE OTHER

For Carlos Franco

Myself the Other

12th October, Lisbon 1907

I am a golden dagger whose blade has grown dull.

My soul fits me tightly, it vibrates with the desire to burst forth. Only my body is heavy. My soul is imprisoned in a narrow hallway.

I am not a coward when it comes to fear. I am only a coward about myself. Ah, if only I were handsome . . .

I feel ashamed at my own feelings of greatness.

I am so great that I can only tell my secrets to myself.

I never had any doubts. I have always felt cold.

1st November

The open windows remain closed . . .

13th November

It's terrible the way I spend all my time wandering. In myself and amongst others.

I always stayed on, I never moved, even when I lost myself.

Sometimes, even now, I decide that I will leave. And I do. But I never manage to go through with it. If it is not my fault, then it is the fault of the others who beckoned me on.

If they did beckon to me, it was because they assumed that I would never follow them; they did so because they wanted to suffer. And since I did eventually respond to their gestures, they became disenchanted with me and they fled, mocking me. I detached myself from them.

I am only allowed to be happy on condition that I am not.

2nd December

It's unbelievable!

Almost everyone is quite contented with themselves; *they are fulfilled*. They live and they progress. They start families. People kiss them.

139

How disgusting! *Not even to have enough genius to want to be a genius!*

Poor wretches!

30th December

. . . And the open windows are still . . . still closed . . .

I have run aground inside myself.

I can no longer imagine myself.

20th June, Rome 1908

Ah, cities, cities!

I exhaust myself with activity. It's the only way I can get myself to close my eyes.

I have been travelling around Europe for six months now . . . I stay nowhere for longer than a week. That way I manage to keep one step ahead of myself . . .

. . . .

But alas, I soon catch up . . .

12th October, Paris 1908

The grey ruins of golden statues; blind, purple sphinxes; thrones without steps and the great marble staircase carpeted in sackcloth! . . .

But why do I look at myself like that, why? . . . It is this longing to go deep into myself that causes evening to fall inside me. And yet I feel so proud to have made that crossing . . .

Ah, if only I were who I am . . . What a triumph that would be! . . .

13th October

What it comes down to in the end is this: I am too much for myself.

15th November

Perhaps I am a whole nation . . . Can I have become a country? . . .

Possibly.

One thing is certain, I feel that inside me there are city squares.

16th November

That's it, that's it!

I have become a nation . . .

. . . Vast deserted roads . . . trees . . . rivers . . . bridges . . . a lot of bridges . . .

I cannot fill myself. I am too much for myself. I rattle about inside.

14th December

My spirit slipped and fell.

I overstepped the mark.

I stand coldly face to face with myself and I am almost happy.

22nd December

Peace . . . peace . . .

5th January, Paris 1909

Today I met *him* for the first time.

It was in the café. I suddenly saw *him* sitting opposite me . . . The café was full. That's why *he* came and sat down at my table.

But I didn't see him sit down. When I noticed him, he was already sitting opposite me. No one had introduced us and yet we were already chatting to each other . . .

He's so handsome!

And what about the triumphal look that lights up his lean, gaunt face? His long hair falls in ringlets. His hair is reddish blond. I felt like kissing him hard on the mouth . . .

Yes, he would know how to be me.

10th January

We meet every night now. We spend long hours together.

I don't know who he is nor where he came from.

We constantly misunderstand each other. We never agree.

141

Again and again he humiliates me, shakes me. In short, *he puts me in my place*.

He doesn't see anything the way I see it.

He is a different colour entirely.

His company is a torment to me. Yet I seek him out everywhere. When he fails to appear at the meetings we arrange – which happens often – an infinite sadness fills me.

The odd thing is I have never seen him *arrive*. By the time I realise he is there, he is already sitting opposite me.

Sometimes he arrives very late. When he does finally turn up, I feel terribly tired, exhausted, as if I had just made a huge physical effort.

I have never heard his footsteps.

He told me that he is Russian, but I don't believe him.

18th January

Our conversations cover all kinds of topics, but we spend most of the time talking about our souls. I reveal mine to him entirely. And he seems to believe me.

He has such long, long fingers . . .

27th February

For the first time since we met, I went a whole week without seeing him.

Only then could I assess what it is that binds me to him.

It isn't affection, although I do sometimes long to kiss him. It is hatred, an infinite hatred. But it's a glorious hatred too. That's why I seek him out and why I am only truly alive when I am with him. That's the truth: I am only truly alive when I am with him.

12th March

My friend is becoming truly unbearable. He makes me his plaything. He takes every opportunity to show how he despises me.

Every day his opinions are more repellent and more beautiful.

28th March

Today someone told me terrible things about my friend.

3rd April

Yet how powerful he is!

He may be perverse, but he is worth more than all the others put together.

He is all intensity, all fire.

When I am with him, I see what I would like to be, *what I also, coincidentally, am.*

If I were him, I would not be too much for myself.

Basically, his opinions are mine.

It's simply that I do not wish to believe what I think. I have my pride. That is perhaps what he lacks.

I am greater than he is. *But he is beautiful.*

He is as beautiful as gold and as vast as the shadows.

The open windows only opened up for me within him.

15th April

Should I kill him?

30th April

I should do something. I feel I am losing my personality.

Little by little my soul is shaping itself to his.

I have genius enough to admire him. This may be my perdition.

Let us at least be ourselves.

Let us suffer, but let us be ourselves.

I no longer believe in my sufferings . . .

5th May

He talks a lot to me about his lovers, but I have never seen his lovers.

I don't know where he lives.

18th May

I can never forget him. His words always come back to me. What I can never remember is the sound of his voice.

As for his footsteps, I have yet to hear them.

12th June

I am definitely going to run away from him. Enough is enough.

19th June

At last! The spell is broken . . . I am leaving this morning.

20th June, Lisbon 1909

I'm back. But how everything about me has changed . . .

22nd June

My friends say that I have changed a lot. They say my voice is different, my attitudes, my physical appearance.

I return home filled with fear.

I look at myself in the mirror . . .

And to my horror I discover on my face, as if in a caricature, the rictus of disdain on *his* face.

I say something out loud . . .

And for the first time I remember the sound of his voice . . .

I stride around the room . . .

I'm trembling all over!

For the first time I hear his footsteps . . .

30th June

I must rid myself of this obsession.

1st July

My God, my God, I no longer have the same gestures, the same thoughts as I used to have! Everything about me has changed. Everything about me rings false.

And everyone looks at me oddly . . . they all flee from me . . .

All of them . . . I hate them . . . I find them utterly inferior . . .

But he, yes, he is great! *He, undoubtedly, is great.*

This hallucination of mine is such torment.

I no longer know how to defend myself against it.

I speak. And suddenly my words diverge from my thoughts.

When I speak, it is he who is doing the thinking . . .

25th July

I sit down at my work table.

I am going to begin writing something I have pondered for a long time.

I write the first lines.

Disillusioned, I get up.

I cannot accept my ideas.

They seem commonplace to me.

I don't believe in what I write.

I doubt if I am, in fact, an artist.

The *other* is right.

If I were an artist, I would be beautiful.

And I would have long fingers.

And I would be pale.

And I would never know what time it is.

I tear up everything I wrote.

I feel sickened by myself.

26th July

Before, I used to kiss myself in mirrors.

2nd August

Today I wrote a few pages.

These pages I do believe in.

They are true works of art.

I read them out loud, glowing with pride.

. . . .

Then I suddenly fall into a rage.

I tear them up too.

They are not mine.

If I had never met him, I would never have written them . . .

6th August

He used to wear a strange gold ring on his left hand.

One day he told me that he had found it in the sea, when he was a child.

And that he was kidnapped by sailors on a schooner.

20th August

I am surrounded by the ruins of myself.

Golden threads draw me towards the abyss.

25th August

But I don't want to, I don't want to, I don't want to!

2nd September

The truth, the terrible truth is this: hour by hour I am slipping away from myself. I overflow my borders.

I suffer so much.

8th September

A mystery!

I did not give him my address; I did not tell him where I was going and today – yes, today in my house – I received a telegram from him. He arrives tomorrow.

Damn him!

9th September

This is what happened:

I decided to shut myself up in the house, giving orders to the servants not to open the door to anyone.

But a terrible fear gripped me.

I went out . . .

And suddenly *he* was walking by my side! . . .

10th September

What is to become of me? What is to become of me?

15th September

He never leaves me . . .

18th September

My senses are beginning to change. Sounds have different smells now. I feel colours in quite different ways. The light pierces me.

26th September

How I have struggled!

27th September

Ah! . . .

28th September

The end!
I no longer exist. I have hurled myself into him.
I have lost myself.
We have ceased being us. We are one now.
I knew this would happen; it was fated . . .
Ah, how I hate him!
He sucked me in little by little.
His body was porous. He absorbed me.
I no longer exist.
I have disappeared from life.
I have formed a cyst inside him.
Ruins!

2nd October

The most painful thing is that he does not even know that he has absorbed me because he has no respect for me.
If he had, I would have been the one to absorb him.

6th October

I want to run away, I want to run away!
Can there be any greater torment?
I exist, but I am not myself!
I am another . . . *I am the other* . . . *The Other*! . . .

. . . .

8th October

Where he goes, I go, but I never know where he is going . . .

His ecstasies are my ecstasies, but he alone does the possessing.

His ideals are my ideals, but he alone realises them.

How can I free myself?

12th October

The wretch!

17th October

Anything but this! Anything but this!

. . . .
. . . .

13th January, St Petersburg 1910

At last, success!

I have made a decision.

I will kill *him* tonight . . . while *He* is asleep . . .

. . . .
. . . .

Lisbon, November 1913

THE STRANGE DEATH OF
PROFESSOR ANTENA

For Côrtes Rodrigues

The Strange Death of Professor Antena

The death of Professor Domingos Antena caused a great sensation even amongst the general public. Not so much, of course, because of the terrible loss this meant to the world of contemporary science, but because of the air of mystery surrounding his death.

The ghost car that had suddenly appeared and then, skidding wildly, disappeared without trace, as if by magic, and despite exhaustive police investigations – including the imprisonment of a few chauffeurs with cast-iron alibis – this obviously made it prime material for the newspapers since it sounded for all the world like a trashy serial, combined with the fact that they had little other exciting news with which to fill their pages.

Besides, Professor Antena was a well-known figure. There was something indefinably odd about his appearance: his smooth, pale, lean face; his eyes always obscured by square, blue-tinted spectacles; the black overcoat and the unexpectedly large felt hat – like an artist's – that he wore winter and summer; his long hair and the silk cravat tied in an extravagant bow; all this had fixed his image on the foolish retina of the hoi-polloi. And yet, in the streets and squares where he was a familiar sight, he was never once the object of any uncouth remarks – so typical of that Portuguese, provincial, vulgar, regionalist rudeness that enjoys free rein even in apparently sophisticated Lisbon (indeed, there it is better honed and more widespread). Unlike more conventional men of science and unlike those feeble artists who, out of a senile fear of noise and agitation, shun the common herd along with all things European and progressive, Professor Antena, on the contrary, enjoyed all that, especially when he was in the marvellous throes of creation. For the fact is that a great scientist is a creator, he relies on his imagination as much as or more than any artist. Science is perhaps the greatest of the arts, the most

151

supernatural, the most unreal, the most touched by mystery. The artist divines. To create art is to foresee. That is why Newton and Shakespeare are peers.

And then, of course, people like nothing better than a good legend, and Professor Antena was surrounded by a golden veil of mystery. It was widely reported that this eccentric man had more than once been on the verge of discovering something vast and unimaginable; his laboratory, with its eccentric apparatus, was, it was said, more like a wizard's cave than the studio of a mere scientist. The newspaper headlines gradually turned him into a popular hero, and this, allied to the extraordinary cures, verging on the miraculous, which he had achieved in hospitals thanks to his unusual use of ultraviolet rays, meant that the man in the street saw him almost as a saint.

That was why his terrible death caused such a commotion. Throughout the city, throughout the land, people talked of little else for weeks on end; the matter was discussed and scrutinised.

How was it that I, his most beloved student – and today, dear God, his heir – and the only witness to the tragedy, how was it that I saw nothing, can remember not a single detail that might identify the car that crushed him? Besides, where the accident happened the road curved and the surface was uneven. The car could not, normally speaking, have taken the corner at that meteor-like speed. I, of course, blamed my blindness on the horror of the moment and people had to accept that. The fact is, though, that despite my unsullied name, despite the close, filial ties that bound me to the Master, I believe suspicion would have fallen on me had the cause of death not been so obvious. Obvious and yet peculiar too, because as well as *real* wounds, such as his shattered cranium, his amputated legs, proof of the terrible violence of the collision, there was another near-inexplicable wound: a perforation, conical in shape, in the middle of his belly, that seemed to have been made by a triangular gimlet, turning at dizzying speed, tearing at his entrails with its diamond point.

Another theory was that the car was being driven by bandits straight out of some melodrama, fleeing the scene of a bloody crime, but no crime had been committed that morning, and so this Holmesian hypothesis was set aside. Thus, since the inexplicable cannot be explained, but must be accepted, the strange death of Professor Antena came to be seen as a simple road accident. Soon no one even talked about it, it was all forgotten and the mystery discredited.

My name often appeared in the newspapers during the enquiry. Many reporters sought me out, as well as correspondents from the foreign press, but I only responded to their questions with my laments, my tears, and a brief description, always the same, of the catastrophe: the huge car, its windows closed, suddenly hurtling round the corner, not even sounding its horn – the noise of metal, clouds of dust, and on the road, the Master's shattered body.

. . . .

Today, almost a year after the accident, I have finally decided to speak out, and I do so only because I now have in my hands documents which irrefutably authenticate my story, documents that at least provide an admissible hypothesis, a strong hypothesis, to explain the strange story that I am about to unfold. At the moment of the tragedy it would have been impossible for me to tell the truth, as everyone will agree when they have read what I have to say. In my position, only a madman would have spoken out; it would have been proof of his madness. Being a sensible man, I said nothing. The greatest proof of common sense is our concealment of the reality of unlikely facts. The truth can only be told in certain very special circumstances. That is my guiding principle.

But to get to the matter in hand . . .

I propose today to set out a true account of the death of the Master, and then to interpret it according to the documents I found amongst his papers. Those documents are, of course, available to anyone who wishes to examine them. Unfortunately, they are far from complete. Being possessed of a prodigious memory – and guarding his secrets more jealously than any artist – Professor Antena only used his notebooks to write down formulae and sketches, often indecipherable telegraphic notes in which he condensed his ideas and the

153

reasoning that led him to certain conclusions. It was these notes which, once developed, later served as a basis for the illuminating volumes he published on each of his discoveries or even on his researches, books that now form a precious library which provides much surprising material, a library which, alas, lacks one volume: the greatest and the most fantastic. Were that not so, humanity would by now have advanced a thousand centuries, we would perhaps have at last uncovered the Mystery . . .

Meanwhile, let us be lucid and brief.

To make my account as clear as possible, I will arrange my narrative thus: I will first establish the truth about the accident. Then, in a summary, I will condense – as far as possible in a clear and orderly manner – all the disparate notes encountered amongst the Master's papers. Quite apart from the amazing things they allow us to glimpse, these notes, when taken as a whole – with some adjustments and with the lacunae filled in – provide us with, if not a definitive, categorical explanation, at least, as we have already said, with a convincing hypothesis about Professor Antena's strange death.

★
★   ★

One April morning last year, the 20th, to be exact, I went to visit the Master, as I did every day. His maid, an old woman, handed me a letter. Startled, I opened it and was even more surprised when I read the few lines that it contained:

Wait until I call you before visiting again. I need to be alone, entirely alone, for some time. But don't worry, you will be the first to know. Goodbye, and forgive me. Tell no one else.

PS. Expect to hear from me at any moment, and come as soon as I call you.

Accustomed to his eccentric behaviour, I folded up the letter, put it away and withdrew.

However, in the days that followed, I could think of nothing else. I was assailed by a terrible curiosity. What lay behind his sudden desire to be alone, a desire that was contrary to all his usual habits? He must have made some new discovery.

Knowing him as I did, and knowing, therefore, that I could do nothing about it, I resigned myself to waiting.

Yes, it must be a new discovery of his, for I recalled that, lately, especially since the beginning of the year, the Master had seemed preoccupied with some new problem that demanded all his concentration. His air of distraction, his often vague replies to my questions and, in recent days, the look of triumph, of apprehension that illumined his face, all indicated that his brilliant mind was again about to surprise us with some new marvel.

At last, in the early hours of the morning, after two weeks had passed, the door bell rang loudly. It was an urgent telegram from the Professor. It said: 'Be here without fail at six o'clock.' I was so impatient, I barely had time to get dressed and heat up a cup of milk.

At six o'clock on the dot I was knocking at his door. The old servant was already up and it was she who opened the door to me:

'The Master told me to have you wait in the living room,' she said.

This was another bizarre novelty. Normally, as soon as I arrived, I would go straight to his laboratory installed in a large pavilion in the middle of the garden.

Meanwhile, the talkative old woman was whispering to me in urgent tones:

'Ah, do you know, he hasn't left that shed of his for two whole weeks, except for an occasional bite to eat.' The 'shed' was what the good woman called his laboratory. 'And even then, he won't let me go down there to call him! He ordered a bell to be fixed up, imagine that. Look, shall I show you?'

She pressed a button that had been installed in the entrance hall.

Only a minute had gone by when the Master rushed out and embraced me.

He looked different. During the two weeks since I last saw him, he had changed enormously. He had perhaps grown thinner, but that was not the main change that had occurred, it was more bizarre than that: the expression on his face had not

155

changed, it had shifted. It was very strange, but that was how it was. And his eyes glinted through his glasses with a different light, as if there were a nimbus around them.

He cried:

'At last, at last! I'm not sure yet, I'm not absolutely positive, but I am supremely confident . . . You'll see, you'll see . . . you can't imagine . . .

All my work up until now has been as nothing! The most amazing secret! The great mystery! I'll say nothing to you just yet . . . but come with me. I am ready to conquer or to be conquered, I'll tell you everything later. Come with me. I want you by my side at the Supreme Moment. That's why I called you. I promised you that you would be the first, the very first to know! Wait here a moment!'

He went out and reappeared swathed in an ample, fur-lined cloak. It was May by then and, although the morning was rather cool, I was surprised to see his eternal black overcoat replaced by that extravagant cloak which I had never seen before. On his hands he wore thick grey fur gloves. He wrapped a long shawl about his neck, up to his chin.

As soon as we went out into the street, the Professor stopped and looked around him. He hesitated. Then he drew out of his pocket something that looked like a watch; he consulted it. Seizing me brusquely by the arm, he dragged me off without a word. Only then did I notice – and I am amazed now that it took me so long – that the blue lenses of his customary square glasses were a different colour, they were a very odd dirty yellow, a repellent colour that made one feel afraid. It's true; when I looked more closely at the lenses, that was the impression that shook me; foolish I know. The colour did not seem like a colour. My eyes felt it rather than saw it. Yes, when I looked at that colour, the message transmitted to my brain was one of touch – looking at it was like touching something viscous. And it was those strange lenses, I realised, that had provoked the change I had noticed in the Master's face: it was the lenses that gave his expression that dislocated look.

During our walk, he consulted his watch again several

times, although at one point I realised that it was not a watch at all. I did not have time to study it properly. I saw only that the face was purple and that the numbers representing the hours had been replaced by coloured marks. I did not dare to question him about the strange object, for Professor Antena had already warned me that he would not answer any of my questions. Besides, I would know everything soon enough . . .

Whatever it was, the mysterious watch must have served as some kind of compass, because he seemed to be using it to orient himself.

We walked for two hours. We were far from the city centre, on a fairly unfrequented road on the outskirts. Even so, two cars had already passed us. The Master walked on in silence, apart from the occasional muttered monosyllable. He let go of my arm. I followed slightly behind him.

I was in a very interesting state of mind. I felt as if I were hypnotised and were following magnetically in his path. If I had wanted to stop while he continued walking or to move when he had stopped, I would have been unable to do so. My steps were a function of his steps. A shudder ran through me, as if we were both in great danger. I sensed that we were being drawn along by a cloud of Mystery.

Suddenly, a kind of incoherent chill froze my fingers, and yet it was quite late on that beautiful May morning and already quite warm . . .

. . . .

We went round the narrow curve of the road. A great silence surrounded us. Then, in the distance, a village bell struck ten o'clock and suddenly – oh, terrible, prodigious moment! – I saw the Master stop short. His whole body shook as if in some kind of trance. He raised an arm. He pointed to something in the air. A rictus of fear crossed his face. He clenched his hands. He wanted to run away. He struggled, but he could not move a step, he fell to the ground, his cranium shattered, his legs crushed, and with a strange conical wound in his belly.

I had witnessed this astonishing mystery transfixed, unable to utter a word, make a gesture, make a movement. My breath came in stertorous gasps. I felt that I too was ready to fall down dead, destroyed. Suddenly, somehow, I managed to shake off this stupor and let out a scream: a shattering, terrifying howl . . .

. . . .

First to arrive were two labourers working nearby and they immediately started loudly cursing the motor car. After only a few moments, a small group had gathered round the body.

Meanwhile, I had regained some measure of composure and realising that I could not possibly tell the truth, the astonishing truth, I decided to accept the explanation of the car, especially since there were deep tyre tracks on the road, doubtless left by the two vehicles that had passed us some time before.

Someone went to call a customs officer who worked locally, and I told him the version of events which has, until today, remained the official version: the huge car hurtling round the curve of the road, the clank of metal, the clouds of dust . . . and a corpse . . .

. . . .

The rest is well known: the removal of the body to the morgue, the great funeral, the fuss made in the press, the fruitless police investigations . . .

Other details, however, were not made public. For example, still barely recovered from the shock, I ran back to the Master's house once the corpse had been removed in order to tell the old servant the sad news and to make whatever preparations were necessary. When I knocked on the door, the good woman opened it; she looked pale with fright and was trembling all over. She told me that there had been a tremendous din coming from the laboratory, that she had wanted to go and see what it was, but had drawn back in terror, because of the great wave of heat issuing forth.

I hurried at once to the laboratory. A mysterious noise, like the buzzing of fantastic bees, was indeed coming from inside. I did not hesitate for a moment. I opened the door – the lock, at first, proving unusually recalcitrant – and went in.

On the table, in the middle of the pavilion, sat an apparatus I had never seen before. That was the source of both the strange noise and the scalding heat. It looked like a small engine, the fly wheel of which had been replaced by a helix formed by a system of three glass vials. These vials contained a purple substance and emitted a kind of halo of black light. No, I am not raving. The luminous rays projected were indeed black. Let me explain myself better. The laboratory was lit by electric light and the black curtains on all the windows were drawn shut. Around the apparatus there was a halo of a different kind of light, one that cast no shadows only light, in short, black light. It was like a torrent of black agate, for like that particular mineral, the terrifying black light, that ghost light, had a similar sombre brilliance. And within that luminous black nimbus, a gold and purple twilight curled and crackled and glittered. Then – and this was the heart of the Mystery – the vials did not merely project light as they moved, they also gave off a grating, smoky sound and a dense, opaque, sonorous perfume. Every now and then, I heard a series of dull explosions creating a circle of echoes.

I was afraid I might be struck down by the strange fluids, suffocated by the hellish temperatures and I really do not know what would have happened had I not summoned up the courage to run over to the switch supplying the current operating the apparatus and turn it off. The machine immediately stopped. I looked at the vials. The purple substance had disappeared, as if it owed its existence to that movement . . .

. . . .

As for the precision instrument that the Professor had consulted several times during our walk, it was found in pieces in one of his large waistcoat pockets; his peculiar glasses were also shattered. Thus, all that was left to me of that awesome incident were three empty vials and a machine which, in itself, seemed perfectly ordinary.

I promised myself, however, that I would get to the bottom of his death and, as soon as I received the money left to me by the Professor, I impatiently began my search for any clue that might reveal to me a little, however little that might be, of that formidable Enigma.

Today at last – having first set out the whole truth – I

publish below the results of my research, in which you will see how the Mystery – using an admittedly abstruse logic – can be explained in simple scientific terms.

★

★   ★

'It is terrible how little we know of ourselves. We are surrounded by silence. What is life? What is death? Where *are* we, where did we come from, where are we going? A Mystery. Clouds. A fantastic shadow. And what intelligent man can bring himself to believe in ghosts! But are we ourselves not merely ghosts? And the Mystery? Look at them: the Great Secret, the Greater Mystery . . . we are them. When we stand in front of a mirror, we should always feel afraid! Let us forget about the future, forget about tomorrow, heroic dreamers of the beyond. Let us, instead, look back into the past, let us try to pierce through it, to know at least who we were.'

Like all great scientists, Profesor Antena had dallied with spiritualism and magic in the past, but the direction he was now taking was entirely new, thanks to an extraordinarily lucid insight: he was not interested in trying to break into the future of the soul, our life beyond death, but in plunging, rather, into the past, our life before life. In fact, it does seem more logical, easier, even more interesting, to know about the past rather than about the future, given that we know nothing of either.

What happened in the past must have left some trace.

And thus, departing from that axiomatic truth, the Master started looking for those traces.

Where should one look for them?

Inside ourselves, of course.

Now, what is the single most remarkable thing within our own personal mystery? The intelligence or, rather, the imagination. For how is it that our brain, which has no particular wish to accept the inexplicable, at the same time is capable of accumulating endless fantasies, indeed it creates them constantly and quite involuntarily? If our brain only accepts what it sees, what it feels, *what is*, how is it possible then that it is equally able to dream about what does not exist? How is it

160

that since there are no fairies, or enchantments, or gods, or miracles, that men are capable of conceiving of all these unrealities?

What is the foundation of all true art?

Fantasy.

What is genius in essence?

The creative faculties. By that I mean, fantasy developed to its highest level.

Yes, if our reason can only accept what it can actually touch, why does it bother to imagine things it cannot touch?

There is something worryingly incoherent here.

Incoherent? Or does it only appear to be? Let's see. One day, we glimpse a particular landscape which we then leave behind us. Since we have already seen it, we are able to remember it later on, when we are far from it, that is, we can see it in immaterial form, but only because we once saw it in material form. That is the only possible explanation. Now, if that is true, what is to stop us assuming a parallel explanation that also has every appearance of being true, that is, that the imagination has a similar origin?

According to this way of thinking, fantasy would be no more than a collection of reminiscences, of distant reminiscences of things that we do not remember having seen, but which everything, in fact, leads us to believe that we did once see, since we are able to re-see it. And here is the ultimate proof: *the imagination is not limitless.* Any artist wanting to create a work can only do so within a very restricted range of arts: he can be a painter, a poet, a sculptor, a musician or an architect. However lofty his genius, he will be unable to create anything that is not a poem, a building, a musical score, a statue, a painting. If the imagination were free, that is, if it were merely imagination, if it were not dependent on something else, such restrictions would not exist. The artist would accumulate other works, other arts and the name of genius would be applied only to someone who triumphed in some astonishing new art.

Apart from that, even outside art, in the simple life of aspiration, there are only about three or four types of anything, everything is prone to synthesis. Think only of the orgasm. Even the greatest onanist would be unable to lose himself in creating a new orgasm, which was not an orgasm, but something else, something excessive, all-embracing, of an entirely different and more thrilling colour, *a colour that it had never before been.*

But to conclude, fantasy, man's most mysterious attribute and that which most clearly marks us out from the other animals, must, since it is restricted, be dependent on something else, and it must inevitably be dependent on memory. Therefore:

We can only imagine that which we saw or that which we remember.

If it was something we saw, the fantasy is called a memory. If it is something we can only remember but cannot recall having seen, then it is pure fantasy.

The man with the most reminiscences will be the one whose fantasy has gone the furthest. Geniuses, therefore, will be those who have forgotten least.

If we accept that perfectly feasible hypothesis, it is only right that we should conclude that we had another life before our present one. Fantasy would then be the distant, vague, veiled memories that we have of that other life. If that is the case, it cannot come as any great shock to us to propose that our present life is merely the death, the other world, of our previous existence.

But how can we pass from one life to the other, bearing in mind that we retain distant memories of the previous one?

According to the Professor, it would all be a question of making a simple adaptation to various environments. The organs of life A, as regards time or any other large concept, would gradually become atrophied in relation to that life, that is they would become modified, until the change was complete. Then that life would die. At the same time, those organs would have adapted themselves and become sensitive to another existence. And when that happened, we would be born into life B. That means:

All souls have an age. And the various different lives — since nothing indicates that there is a limit on their number — would be nothing more than the several environments to which successively, and according to their ages, the souls would mould themselves.

We should also remember that amphibians, who are now mainly terrestrial animals, started out as larvae adapted to living in water. They changed their form and they changed their organs. They had gills, now they have lungs. They live, as we can see, two different lives in two different environments. Therefore, it is not so very daring to formulate the following hypothesis:

In the life of yesterday and the life of today, we are nothing more than successive metamorphoses, differently adapted, of the same astral being. Man is a chrysalis with a memory.

We are going to try if not to demonstrate this proposed hypothesis, at least to provide some evidence. Let us search within ourselves for the most convincingly mysterious phenomena and see if they fit the hypothesis in question. We need go no further than dreams or epilepsy. Is there anything more disquieting than the real or, rather, insanely real visions that arise in dreams and during epileptic fits, and which are like a temporary death, a dive into something beyond ourselves?

Dreams.

Let us take as proven that man does have memories of another life, of another metamorphosis, before this one. If he has memories, that means that he preserves traces of the senses, of the organs of that other life. (Amongst amphibians of the order Urodela, there are traces of the original gills in the the branchial flaps and the spiracle, indeed, in that extraordinary creature the olm, adapted to two simultaneous modes of life, they persist, functioning alongside the lungs.)

During sleep, our present feelings are anaesthetised, but the twilights of former senses remain awake, since they would not be susceptible to the sleep of this life, which is not that of theirs. Meanwhile, in our contemporary, sleeping senses, whilst images of our present life stagnate, they are not completely anaesthetised. They will not, however, be so intense as to suffocate the lingering traces of former feelings, as happens when we are awake, and thus they will both work together. That explains the incoherence of dreams, the disordering of reality, since the feelings will be mere shadows of stagnant feelings, interpreted through hints of senses belonging to another life, transmitted to our brain through our drowsy, vacillating, present-day senses. Or, to put it perhaps more clearly: during sleep, our sleeping senses will be activated by senses from another life, whence, the sum of arbitrary fragments which translates into the incoherence and lack of proportion evident in the phantasmagoria of nightmares.

Often, when we dream, we have the clear sensation that we are dreaming, and if we have a frightening dream, we make a violent effort to wake up. This is merely an indication of the struggle between our real, anaesthetised feelings and the active remains of our ghost-feelings.

The more heavily drugged our senses are during sleep, the more clearly will we remember our dreams. Not to dream means that our present-day senses have gone to sleep entirely and so we can have no memory of anything experienced by what remains of any former feelings.

Parallel to this is the case of epilepsy.

For some physical reason, in epileptics, the adaptation of the organs to present-day existence is only intermittent. There are lacunae in this life. During a fit, the epileptic will return to a previous life, although he or she is unable to tell us or remember anything about it (not even about the gap left in their present life) since the adaptation of their organs to the life of yesterday and their respective maladaptation to the life of today will have been complete. Thus, during the fit, they will retain no points of reference that might allow them to remember in this life what they experienced in the other.

There is no proof, however, that there are only two existences. On the contrary, everything points to the fact that we live an infinite series of lives, or possibly a closed circle of serial lives, which, without much difficulty, one can conceive as representing the immortality of the soul.

Still according to the Professor's notes, madness would be

no more than a premature, imperfect adaptation to a future existence. It is also highly likely that we already contain hints of senses from an immediately future life, just as formerly, in the life of yesterday, there would already have been indications of this life, of today's life. That would explain the peculiar phenomenon of *déjà vu*, that feeling of having already witnessed something, of already knowing the place where a particular scene we are living through now, for the first time, is happening.

In fact, it could very well be that in our former metamorphosis, probably during our latter years in that period, there were already in existence embryonic future senses sensitive to our present-day environment, and these would have retained a faint impression of that other landscape, ghostly memories that flicker when we stumble across it now.

'Thus,' the Master writes, 'when I look behind myself, I have a clear notion of – I can, in fact, remember – the colour of certain eras, in particular, that of the romantic period, a time in which I would have been an old man in my previous life.'

There is another essential point to examine, one that will allow us to formulate hypotheses about certain circumstances of the life immediately prior to this one.

Let us see: in this present-day existence we are not the only living beings. However, the only living being with the gift of fantasy is man. That is, man is the only being with memories, the only chrysalis capable of remembering.

Why is that?

There are two possible hypotheses: in the life of yesterday there must be various species, each of them *dying* differently, that is, de-adapting themselves from life A and adapting themselves to life B in different ways. A single species would retain traces of senses from that life A which, in life B, would be the preserve of man.

This second hypothesis seemed to the Professor much more probable and much more interesting. In that previous life there would be one being, *but many dead*. According to how you had died in life A, so you would be born into life B, and the being who had had the most perfect death in life A, would have the least perfect life in life B. Thus 'the fate of beings from that former existence would not be the same in the next'.

And that could very well explain the origin of that extraordinary human concept: Heaven and Hell – Heaven for those who had behaved well, Hell for those who had behaved badly. It would reside in the unconscious adaptation of a conscious truth known in the other life and of which, in this life, we have retained only the faintest of reminiscences. In the life of yesterday, we would know that our future in the life of today would vary according to how we had lived in the previous life. And in just the same way, we would suppose – as we developed in our present-day life – that our destiny tomorrow would be different according to how we proceeded today, choosing good and evil as factors from various fates. Now, being good or being evil requires a different orientation, a different tension in the spirit, which could, logically speaking, influence the adaptation of our organs to our future existence and their respective disaffection with the present one: 'In the life prior to our life there would be a single being who would die more or less perfectly and would enjoy a certain fate in this life according to how he or she behaved, how he or she was; of course, that has nothing to do with being good or bad, ideas which only have meaning for our present-day senses.'

Fantasy is made up of memories. If man imagines different fates for himself later on, it is because those memories exist in him in some real, parallel way.

That is where all these conclusions lead and that is why Professor Antena thought his second hypothesis to be the most feasible.

However, I have still not touched on the most disquieting aspect of the problem.

If you accept the hypothesis of successive lives, and if we take into consideration only the life of today and the life of yesterday, where will those lives take place, what would be their *environments*?

'Those lives exist superimposed on each other, as do their environments.' That seems to be the Professor's conclusion. Except that those beings who were adapted to one life would be insensitive to the next life. Thus, they would be unable to see it, or feel it, even if it passed through them, intersected them.

'Do these existences not fill the various planets?'

That's very possible, except that the Professor doubted the existence of other planets. According to his notes (we will never know, unfortunately, by what reasoning, observations or experiments he came to imagine such a system in the universe), the planets would only be like various *stages* of the same period of time – or, rather, of the same undefined quantity – and the lives would be the age, the different stages of metamorphosis of the same psychic being who is gradually adapting to one or other 'stage' of that undefined quantity.

This is not pure fantasy. If we look around us, we immediately find parallels; they are distant parallels, but still comparable. For are there not three different environments around us: solid, liquid and gaseous? And are there not individuals especially adapted to at least two of those three environments?

Right then. Let us accept for the moment that a fish would not have organs sensitive to terrestrial life, that when it rises to the surface of the water, its eyes would not notice the cliffs or the rocky coastline, that its body would be porous and transparent to everything belonging to that life. Suppose that the same were true of terrestrial beings as regards the aquatic environment. Then we would have two mingled, entangled lives, but each life would be lived separately, existing only for certain individuals.

So that is what happens. We have only to look at each other to see and feel areas where we cannot exist. Let us accept, then, that those environments that we can see are, although different, of the same order, whilst others exist in other orders where the differences will be enormous. None of the beings belonging to a particular group adapted to one of the environments will be sensitive to the environment of any other group, and that is the Master's hypothesis. Let us suppose further, to complete the hypothesis, that just as a toad, in its larval form, is adapted to the water, and in its adult form, is a terrestrial animal, so too a psychic nucleus living originally in life *A* in environment *a* would gradually adapt itself to environments *b, c* and *d* in which lives *B, C* and *D* would exist, each of these environments, of course, growing in sensitivity as they metamorphosed or aged.

There is more though. There is another better, more convincing parallel – plant life.

Vegetables are *living things*, and yet they share no sense, no organ, in common with that of animals, in fact not even their environment is the same, since both groups make use of different elements in the same environment. Vegetables cannot see our lives, they cannot feel it. The proof of this is that they lack any instinct for self-preservation. *They do not run away when we try to pick them.* Our life 'crosses' their life, but they never sense that it is there.

So why should the same thing not happen with us?

Why should there not be living around us other beings – our relatives, our antecedents, our future selves – who can see and feel us even though we can neither see nor feel them?

It would be going too far to propose the contrary. (We know so little, so infinitely little, that we should never guarantee anything.)

In that case, we should find the comparison unsurprising, as unsurprising as the proposition that the diseases that kill us are merely the *harvests* that those beings from another life make of us and from which we cannot flee because we do not know that they are there.

'Also,' the Professor notes in parenthesis, 'all these comparisons with the vegetable kingdom could equally include the mineral world as well. We have no proof that minerals are not alive. They may simply live a life that we do not understand. They could not live alone, but they can live in a group: they may have a group age, and each 'era' of that age will be represented by a mineral species.

However, we must not forget that these are mere comparisons, crude parallels. The fact is that for all of us – animals, vegetables or minerals – the environment is essentially the same, only the adaptations to and the ways of using that environment differ radically.

'Together, we all form a group. We could, perhaps, all see each other; at least those superior in organic complexity could see those who are inferior. There will, therefore, be various groups. Naturally, no one group would be capable of unveiling the mystery of any other group.'

And that was the extraordinary enterprise on which Professor Antena decided to embark, despite all the obstacles.

Unfortunately, we cannot know how he managed to attain a practical result, since, as we will see, his strange death seems to indicate that he did, albeit in vain. From his papers, though, we know the theory behind what he sought to achieve.

If we accept as true a system of successive, intersecting lives, each of them sensitive only to the group of beings currently in existence, the person in one of those lives who could, nevertheless, manage *artificially* to make his organs sensitive to another life would be able to travel from his existence to that other existence: for example, a vegetable that continued to be a vegetable whilst, at the same time, being an animal.

We do not know, we cannot feel, what the existence of a tree might be like. If we could experience it, *without forgetting ourselves*, we would know that. 'Without forgetting ourselves', that is, without ceasing to be ourselves, since, if the transformation were complete, we would still know nothing, because then we would know only our vegetable life.

Again, according to the Professor's hypothesis, an epileptic who has a fit might descend into another world, but since his organs become momentarily entirely maladapted to *this* life, he cannot, when he returns, tell us what he experienced in that other life. *He travelled there with all his senses blindfolded.*

To sum up, the Professor proposed the following: we would have to adapt our senses to another life (to the life we lived immediately prior to this one) whilst, at the same time, keeping our present-day senses alert. This truly was an ambition worthy of a god!

We publish below these curious notes, taken almost word for word from his notebooks.

'Let us suppose that various planets do exist and that on each of them there is a life and an environment. Not even that would disprove my hypothesis about superimposed worlds.

"How is that possible?" people will ask. The planets must be separated by space and you can only cover space by movement. Ah, but who says that movement exists? Can we be sure of that? We cannot. There have long been doubts about it; Zeno of Elea denied its existence. What is most probable, almost certain, is that movement, time and distance (or rather, the measurement of time and distance) are merely sensations proper to our present-day organs, *sensations that define them*, and the reality and unreality of things are merely sensations too. In the universe nothing is real or unreal, but something else which can only be known by the perfect individual who has adapted from one life to all lives, living them universally. And that triumphant person would surely merit the name of God.

Would the well-known phenomenon of *déjà vu* not support this hypothesis of the existence of superimposed environments? If existences were crystallised separately at a great distance from each other and if that distance were a reality, we would presumably be incapable of snatching premature glimpses of feelings (which are, anyway, only very vague) of what another life was like and incapable of peering into it, occasionally recognising ourselves in vague memories, shadows, landscapes, twilights.

When I was small and I stood before a mirror, I would tremble because I did not recognise myself, that is, I was afraid of my own mystery. Now I realise that the feeling I experienced then was something else. It seems to me that it was not that I did not recognise myself, rather, that I knew who I had been before, but had now forgotten, and, try as I might, I could not remember.

That merely supports my theory of reminiscences, the idea of successive lives that leads on to the concept of the eternity of the soul. We should, in fact, be spiritually eternal, and one indication is that when we think of what we call the Beyond, we always get the feeling that even if death meant total destruction, we would still *know* something – since we would have known nothingness, would have seen or felt nothingness.'

. . . .

★

★   ★

That was all I could extract from the Professor's vague notes. From now on, I can only make suppositions about them.

Professor Antena must have given deep thought to these notes, which date back some years, and made various adjustments to them. He obviously found authentic proof for his theories, but had not as yet added anything further, since, being still immersed in the matter and determined to work it through to the end, that would not be necessary. In fact, when he was working on a particular problem, he only used his notebooks to jot down ideas about other problems he might tackle later on.

Confident that his system would work, he set out to demonstrate it, that is, to penetrate into another life, probably the life immediately prior to ours. How would he do this in practice? That remains a secret.

Amongst other bundles of papers there is a series of calculations and chemical formulae which may be related to his search for the marvel. Most of these calculations are indecipherable and the formulae illegible, since familiar symbols are accompanied by many unidentifiable ones. The most common formula is this:

$$W^3Y^2X\,N^4R_0 \,.\, a$$

Doubtless the strange vials containing the purple substance that I had seen in his laboratory had something to do with the discovery, as well as the mysterious watch which seemed to orient his footsteps during that last tragic walk. We know nothing more.

Now, as I said at the start, in all this lay proof of the

verisimilitude of Professor Antena's extraordinary death, whose truth I have only now established. Let us see how.

It is really quite easy if we accept that the Professor solved the Mystery, as his fantastic death seems to indicate.

Whilst maintaining his organs in a state of sensitivity to this life, they would have, in fact, awoken in another life. In that Absolute moment, the Professor's body had ceased to be porous, insensitive, invulnerable to that other existence, but when that happened, something in that world must have run him through; the same thing might happen to an epileptic who descends into that other life during a fit, some object in our existence could easily mow him down (a car, the wheel of a machine) if we could not see his body and protect it.

Thus, by some disastrous coincidence, Professor Antena, at the very moment of conquering the Mystery, emerged into that other life in the middle of a square packed with cars, or in a vast workshop, in the midst of terrifying, pounding machines that crushed him.

(Obviously, the terms I use are merely vague parallels, because in that other existence there would be no machines or squares, but other things, entirely new things, which the Professor, coming from our life, would have witnessed for the first time.)

That is the hypothesis that I propose. Anyone who wishes to can formulate others, they may even take up his theories and try to put them into practice, which is why I am publishing this. It would be a crime to hide them. They tear at the shadows, they make us tremble with Mystery, as no other theories do. However incomplete and muddled, they are still astonishing.

And in memory of Professor Domingos Antena we should remember always, in awe, the person who, for moments, was perhaps God – God Himself – the person who became, for an instant, the God whom we men are eternally creating.

Lisbon, December 1913 and January 1914

MYSTERY

For José Pacheco

Mystery

I

The pain was so intense that when he placed a hand on his forehead he could sense his whole skeleton beneath the skin.

The tram he was riding in clanked and clattered its way down the broad avenue, and that acrid noise, together with the brilliant light that beat against him as it flickered zebra stripes through the chattering windows, was an accurate rhythmic equivalent of the present state of his soul. His soul today was all broken glass and leprous scrap iron.

Distractedly, the artist looked about him. He concentrated on the panorama surrounding him and incorporated it into his own delirium, following it in all its multiplicity. For the scene inside the tram was inconstant, it varied from moment to moment according to the external landscape. When the tram went round a corner, the great buildings and the trees would slither across in a semi-circle and the zigzagging street-lamps would bend and clasp hands overhead, somersaulting in through the windows.

The figure of the man who had been waiting for the tram in a doorway and had got on while the vehicle was still in motion, would still seem to be framed by that doorway; just as the charming European girl who had sat down next to him was still vibrant with moonlight, still pearled with movement, for she had fled her companions who could still be seen far off, tinged with platinum by the nostalgic December moon, as they stood laughing and biting into bitter Spanish oranges.

When he looked more closely, by dint of intense concentration, he could distinguish in all this mobile atmosphere cascading buds of air that jostled and foundered, pale vertices of light, hemispheres of colour, planes that span and then stopped, creating bizarre harmonies, and also perhaps – along with the things that they sustained or penetrated – a new beauty worthy of some immortal painter.

Turning his attention to the material forms about him, the artist saw the trembling, garish oscillations of the red seats in the deserted first-class compartment and the multiple physiognomies of the passengers whose faces became overlaid by those of the passers-by slipping along the street parallel to them, and who only recovered their own faces when the tram stopped.

Ah, movement, the great renewer that multiplies everything, that vibrates and dreams . . .

Why did he feel so desolate? Precisely because his life was an existence in which both body and soul had grown stagnant, an existence in which nothing ever happened. *It was as if his life did not exist.* That is why, one evening, consumed with anxiety, the artist had taken the vehement decision to make a fervent attempt to seek life out, to build it with his own anointed hands, by sheer determination. Since then he had hurled himself passionately upon the world, upon life, leaping, running, kicking . . . but up until now, he had failed to build anything out of it for himself. His body and his soul appeared to have the strange ability to repel the hours, just as, inversely, a magnet attracts metal. Everything span about him and fled; he was always the sole centre of an enormous circumference. He kept moving forwards, body and soul, in the hope of coming close to what fled at his approach. The same thing happened with time – his position remained constant in relation to the thing which, however hard he tried to clasp it to him, stole away from him and bounded into the distance. He was the one who had no incriminating papers in his drawers, who had no confidential letters to conceal. He was a creator. Perhaps that was why his life did not exist.

Pride, pride! But the price he paid was this dull death agony. Meanwhile, he had reached the great square. He made an effort to collect his thoughts and, however painful the experience, he began to see himself with utter lucidity.

How discomfiting! His soul was a vast house in winter, cluttered with furniture draped in sacking, and with open

176

windows through which the sibilant wind rushed in . . . and there was thick dust, lots of dust, covering the great stacks of books and manuscripts.

Nothing attracted him or filled him with enthusiasm; if he came close to the few things that he did not actually have, he fled from them feeling deeply disappointed, just as today he had fled from the blonde girl with whom he had lunched.

Lastly – and this was the latest torment – there was the breakdown of his soul which he now experienced like a physical pain translated into an endless torpor, an invincible drowsiness, an insatiable desire to live with his eyes closed. And the drowsiness that penetrated him was like an alcoholic drink that brought him to his knees: it numbed not only his brain, it made his whole body drunk. He could feel that moral drowsiness in his very flesh. Every inch of his flesh simply wanted to close its eyes.

Maelstroms of thoughts provoked by the slightest thing whistled through his constantly whirling mind and even when he wasn't really thinking about anything, he could still feel his brain working. Only his hearing remained untouched by the fever. It was an unceasing, nameless torment!

Ah, if only he could rest . . . And he imagined the gleaming white hospital room where he would lie down in a large, white bed, never to rise again.

At other times he was harried by ridiculous ideas, especially by vague memories and insignificant recollections that arose for no reason. Right now, a vivid memory suddenly surfaced of a rainy day in his childhood that he had spent on a beach in the north, in his own country.

It had rained all day, a sinister, torrential rain. The sky had remained black as night, there had been lightning, thunder, high winds, a terrible wind that had screamed, desolate and frightening, along the paths of the small chalet garden. It was autumn and the dry, yellow leaves had whirled about for a long time, hurled mercilessly against the window panes.

In the afternoon, though, the storm had died down. The wind dropped, it stopped raining, the sky grew blue again, and the sun came out, the sad, nostalgic sun of autumn afternoons, fond and comfortingly golden. Then, with his father's old nursemaid, he had gone to buy corn bread, hot and golden, straight from the great provincial oven. And he remembered so well the narrow, grey, rain-drenched streets, their chill smell, the penetratingly damp air lit by the weak sun . . .

Why had that banal childhood afternoon, all dampness and rain, surfaced in his memory now? Why? Because today – he realised with horror – he had the same sense of stagnant discomfort; yes, in his soul today there was the same penetrating dampness, thin and grudging, that had desolated one country afternoon in his childhood.

A beggar asked him in a feeble voice for alms. He was an old man with a full beard, tall, stately, shivering with cold. The artist put his hand in his pocket, he selected a few copper coins and held them out. The old man thanked him. And just as he had often wept tears for the childhood of old people he respected, he began to feel tormented now by a sense of infinite pity, pity for all those who suffered and even for those who did not: the happy, the mediocre, everyone. Such was his egotism, he almost swooned with compassion and tenderness.

Still immersed in these oppressive thoughts, he reached his room. It was a vast room in a good hotel, carpeted, comfortable, in which, nevertheless, he spent as little time as possible. This was because when he was in that room, especially during the day, the furniture and the curtains seemed threatening and he felt as if the walls themselves were pulling obscene faces and closing in to crush him. One night he had woken up in a state of terror: the whole place had gone mad and he was convinced that the chairs and the mahogany wardrobes would have strangled him if he hadn't fled down the corridor. Obviously, it was just a nightmare which, however frightening, was so bizarre that he laughed out loud when he remembered it.

He lay down at once and, before going to sleep, he thought: 'My suffering has but one cause: I am an anchorless ship being carried drunkenly along by whatever current takes it. If only I could drop anchor somewhere . . . But where . . . where?'

The following morning, after sleeping for ten solid hours,

he woke up exhausted, ready to live another identical, empty day of his life . . .

The first thing he thought that morning was: 'What a strange feeling yesterday when I placed my hand on my forehead. I could feel my whole skeleton. But I felt it in a very odd way. I felt it as if it were a shadow. That's it, when I placed my hand on my forehead, I could feel beneath it the gaunt shadow of my skeleton stealing away. That, I realised, was an expression of the most terrible pain. But why, why? Could I be going mad?'

The artist often considered suicide, as a cure for his anxiety. And then he would be torn apart by an infinite tenderness, a limitless pity for himself. Did he really have to destroy himself? Yes, it was perhaps his only salvation. How sad! And he imagined himself as someone crossing a bridge carrying a precious bundle which, when he was already close to his destination, he had to throw into the river in a final gesture of despair, since he lacked the strength to carry it any further.

He had more than once decided, positively decided, to put a bullet through his heart. He had even got as far as buying a gun. In the end, though, at least up until now, he had always given up the idea with a feeling of great joy, a joy that soon dissipated: even if he didn't commit suicide, he would have to die one day. *If only not committing suicide could save him from death . . .*

II

Yes, he needed to drop anchor somewhere because he had to live in order to write.

Only a short while ago he had received a letter from a close friend. In response to his laments, to his cries of desolation, the latter had said, after many circumlocutions in which he apologised for counselling such a cure for a remarkable soul such as his, that perhaps (indeed he was sure) the hours would weigh less heavily on him, would wash him clean, were he to seek a kind, affectionate companion who would understand him a little and to whom the artist could give his life, that is, someone who could provide a purpose for his mad existence.

It was true; up until now, his life had been a constant struggle. Flushed and sweating, having seen all things but known none of them completely, he felt like a child anxious to play with all the toys he has just been given, who hurls himself upon them, playing a little with each of them, and then growing weary, disenchanted, having discovered what each of them does without really having played with any of them.

A companion . . . a companion . . . Perhaps even a lover. Yes, in certain tender moments, he had sometimes felt a longing for a pair of white hands that would clasp his fingers . . . a mouth that would bend to kiss his . . . and blonde tresses smelling of youth and love.

The paths of a large garden; healthy, golden air, trust, simplicity, peace . . .

That's why he wrote back to his friend saying that there was no need to apologise for offering such advice. If only that companion existed . . . if only he could find her . . . Yes, perhaps that was the remedy for his life.

Looking for her was another matter.

Why bother?

If he were like everyone else . . . but he wasn't. He required love to be love. And love doesn't exist.

It wasn't that he dreamed of passionate affairs, strange affectations or abstruse perversions. All he wanted was to know another soul entirely, a soul that would in turn know his soul. If that were the case, they would be joined by a great affection. He set to imagining a fantasy existence: he, the Artist, producing his immortal works slowly, calmly, steadily, piling dream upon dream, whilst below, when he looked down from the mountain peak, would be a life of new beginnings with a genuine companion, spontaneous, petite and blonde, to ease and warm his existence . . . Bare arms and a shedding of white rose petals.

Deep down he really loved life. Don't go imagining someone daydreaming about other lands, shut up in an ivory tower built somewhere beyond the skies. He loved life, but only when it was stripped of everything that sickened him, and what sickened him was the everydayness of other people's lives.

No, he was quite sure, he was not made to be happy.

The remedy lay elsewhere: he must resign himself and live, or else rise above life and die.

He had only rarely, and then only vaguely, sought a loving companion. However, he had always fled in terror from the abyss that opened up between him and the enchantress the moment they began to grow closer. The words he wrote to one could have applied to all: 'In your life, my love, I was never more than a passer-by, someone who appeared momentarily and then vanished.'

Lack of understanding was the barrier he always bumped up against and which he always would; there was no solution, he knew that all too well.

Besides, that barrier lay between all men, who were doomed to perpetual isolation. The majority were content to exchange glances and vague signals from either side of the abyss and not one of those souls ever attempted to get close to another soul on the other side of the precipice. *It was as if it were impossible.*

If, after living an unclouded day-to-day existence together for many years, two spouses looked closely at each other, if they looked deep into each other, they would find – they were bound to find – two strangers separated by a thousand trivialities, a thousand tiny lies, a thousand insignificant disloyalties. Their souls never really knew each other, however sincerely they believed in their friendship and their love.

In normal life, friendship is nothing but a false idea, a convention we gradually grow accustomed to. And love . . . that was just sundry fragments taken from cheap literature mixed together with a few clammy pleasures to liven up the cliché and anoint it with tawdriness.

Moreover, the artist knew how difficult it was to reveal one's soul. Even when we want to open our heart to a dear friend, a few details always escape us, details we can't explain, perhaps because we lack the words, and which we feel would be exactly those that would most precisely describe our feelings. We thrash about, we beat against a dense veil we cannot tear, *a veil that would only be sundered if our friend were to understand us through some means other than words*.

And that is why the artist sometimes wondered fearfully: 'Perhaps our souls are secrets.'

Ah, if only he at least suffered . . . Yes, in the final analysis, it was possible that he might find some meaning to his life in suffering, might find the root. He sensed as much one night when he was walking alone along a narrow street and suddenly felt filled by a deep sadness; for he found that he felt much happier, that his life seemed much fuller and more beautiful than it had only a short time before when he was walking across a broad square, before that feeling of bitterness had surfaced in him. Perhaps that was why he had unconsciously further refined the feeling by scorning certain rare moments – tinging them with suffering in order to sensitise them – moments which, were he to allow them to blossom, might preserve their golden warmth. Yet, even though he longed for tenderness that afternoon, even though he bemoaned the fact that nothing ever happened to him, he had rejected the sweet girl who had smiled at him on the boulevard, so spontaneously, so sweetly . . . Instead of clasping her

182

hands, he had talked of fantasies, had said goodbye without even a caress, had lost her forever . . .

The truth is, he did not even suffer. In his mind everything became tainted with literature. Out of any genuine pain he might feel and out of his imagined sadnesses he carved only masterpieces. Faced by the marvels both these states provoked in him, he immediately stopped experiencing them in order to bless and admire them.

His pain was, at most, only the melancholy we feel after reading a great but troubling book.

His feelings were at their most intense that lovely winter afternoon. The boulevards of Paris were packed with people – a very modern, ultra-civilised, Latin crowd. And he, who had always delighted in the flow of contemporary life, let himself be carried along on the current, feeling almost happy. The urban hurly-burly went to his head, like some intoxicating draught.

Borne up on a blue wave of enthusiasm, eager for happiness, he set to daydreaming, as if he were sitting amidst clouds of opium. He had finally found his soulmate, he had found her one sunset-red evening in the marvellous gardens of a great royal palace, battlemented and historic. It was pure fantasy . . . He had met her by chance and immediately, after they had exchanged their first words, he had trembled in recognition . . . Then, in a succession of loving afternoons, amazed, incredulous, he had come to know her soul . . . No, it wasn't a mistake! He had found her at last, he at last had her by his side! Her soul would be able to plumb the depths of his soul, just as hers no longer held any secrets for him. It was like a dawn, a new dawn!

He experienced a thousand sweet episodes, creating them as he went, each one banal and commonplace, until he had realised his desire in its entirety: he wandered the country landscape in which his happiness would bloom, he traced the profile of the enchantress, saw her long hair, her jewels, her bare feet in the cold water of a stream, the blush on her

183

cheeks, her kisses and her smiles, her veils, her wild fingers with their red, polished nails . . .

A sudden, dissonant noise brought him back to reality and then a strange anger gripped his mind. How could anything like that possibly happen, if he just imagined it all? He had only to have dreamed the background, the plot and the main character beforehand to ensure that he would never travel through that landscape, live through that experience, meet that person. Dreams never come true. And he had dreamed everything . . .

Nothing repelled him morally, only physically, which was in a sense worse. He knew he would be capable of stealing, but not of killing.

That was perhaps what lay behind his arid life, why, perhaps, his life was restricted to the moral, that is, to the unreal.

The most troubling aspect, however, was that what he was left with was a real and insuperable anxiety, but at the same time a sense of glorious pride, of immense pride, so ardent and so golden that he wondered if perhaps it was he, in his imagination, who created all the difficulties.

Suddenly, how he didn't know, he found himself in a large, romantic, traditional garden. He walked round it, filled with tenderness, watching the children, their cheeks flushed, their legs bare, running about in the damp, healthily perfume-laden air, and blonde young women reading books of poetry or chatting and holding hands with their young men, as young as they were. Ordinary people, happy people . . .

The children . . .

Now he was swept up in a whirl of activity. Nearby a barrel organ was groaning out music. He went closer and stopped in front of a carousel for children. The machine raced dizzyingly around – all the fun of the fair – transporting a swarm of laughing children who were riding elephants and doves, lions and bees, panthers and swans – as if they were real.

Looking back at his own childhood, the artist was filled by nostalgic longing, a terrible tenderness . . . It was only in that uncertain period that he had been happy, that he had had everything. And why? He understood the reason clearly in that moment – the facts were there before him. In childhood we do not yet have any sense of impossibility: *we can as easily ride a lion as a bee.*

III

Night after night, the artist's suffering increased. More than ever, he felt a fierce need to find a harbour. In a moment of extreme *ennui*, he had looked at his own existence and had experienced a feeling that was both incoherent and bizarre, as if he dragged the hours behind him in his crazy path, but meanwhile remained always fixed in the same moment . . .

If he looked hard at himself, if he took his own measure, he found himself immersed in a great bitterness that he did not have the strength to combat. So, he concluded, this was to be his future: to accustom himself moment by moment to the idea of suicide. This much was certain, one day he would find the strength to destroy himself, to be conquered, since he could not conquer; in short, he would one day have the strength to put an end to that intolerable situation – damp, stagnant, viscous . . .

And from then onwards, that was his one hope, but it was a sad hope that he did his best not to think about, forgetting about himself, anaesthetising himself with everyday life . . .

He was wandering, alone, through the broad streets, as he did every evening when, suddenly, someone held out their hand to him in an expansive gesture . . . It was a banal acquaintance he had had little to do with, someone he hadn't seen in ages, with whom he had barely exchanged more than a few words.

. . . .

And that night, early, when he was walking home, the artist thought about the pleasant hours he had spent with that distant stranger, how he had found in him an open soul, generous and intense . . .

They had started off speaking about art and then slipped almost at once into a sudden intimacy and a description of their own souls. They had found so many points of contact: like the artist, the stranger had grand, wild ideals, but also suffered from terrible periods of torpor and nausea. He even confessed that sometimes he was gripped by an ardent desire

186

to go mad as a way of putting an end to his life or, at least, of ceasing to think about it. The idea of suicide repelled him, he had always felt proud of his love of life . . . Were he mad, he would still exist, albeit calm, drugged, dead to desire; for however convulsive his madness might be, it could never be as bad as his life of aspiration. The artist agreed with him. To go mad, that *would* be a victory . . . And he began talking about himself. He explained how he felt as if he were drifting with the current like an anchorless boat, drunk with gold on the deep, muddy, bitter waters. He described to him his anxiety. He told him about his idea that perhaps all souls are secrets. And the stranger remarked:

'It's desolating, horrible. Two souls, however loyal, however united, are always separated by a whirl of tiny things that gather in a cloud impossible to penetrate. *But, alas, perhaps that is precisely the reason for their existence . . .*'

He, who for so long had found no one, had discovered a wonderful companion. And their friendship would grow . . .

He did not see him for a week. During that week his anxiety was at its painful worst. He seemed to reach new depths.

To go mad – ah, if only he could achieve that triumphant state . . .

Obsessed, his imaginative mind, his literary mind, immediately began working on that idea, imagining a man who, in his desire for madness, goes out into the street and shoots the first person he passes, a complete stranger. He would choose an elegant young girl, soft and blonde, because one always makes choices whatever the circumstances. There would thus be a touch of tenderness about the tragedy. By killing someone he did not know, that man would have committed an unjustifiable act, that is, *an act of madness*. He would be arrested, he would explain his crime: he had committed that incomprehensible act of murder because he wanted to go mad and he would add, as a tender detail, the reason behind his choice of victim. At first sight, the man was no longer a madman, there was a motive for the crime – the desire to go mad – but, good

God, such a motive would be still further proof of his madness, such an idea could occur only to a madman. The murderer would thus be deemed not responsible for his actions and shut up in a madhouse . . .

However, on finding himself in such a paradoxical situation, was the man mad or not? A mystery. He had got into that *coherently mad* situation through a logical, conscious and correct reasoning process.

Meanwhile, placing himself inside his character, the artist immediately concluded that, *even if the man wasn't mad*, he would doubtless end up going mad – at least once he had entered the madhouse – in his desire to find out if he had or had not triumphed.

Yes, he would be gripped by such a fiery maelstrom of ideas that they would suck him down until he drowned in the blue, in one final twilight . . .

And after this strange daydream, of course, the artist was left only with another plot for one of his complicated novels. It was what always happened – with his daydreams, with his sadnesses, with his sufferings. *That's why he never took himself seriously.*

The physical suffering, which his moral desolation had long ago become, was now an exquisite torment: the same intoxication, the same drowsiness in every inch of his flesh. Before, though, that impossible desire to sleep, that feverish desire in his tortured soul, used to spread throughout his whole body. Now, amongst the drowsy flesh, there were small sections, clear interludes, of lucid consciousness. What once suffused him with anxiety now wrapped the faded fears of that hellish prostration in a nervous torpor.

A few days went by. He met the stranger again.

A wonderful friendship grew up between them; they would spend a few hours of almost every evening together and one day his friend invited him to have supper with him at his house. He lived with his family – his father and two sisters – in a lovely villa on the outskirts of the dazzling city. He wanted to read him a poem and to show him his books and the flowers in the garden. He was so insistent that the artist, who would have preferred to refuse, accepted.

On his way there, he realised that this was the first time anyone had invited him to supper at his house, with his family . . .

IV

And now, in the perfumed evenings, he would review that whole ethereal dream, a very real dream now that he had by his side his loving female companion in the simple garden of the villa where the bride and groom had gone to live in a country in the south – the country of the artist, a country full of light . . .

It was wonderful, wonderful!

When his friend first introduced him to his eldest sister, who could have guessed that in that small, pretty, carefree body lay the realisation of his dream? Afterwards, though, little by little, incredibly, moving from enchantment to enchantment, he had discovered in that soul the subtle, veiled woman he had despaired of ever meeting. Finally, as he moved from fantasy to fantasy, reality had surfaced, saving his life through this incomparable adventure. Now, that blue victory was his! He had *someone*, someone whom he knew almost completely, someone who was not a stranger, an astral stranger; someone who, in turn, understood him, knew all his secrets.

What joy! He had built a bridge across the insuperable abyss; he was the brilliant conqueror of shadows and, for the first time, two souls were there, face to face, free from mystery! . . .

It was just a question of tearing one final, tenuous, golden veil and his glory would be complete . . .

. . . .

He was radiantly happy now!

He had the palms of healthy, white hands in which to plunge his anxious fingers, he had golden lips to kiss, the sensitive flesh of another's body to explore. He felt life stir inside him, he who had always lived in death. He *had* someone, he who had never had anything. Now, when he lay trembling on the sweet body of his young lover, of that young wife who surrendered herself to him with every inch of her pink-veiled flesh shimmering with roses, a feeling of infinite pride filled him because he could feel, beating under his hands, amidst the ecstasies and the lilies, not just her body – he had experienced that in earlier sad embraces – but her soul. And when he touched that body, he bound its soul to him too, yes, he possessed it carnally, in brilliant desire, in moonlight spasms, in fluid agony, in a tremor of pale glory, subtle with transparent sound . . .

Night after night, his triumph grew clearer, more tangible. Something was still lacking though – a tiny light – in order to reach the end, the 'beyond' that he could clearly glimpse, oriental, musical, echoing with the slender timbres of rhythmic perfumes.

Yes, he had arisen! He had ceased to be a stranger, nothing separated him now from that other tremulous soul! Their two souls had shared mutual ideas, heroic and profound. And even more wonderful than having finally penetrated someone else's mystery was knowing that someone else knew his every secret.

Ah, how he had suffered before in those terrible moments of wounded tenderness, in his desire to throw himself – a poor, sad creature – into the arms of someone who, *without words*, would understand him a little, feel his pain a little. And in the face of total incomprehension, even from certain loyal friends who truly admired him and who, nevertheless, so often hurt him, how often had he suppressed a fierce desire, a perverse desire, to hurl his soul at them like someone hurling a golden globe, scintillating with lights . . . and to have them sully it, trample it, yes, trample it!

Today, however, he had won through. It seemed unreal: he had what he had dreamed of! He had a sweet companion into whose arms he could silently entrust himself and who, in silence, would intuit the secrets of his soul – the tiny veiled things that no one can express; at last, someone who *experienced* his soul the way one might *experience* a work of genius.

For the first time he was not alone. Indeed, since he had never existed in relation to another person, he had always been alone, even in the company of his colleagues he had always felt absent. He had only felt a little less alone when abroad, during long periods of isolation, due to the concentration of his mind which, the more intense it grew, the less it was touched by daily life and thus made him think more about himself, made him live more inside himself. Now that he existed in relation to another soul, *now that he found his soul perfected*, he felt at last that he had a companion.

The artist had often sensed that he lacked something that others had, but had never known what that something was. Whatever it was, though, he was certain that it would be some kind of point of reference. The vacuum had been filled. That was all there was to it.

The truth was that only now did he know himself – *because someone else knew him*. He had triumphed. He was no longer isolated, in the true sense of that phrase, not in the hypocritical way other people use it.

In that warm, affectionate atmosphere, his body unravelled, that was exactly how it felt; before, he had always had the feeling that his body was contorted, twisted, confused.

If he daydreamed now he saw at once, in a flash, how much the scenery of his soul had changed. Dawn had broken inside him and become glorious morning. All the clouds had scattered, leaving the sun to shine on the gold. The pile of grey objects had crumbled into blue ruins. The sacking had been whisked away to reveal furniture made out of ivory and silver . . .

Now, inside himself, he strolled along broad avenues where before he had stumbled down alleys, into narrow hallways.

He no longer felt the desire he once felt to lie down in the streets of great cities, perhaps because that was the position of the dead beneath the earth.

His soul, which had always been a narrow channel, viscous and stinking – or at best a moonlit quagmire – was now a white tower rising out of the sea.

His life had at last dropped anchor in a vast, lively bay, full of sunlight, flags and noise, swaying with masts and sails.

His future now was all horizon.

. . . .

The villa where the bride and groom had come to live was a fitting adornment to such miraculous happiness. It resembled a sensible English cottage with walls covered in a blanket of glicinias. It was surrounded, as if with a ring of coolness and health, by a lovely garden, very green, all grass and perfumes. Beyond, there was nothing, apart from another villa about a hundred yards away, almost directly opposite, that was inhabited by a mad poet and his nurse. A gardener and an old maid took care of the two newlyweds.

The capital could be seen as a distant tumult of lights and heard like a vague echo of movement and civilisation that only added to the peace and isolation of the enchanted place.

.   .   .   .

Yes, his life would have an end, but he would live his future existence as a tranquil present: new smells, new sounds, different colours, against the same eternal backdrop of gold and blue. His works would create themselves, effortlessly, smoothly, peacefully; the only fever would be in his imagination and he would always have a gentle shoulder on which to lean his sacred brow.

He was ready now to go beyond the ultimate triumph – complete communion between two souls. And so great, so urgent was that happiness that he even felt a strange desire to die alongside his rosy companion. Of course, that desire was soon swallowed up in a desire for life, in the joy of the cool hands that clasped his fingers.

Then, when his ideas about death had also become a distant doubt, he was seized by another: *Could one truly break down all the barriers between two souls?*

He would find out that night. Yes, that night – he was sure – he would reach beyond his happiness. The tenuous golden net which, however translucently, still separated their two souls, would finally be torn, dissolved.

When he went up to his bedroom, embraced the wild body of his splendid lover and kissed her hard on the mouth, mingling with her body in the same shadow, his glory seemed boundless . . .

V

The madness of the poet who lived nearby was the calm, ethereal madness of one shipwrecked in unreality, which was why his friends had taken pity on him and, rather than send him to the madhouse, they had installed him in that delightful house far from everyone.

However, he spent that particular night in a state of great agitation. Trembling with excitement, he insisted on standing on the balcony of his room, leaning on the balustrade and staring out into space.

At about three o'clock in the morning, he got out of bed and ran over to the balcony again. Suddenly – according to what the nurse said the next day – his eyes grew vacant, his whole body trembled and, pointing to the villa opposite, to the window of the newlyweds' bedroom, he had let out a loud cry. Later, he spoke wildly of seeing a flame leap from that window, a vast, strange flame or rather, a luminous shape that leapt the windowsill and, in an arching spasm, a diffuse wave, rose up and flew away . . .

. . . .

The following morning, since it was eleven o'clock and the master and mistress had shown no sign of life – and they tended to be early risers – the old maidservant decided to go upstairs and wake them. She knocked at the door, she called, she shouted . . . Getting no reply, she tried to open the door. The odd thing was, the door was locked from the inside, when normally they left it half-open to let the air circulate. Frightened, she ran to tell the gardener the strange news and he, in turn, went up to the newlyweds' room. He called and when no one answered, he tried to force the door, the key of which was still in the lock, on the other side . . .

. . . .
. . . .

The two lovers were sleeping serenely in the big bed, but

194

their bodies were stiff and cold. There was no sign of violence, though, not even a scratch.

There was no evidence of a struggle in the room. Everything was in its place. The jewels were on the dressing table. There was no weapon, not even a bottle that might have contained some toxic substance. Nothing. Not a trace, not a footprint. The door had been locked from the inside. The window stood half-open, but the window was on the second floor. It would have been impossible to lean a ladder against it without leaving some trace, without crushing the glicinias.

And during the police investigation, all they could ascertain was that the mad poet had been unusually agitated that night and claimed to have seen, at dawn, leaping from the window belonging to the two dead lovers, a flame, a great, strange flame, or rather a luminous shape which, in an arching spasm, a diffuse wave, rose up and flew away . . .

A triumph? Pure superstition?

A mystery, a troubling mystery . . .

. . . .

Lisbon, August 1913

THE MAN OF DREAMS

For José Paulino de Sá-Carneiro

The Man of Dreams

I never knew his name. I think he was Russian, but I'm not sure. I met him in a cheap restaurant on the Boul'Mich, during my time in Paris as a failed medical student.

Every evening we dined at the same table and one day we fell into conversation.

His was a truly original and interesting spirit; he had bizarre opinions, strange ideas, as strange as his words, as extravagant as his gestures. That man, I felt, was a mystery. As I learned later on, I was not deceived, for *he was a happy man*. I mean it, he was an entirely happy man, so happy that nothing could destroy his happiness. I often tell my friends that the most singular fact about my entire life is that I have actually met a happy man.

I learned the nature of his mystery one rainy night, one dark, icy night. I had begun by cursing life and then my friend, in a tone of voice unusual in him, said:

'You're quite right, of course. This life is a terrible thing, so terrible that no one can make it beautiful. Take the man who has everything, health, money, glory, love. He cannot possibly want anything more, because he possesses every beautiful thing there is. He has achieved the maximum good fortune and is, therefore, the most wretched of men. For there is no greater misfortune than to have nothing further to desire!

And, believe me, it is not so very hard to reach that miserable state. Life, after all, contains so few things, there is so little variety. Take any area of life. Tell me, are you not already sick of the meals that have been served up to you ever since you were born? It's inevitable, you never refuse a meal, because you're a man, and it is not in your power to control life. Call in the most wonderful cooks and what will they give you? Vegetables and meat – half a dozen different types of vegetable, half a dozen varieties of meat. Even on earth, anything that isn't animal or vegetable is inevitably mineral. There you have the inconceivable penury of nature!

And as for feelings, name one which, when it comes down to it, cannot be reduced to either love or hate. And sensations? Again there are just two, joy and pain. In life, everything goes in pairs, like the sexes. *And can there be any more desolating fact than that there are only two sexes?*

Returning to the matter in hand, though, show me an entertainment that is not religion, art, theatre or sport. You can't, I'm sure.

Certainly the best thing in life is movement, because if you walk along at the same speed as time, that helps you to forget it. A train in movement is a machine for devouring moments, which is why it is the most beautiful of man's inventions.

To travel is to experience movement. However, after a short time spent travelling, the same feeling of terrestrial monotony assails us, with boring inevitability. On every side we see the same scenery, the same accessories – mountains or plains, seas or meadows or forests – the same colours, blue, green and sepia, and in the polar regions, blinding, limitless whiteness, the ultimate expression of monotony. I had a friend who committed suicide because there were no other colours, no other landscapes, beyond those that exist. And, if I were him, I would have done the same.'

I smiled and remarked ironically:

'You didn't though.'

'Who do you take me for? I have seen other colours, other panoramas. *I know what I want, and I have what I want!*'

His strange blue eyes glinted, he leaned closer to me and cried:

'I am not like other men. I am happy, do you understand, *happy*!'

His attitude was so singular, his tone of voice so peculiar, that I judged I must be listening to a madman, and I had a strong desire to put an end to the conversation. I could think of no feasible excuse to leave, however, so I had to stay, and, without pausing for breath, that bizarre man then vouchsafed to me the following extraordinary confession:

'It's true. I am happy. I have never told anyone my secret, but today – why, I don't know – I'm going to tell you. To think that you assumed that I lived an ordinary life . . . You must have a very low opinion of me. I thought you held me in higher esteem. If I had lived that life, I would have long ago died of it. I am a proud man and the worst possible fate would be to have to live life as it is. I never tire of telling people: human life is impossible – there's no variety, no originality. I compare it to the menu of a restaurant where the dishes are always the same; they look the same and they taste the same.

Well, I have succeeded in varying existence, in varying it daily. I not only have everything that exists, you understand, I also have everything that does not exist. (Besides, only what does not exist is beautiful). I live hours that no one has ever lived, hours made only by me, feelings created only by me, sensual experiences that are mine alone, and I travel through far-off lands, through mysterious nations that exist only for me, *not because I discovered them*, but because I built them, because I build everything. One day I will even build the ideal, not just achieve it, more than that, I will construct it. I can already glimpse its fantastic form, tall and slender, merging with the blue heights, carved out of victory, glittering with gold, no, not gold, with a metal more golden than gold.

Obviously, I have no words to express these marvellous, non-existent things. Ah, but the ideal, the ideal! I will dream about it tonight. For it is in dreams that I experience everything. Do you understand? I have learned to control my dreams. I dream what I want to dream. I experience what I want to experience.

I have made some marvellous journeys . . . I will tell you about some of them. The most beautiful, because it was also the most terrifying, was this.

I had grown weary of light. Every country that I had ever travelled through, every landscape I had ever contemplated, was always flooded with daylight and, at night, with the light of the stars. I found that eternal, irritating light so enervating, so monotonous, for ever stripping everything of its mystery, that I set off for an unknown land, lost in a world beyond reality, where cities and forests are perpetually plunged in utter darkness. There are no words to express the beauty of what I saw in that extraordinary place, because *what I saw was the darkness*. Your intelligence cannot, of course, conceive of this, nor can anyone else's.

It was an immense capital city. Its boulevards stretched, ever onwards, for miles, and were lined with vast trees; silent, milling crowds packed the streets and all the vehicles – the carriages, the great buses, the cars – travelled along together in a gloomy, muffled clangour. *Out of the silence came a music.* A strange, fearful shiver, delicious and new, ran through me, scattering through my body. Before my very eyes a mysterious life was finally opening up, for there was no light to illumine it. A proud and fearsome spectacle . . . I could see the darkness! On the corner of some lost street I found two lovers locked in a passionate embrace. Ah, how wonderful those deep kisses must have been amongst the supreme blackness of the dense dark! Further on, I witnessed a scene of violence, daggers were drawn, there were cries of pain. I have never experienced anything more frightening. And on the outskirts, there were vines laden with fruit, fields of ripe wheat, cornfields and orchards swaying in the wind . . . all of life, in short, all of life, but carried on in impenetrable darkness. What a triumph, what a triumph!

I achieved perhaps an even greater triumph on my journey to a perfect world where there are not merely two sexes. I saw labyrinths of intertwined bodies possessing each other in a chain of continuous orgasms, successive and current, that melded together like a long fugue. Infinite, infinite! It was a glorious dawn chorus of the flesh, a sublime score of voluptuousness that thrilled through each of those various turbulent sexes. And life, all the while, slipping by in waves . . . !

It would be impossible to recount all my journeys to you, but there is one other country I would like to tell you about.

What a strange country that was. Everything in it was the same colour, a colour which I cannot describe to you, because it does not exist – *it was the colour of no-colour*, and therein lay its supreme beauty. The atmosphere of this world was made not of air but of some other gas, in fact, it was not an atmosphere, it was music. *In that country, one breathed music not oxygen.* More bizarre still were the inhabitants. They had a body and soul like people on earth, but what was visible and definite and real was the soul. Their bodies were invisible, unknown and mysterious, as our souls are invisible, mysterious and unknown. Indeed, like our souls, they may not even have existed.

What divine feelings I experienced in that country. My spirit broadened out. I felt as if I could comprehend the incomprehensible. I must return there one day, to that peerless country, to that country of the soul.

In short, my friend, I make whatever journeys I choose to make. For me there are always new panoramas to explore. If I want mountains, I have no need to go to Switzerland, I leave for other regions where the mountains are higher, the glaciers more resplendent. I can choose from an infinite number of mountainous scenes, each one different, as well as seas that are not seas and vast areas of land that are neither mountains nor plains, but something more beautiful, higher, flatter, in short, *more subtle.* I have transcended the world: it is a universe, but a universe that is constantly growing and expanding, by that I mean that it is not exactly a universe at all, it is something else.

There are no barriers for me in the spiritual sphere either; I have gone beyond love and hate and have known other feelings which I cannot define, of course, because only I have felt them, and I cannot explain them even in words, even by comparison. I am the only person whom those feelings excite. It is unnecessary, therefore, to seek some word to translate them, since I could never communicate them to anyone else. Besides, it is the same thing with the loveliest moments I have lived. I can only speak of those that remotely resemble life and are, for that very reason, the least admirable.

Let me sketch out for you some new pleasures.

There is no doubt that the body of a woman is a marvellous thing and that the possession of a splendid, naked body is an almost superhuman pleasure, a dream almost. Ah, the tawny mystery of fondled breasts wet with kisses, blonde nipples that brush against one's flesh provoking in one marmoreal ecstasies . . . sharp, sinewy legs, the distant vibrations of imperial orgies, lips that were made to wound with love, teeth that grind and grip in lofty orgasm . . . Yes, it is beautiful, it is all very beautiful, but the pity of it is that there are so few ways of possessing all that beauty. Bodies may entangle and contort, kisses may cover every inch of flesh, blood may even be shed . . . In the end, though, it is always the same two sexes caressing each other, intertwining and devouring each other, and it will all end in an orgasm that will always be the same orgasm, given that it always resides in the same organs.

Now, I have possessed women in a thousand other ways, I have been shaken by different orgasms that reside in different organs.

Ah, how delicious it is to possess someone with one's eyes alone. Our flesh does not touch, however lightly, the flesh of the naked lover. Our eyes, only our eyes, suck at her mouth and bite her breasts. A scalding river runs through our veins, our nerves tremble like the strings of a lyre, even our hair feels it, all our muscles relax, and our eyes, watching from afar, drink deep of all that beauty, until, at last, sight enlarges us, we see with our whole body, a tremor shakes us and a limitless, shadowy orgasm cuts through our flesh in a moment of extreme desire . . . We experience supreme pleasure. We possess the body of a woman with our eyes alone. We possess her physically, but immaterially, the way two souls can love each other. In that case, the orgasms into which we plunge are sweeter, calmer, but no less delicious for that.

(Another interesting, voluptuous act is the total possession of a woman's body through just one of her breasts.)

So, my friend, understand only this: I am happy because I have everything I want and because I will never exhaust all the things I might want. I have managed to make the universe infinite, what others call *infinite*, but which, for most people, is a narrow, walled field.'

There was a long silence. A typhoon was whistling through my mind and the whirl of fantastic images that the stranger had evoked for me seemed to be trying to shape themselves into something more real. The moment they seemed ready to be fixed, however, they burst like bubbles.

The man said:

'Life is a cliché. I am able to avoid that cliché. That is all.'

And with that, he ordered a cognac.

I did not see him for two days. When I met him again at the same restaurant table, I noticed a different expression on his face. He confessed to me:

'I now know what the ideal is. It is rather less beautiful than I imagined . . . And what have you been up to, my friend?'

We talked of banalities. I wanted to lead the conversation back to the subject of his dream life, but my efforts were all in vain.

We left. He walked with me as far as my house. He said goodnight. After that, I never saw him again.

*
*   *

I thought about that strange man for a long time afterwards. For months and months I was obsessed by the troubling memory of him. I too wanted to know the secret of becoming a master of dreams, but it was no use. I never did manage to control them and, shortly afterwards, I gave up my search for that golden chimaera.

From then on, my madness consisted in wanting to throw some light, however dim, on that remarkable mystery.

And finally, one day, one triumphant day, I guessed the truth.

What became of that man? A secret! I never knew anything about him. He often walked home with me, but I never found out where he lived. I thought he was Russian, but he never actually said that he was.

He was tall, extremely tall and thin. He had long, curly hair of a drab blond, *fugitive* colour, and his fantastically blue eyes were certainly the strangest eyes that ever lit upon me. I can only evoke them through this incoherent description: they were of a shining, brilliant blue, yet they did not shine.

His unsettling voice, at once dull and sonorous, seemed to

issue from a false throat that existed outside his body. When he got up and walked, his long, agile, silent steps gave the impression that his feet were walking on air, not on the ground; his walk was as hesitant – and this is the oddest thing – as his vague, hesitant features. His physiognomy might best be described as 'inconstant'; you could never take in all the different parts together: a great painter would have had real difficulty in fixing on canvas the mobile features of that man of dreams. However long you spent face to face with him, you still never felt that you knew his face, that fugitive face of his was not something that could ever be learned, even after long hours.

The over-riding impression left by his physiognomy, his walk, his gestures, his voice, was this then: the stranger was a creature of fog, indefinite and vague, unreal. *A dream creature.* That idea flashed through my mind with blazing clarity. Yes, the man was just like those people who come to us in dreams and who, in the morning, we can never entirely reproduce, however hard we try, because we lack all the details: we remember their eyes, but forget the expression of their mouth; we can recall the strange colour of their hair, but not the fantastic colour of their eyes. In short, it is never possible for us to reconstruct the whole of that shadowy person glimpsed in dreams. His features escape us, just as the features of that strange man escaped me.

I mean that *the marvellous stranger was a dream character* –and yet real too.

It was at precisely the moment when I stumbled proudly upon that distantly lucid thought that the admirable secret became for me an *idée fixe.* I was afraid I might go mad. I dread to think what would have become of my poor brain, brushed by the wing of mystery, if, in the end, I had not managed to plunge deeper into the blue abyss.

If the man of dreams was a dream character, but at the same time a real creature, he must have lived a real life, our life, my life, the life of all of us. Impossible. He told me that he could not bear this odious existence. *More than that, his attitude to this existence of ours was precisely that of a dream character,* yes, it was that of a hesitant, unreal character with unreal, hesitant features. Therefore, the marvellous stranger did not live *our* life, and if he did *not* live it and only appeared in it vaguely, it was because he was dreaming it.

And that was when I managed to snatch a glimpse of the infinite. The strange man dreamed life and lived dreams. We live what exists; we can only dream of beautiful things. Yet that wasn't the case with him. He had demolished reality, relegating it to dreams, whilst he lived in unreality.

A chimaera of dust rising . . .

Golden wings! Golden wings! . . .

Paris, March 1913

WINGS

For Alfredo Pedro Guisado

Wings

I

The memory of that extraordinary person was engraved for ever on my mind when, one night in a café, Inácio de Gouveia rather indifferently introduced him to me.

How could I forget that inexplicable, slender creature with his long, dull-gold hair, his liturgical face and his unsettling eyes, whom I had seen for the first time near Notre Dame, in the small hours, standing alone and still. For he was not, as would have been understandable, contemplating the cathedral in the violet mists in the early hours of an autumn morning, he was, perversely, standing with his back to it, staring at the sky, deep in thought, enraptured . . .

I stopped for some minutes to study the wretch. His face was contorted, his eyes twitched oddly, his body was shaken by sudden tremors, as if he really were witnessing some thrilling scene taking place in the empty air!

I came across him again, a few days later, in the Place Vendôme.

I could be more discreet this time, because it was the five o'clock rush hour and the stranger was again studiously scrutinising the atmosphere. That day he seemed calmer, in a pinkly tender mood, lowering his fragile gaze every now and again to glance at the rich women climbing in and out of their cars.

And I saw him again, one last time, in the Jardin de Luxembourg, where he seemed to be absorbed in watching the children playing.

It was thus with great curiosity that I greeted him, uttering the inevitable 'Delighted to meet you', although, this time, it was utterly sincere.

I knew now that he was some sort of Russian artist, a vague acquaintance of Gouveia's, 'Petrus Ivanowitch Zagoriansky . . . I think,' the novelist said to me in Portuguese.

Then Gouveia left us, and we stood there alone.

Our conversation got off to a marvellous start; it was as if we were old friends. I spent the whole night listening in astonishment to what the Russian had to say.

What zebrine intensity, what a synthesis of gold!

Face to face with him, convulsed by the beauty of his *new* words, I had the crazy feeling that the artist was speaking not only with his mouth, but with his whole body.

Afterwards, we met often, almost every day. And now, remembering that time, not so very long ago, I recall it as a period touched by dreams, beauty and wonder, by a mysterious disquiet.

I am not writing a novel, I am merely describing a real episode, however secret and disturbing. I will, therefore, not bother to give a dramatic plot to my narrative. It will flow freely, unfettered, relying almost entirely on verbatim reports of our conversations.

I confessed right at the start that I already knew him by sight and that I had been deeply impressed by his rapt appearance and his strange pose, staring into space, outside Notre Dame and in the Place Vendôme.

I remember that Zagoriansky merely smiled one of his unforgettable *triangular* smiles, adding something I didn't understand, some harshly onomatopoeic word, doubtless a Russian word intended as a reply.

However, a few days later, when I spoke to him at length about my art and explained to him the plots of some of my novels, my companion shifted in his seat, lowered his eyes, and said spontaneously:

'This really is extraordinary. I had given up hope of ever meeting someone who thought like that. My friend, you are an artist, an Artist! Everything you have just described to me – I mean this – is an apotheosis of my own sensibility. What a triumph! For the first time, I have found someone with whom I might actually be able to talk about my art. I don't mean that you will understand me – far from it – but you will understand me a little and that is a great deal. You'll see . . .'

And then, in deep confidence, he started telling me his aims, his latest theories:

'It's my nerves you see! My horror of Sameness! Why always do the same thing, when there are so many Other things around us? Give me excess and diversity, ornament and gold!

You remember seeing me looking up at the sky, like a madman, rapt. At the time, I was writing one of my new poems in which I wanted to suggest all the unsuspected beauty of the air. Yes, my friend, the air — that great insidious thing that wraps about and gives life to everything — actually pulsates.

Ah, Notre Dame, that medieval encrustation! Temple vaults, rose windows, cornices and roofs, they all rise into space. But they are merely the steps to the throne, for there are any number of cathedrals successively projected on to the atmosphere, into the Infinite! The atmosphere is a mirror of ghosts and floating there is every statue, every lancet window, every bit of tracery, translated into something more fluid, more tangled, because the air turns everything around, it moulds and scatters, it curls and endlessly diversifies. There is another subtle influence beyond our real existence, that of the airy, continuous shapes of which we are the frame. Who knows, perhaps they are the subtle, volatile souls of bodies from other worlds that have stepped beyond the Void?

And that is something that my Desire has struggled to pin down . . . translucent spectres, visions of ourselves and of temples, palaces, towers and arches. I experience the monuments not only in their immutable, simple, crude stone versions. For a long time now I have sensed and felt them more imperially than that, in their incorporeal, airy forms — transmissible, flexible, penetrating . . .

The great cathedrals! Notre Dame . . . What high reliefs they create in space, what marvellous intersecting planes, multiple, free, disintegrating, planes that intertwine, transmute, founder, swirl!

I want an Art capable of interleaving ideas into those planes!

But listen, listen! I want an Art that is fractured, divergent, inflected, an Art with a centrifugal force, an Art that cannot be proved by arithmetic, an Art-geometry of space, yes, that's it, a three-dimensional Art ... in space, in space ... *Areas and Volumes!*'

I found it hard to follow this whirl of ideas, it made me dizzy. I was lost. This was, after all, an entirely new way of imagining.

Apart from that, there was something distressing about his disjointed sentences, a glimmer of madness; there was a smoky splendour about his eyes; his mouth contracted in a shadowy rictus.

He went on:

'It is necessary too, my friend, that an Artist of genius must know how to individuate, how to animate the Atmosphere ... when it is shattered by great express trains, by the tapering snouts of Zeppelins, by propellers, by flywheels, by factory machinery, by the arms of cranes – such harsh beauty! – when it is sculpted by basilicas, memories, Egyptian ruins ... or tentatively, when it is caressed by a woman's scornful hands, by the games played in gardens by fair-haired children.'

Later on, he said to me:

'Believe me, I grow daily more convinced that the atmosphere is an inexhaustible source of countless beauties. It is up to we artists to learn, hour by hour, to penetrate it ... to understand about Distance, to know the Air and space, which is never still, but always vibrating, wriggling. The tiniest oscillation is, in itself, a motive for art – it is a new beauty: fluttering, creaking, disjointed and buoyant. Imagine a magnificent, naked body stretched out on Indian bedspreads in a luxurious studio. But around it, my friend, around it, everything *is* that body – the essence of that body's beauty! Everything else would perish, would break up, the whole ambience would become focused on that apotheosis of convergent alabasters. Then the body itself becomes so concentrated that it collapses in cataracts of delicate, blond, louche oscillations ... Coiled buds of air push open the breasts, colonnades vanquish the legs, multiple garlands shake the arms: encrustations of kisses beat upon the lips. Everything subsides into beauty! And the

214

body is just a heap of ruins, a detritus of air, that wanders freely, in a vortex, entangling, intersecting, unfolding, convulsing. *The air is that naked body!*

And in the great factories . . . the acid grind of machinery . . . flywheels . . . pistons . . . drive chains . . . the shudder of complicated mechanisms . . . create more movement in the air . . . like fireworks, air fireworks. Helixes, spirals, parabolas, stars, extinct hyperboles, whirl and zigzag and devour each other. Contemporary magic! Europe! Europe!

And at the theatre the whole atmosphere surrounding the spinning figure of a brightly-dressed dancer is infected with colour, caught up in a polychrome jetsam that touches our hands and the faces of the spectators, like the chatter of glass beads.

That, in short (along with the inflections of swords), is what we must, today, learn how to sense and describe in our souls.'

I again exclaimed my amazement at and my reverence for these sublime theories. He was astonished that I should have such an immediate understanding of them – even given my sensibilities and my character. But he was soon convinced of my sincerity, his confidence growing with each day that passed.

*
*   *

When he left Moscow about ten years before, after the death of his father, Petrus Ivanowich had brought his family – his mother and his sister – to set up home in Paris.

From the very beginning of our relationship he had very much wanted me to visit his home, where, incidentally, I later met Sérgio Warginsky who introduced me again to his still very beautiful wife, whom I had met before in Lisbon, in very different circumstances.

I felt a frisson of delight on that first visit, for the moment I went in, I sensed the atmosphere of tenderness and care that surrounded the artist. I immediately identified the faithful servants of his genius, his mother and his sister: Sofia Dmitrevna, a lady possessed of a most aristocratic bearing and a magnificent head of white hair, and Marpha Ivanovna, a lovely young girl full of life, tall, robust and muscular: the picture of rude beauty.

Months later, having noticed Petrus' preference for my company, they began asking my opinion, for they were much concerned about his delicate state of health, and even more concerned about his over-intensity, his complex character, his often bizarre behaviour. One day, they told me that my friend had once suffered from terrible, mysterious attacks, a sort of strange, sinister epilepsy, which no doctor had been able to diagnose. The last time he had such an attack was six years ago, but since then the artist had become even more unbalanced in word and opinion.

I always sought to reassure them. Only now do I see how right they were to worry.

It was not only Zagoriansky's conversations about art that were disquieting – marvellous though they doubtless were, and genuinely eccentric. For example, if he attempted to explain anything about his soul, the strangeness and the vagueness persisted. Our conversations rarely continued in that vein, though; his was a very concentrated nature. Whenever he did open up to me, his psychological perceptions about his most obvious personality traits were as unusual as his theories about art.

He said to me one night:

'My friend, I swear that if I were to recount out loud to myself my own story, even I would not believe it. My life has always developed at a tangent. If I went into any detail, you would think it was pure literature, and yet it is the absurd truth. What is more difficult to believe, however, is that all the people I have ever known, even apparently insignificant people, have all proceeded in accordance with my life. *I have always met the people I was supposed to meet.* No one has ever behaved with me as they would with anyone else – even those who have never met me. So much so that I have come to think that perhaps *I am not just myself, but many people, that I am all the people in my life.*'

A look of such pain crossed his face – albeit shot through with acute irony – such sadness veiled his voice and his bright eyes, that I felt genuinely sorry for him, as well as, perhaps, a touch afraid.

I soon began to notice the abrupt pauses in his sentences, his habit of staring into space or of frequently glancing around when talking, *entirely randomly*, never pausing in his talk – a moment of sudden inattention, inexplicable and frightening.

From time to time, he would make outlandish statements:

'Have you ever noticed the smell of petrol? It's very odd, don't you think? It's a smell with a crust on it, yes, a kind of double smell, a perfumed tone that starts off crudely and becomes sharper, then more spherical.'

And again:

'I've never loved anyone, but I'm sure that if one day I did love someone, my love would be like a deep desire to sleep. I would say to the woman I so ardently loved: "My love, my love, I am sleepy with you!"'

'I am constantly being reminded of tastes I have never known, contrived tastes that rotate and shift in complex ways, tastes that are, I would like to believe, transformations of energy . . .'

'There was a time in my life when I used to invent obsessions. I invented them, I didn't really have them. The most dangerous part was that, after a while, I could not work out if those obsessions were merely artificial ones, created by my artist's imagination, or genuine moments of madness which had, at some point, lacerated my spirit and which now, hesitantly, were resurfacing. I well remember my uncertainty about this double obsession, which, when I thought about it clearly, I knew was nothing more than the complicated plot of a novel I had intended to write, about a man who had convinced himself that his thoughts were translucent and thus, everyone – even animals – would know his thoughts, his desires, his disillusions. On the other hand, he began to see, little by little, in a growing state of distress, exactly the same expression on every face, the same ticks, the same grimaces. He would flee, eyes closed, in a nausea of fear; in vain, for, in the end, he began to see that incurable, obsessive, irritating, fixed expression even in inanimate objects, even in smells.'

Far more disquieting, because it was so painful and intimate, was the debilitating confession he made to me one feverish morning.

I had accompanied him on a visit to a mediocre painter who lived in a small room on the top floor of a hotel near the Odéon. When we left and came out into the street again, he said:

'How I envy him. I will never live in a room like that. Who knows, perhaps my pain consists in that alone. My destiny was a different one. I was always fated to have carpets . . . I will never be able to live . . . *The pain of always having known where I was going to sleep*! I doubt that you share my views . . . But how I would like to be that room. Did you notice? That room is a young Parisian girl. I have never been able to internalise kindness. I have never received a letter that I wasn't expecting. Such aridity! If at least, like a certain distant friend of mine, I could fall in love with a dead woman . . . but it's no use . . . and so, alone, I walk my imaginary greyhounds . . . Sometimes I almost think that a certain episode happened to me, doubtless something someone once told me. Absence, absence! She would be barefoot, one moonlit night, near the lake, asking me to splash her hands and bare arms. Then we would have dabbled our fingers in the same water. And now – imagine how sweet this would be! – I would probably believe that that water was the one kiss we exchanged . . . My lovely, silken spirit, all embroidered in pink . . . But even this autumn is an illusion!'

I listened to him in alarm. I had never heard him speak so incoherently before, and that incoherence was, alas, real, it was not the artifice of some poseur – the expression on his face was too pained and tortured.

He soon changed the subject, however, and his ideas again became more lucid.

For my part, being used to his ways, I had already drawn this selfish conclusion: he may well have been seriously unbalanced, but it was from that imbalance that his great genius sprang. I blithely calmed his family's fears.

In fact, with my usual scepticism, and setting aside any

vague feelings of disquiet, I thought no more about it, apart from once, when he rushed into my house one morning, shouting:

'My friend, my friend, I believe that today I have at last discovered the secret of my existence: *I am the slender hands of a woman with painted nails!*'

He wasn't joking – even so, only a madman would come out with a statement like that.

But what he had said was so beautiful, so golden and so unsettling, that I soon forgot about any danger and, in truth, I admired only the Artist who had uttered it.

II

It was only latterly that Petrus Ivanowitch spoke to me, with utter frankness, of his ambitions as an Artist, about his work. Until then, in fact, he had merely spoken in general terms about his theoretical opinions, but he had never mentioned his poetry, except very obliquely.

For my part, I never for a moment doubted his genius, I believed in it absolutely. However, my certainty was based only on the unforgettable nature of his spirit – his fiery phrases, his gestures, the brilliance of his eyes – and of his whole being. For that, far more than any perfect work, was an unerring indication to me that I was in the presence of an immortal Artist. So much so that, before I thought it through calmly, I was even under the impression that I had already heard much of his poetry.

He first spoke to me about his own work when I made a French translation of a few excerpts from my own books and from the work of the admirable Fernando Passos. Zagoriansky was amazed. He was astonished – he assured me – that something born in such a different country could bear even a vague resemblance to the veiled spirit of his own work. He found certain of Fernando Passos' words particularly moving. He told me how much he would like to meet the Artist one day, but I could only show him his photograph.

Then he talked to me about his plans, about a book on which he had been working for many years.

It had no title:

'Its title,' he confessed, 'would be, at most, a musical phrase and a few touches of colour.'

It would be divided, he added, into several parts, several compositions, but each of them had to be joined together astrally, hypnotically (those were the terms he used) to form a single unity. And then he said nothing more about it that night.

However, some weeks later, he announced to me that he thought he was close to reaching the limits of his book. In fact, he would never publish it until it had reached what he called 'that fluid: perfection'.

He said to me:

'Until now, there has never been a perfect work of art. The greatest are mere excerpts. And I want my poem to be a whole, so far beyond correction that no one could remove a single letter without it crumbling into nothing.'

I said:

'Nevertheless, my friend, don't overdo the torment. Perfection is a very relative thing, very much a matter of personal taste.'

'There is no personal taste. There is only Gold!' he retorted.

'Fine,' I went on, 'but if that is so, how then, my friend, will you know when you have achieved Perfection.'

His reply was instant:

'Just now I cannot guarantee that I will, but I believe that the moment I do, I will know it, possibly *physically*. Water, when it boils, bubbles up. That's how we know it's boiling. Well, I genuinely believe that something similar will happen when I reach the abstract level I am aiming for. Yes, I can imagine it, I really can; the moment I achieve perfection, some physical phenomenon (perhaps some sudden adjustment) will take place before my eyes, in the atmosphere, or perhaps, who knows, even on the pages where my poems are written.'

'That would make a wonderful subject for a novel!' I said, shrugging my shoulders and smiling, then ordering another coffee.

'A fluid art, my friend, a gaseous art. Better than that, my friend, better,' Zagoriansky was declaring to me – we were in his study, where he had first received me, 'an art on which gravity has no influence! My poems . . . my poems . . . but you don't yet know them. Nothing will hold my poems down, I want them to vibrate in the air, free, intermingling, transparent to the light, to all bodies, subtle, imponderable! And I will achieve this! I have not yet reached perfection, and I know that there is still much dross in my poetry, which is why gravity still acts upon it. But soon, soon . . . ah!'

Suddenly, calming himself, he sat down in a great magenta armchair.

'I have never told you the main characteristics of my work. Today, however, I feel that I should open myself frankly to you, reveal to you my secrets. I think I am nearly there, at last, and you, my friend, thanks to your own spirit and to my influence, are ready *to know*. Listen, I do not write only with ideas, I write with sounds. My works use both sounds and ideas, the suggestions of ideas (and then only intermittently). If I read my poetry to you, my friend, even if you didn't understand a word, you would still partially *feel* them. And it would be just the same in the case of a deaf man who could read them, but not hear them. The total effect of my poems can only be obtained by reading them out loud, they must be heard and understood with one's eyes open. My poems must be interpreted with all the senses. They have colour, sound and smell, they might even have taste, who knows? Every one of my phrases has a chromatic or aromatic timbre, relative to, simultaneous with the movement of each "circumstance". That is what I call the irregular stanzas into which I divide my poems, suspended, automatic, each with its own speed, but all interlinked by fluid ties, by gaseous elements, never by anything solid, but by successive ideas. Perhaps I'm not making myself clear. Yet how can I express myself in any other way? Wait, perhaps . . . My work is not a simple individualistic description in words – a simple written realisation. It's something more than that: it is simultaneously a musical, chromatic creation, pictorial if you like, indeed, more volatile than that, it is a creation in smell. Yes, my work can even encompass perfumes! It can, will be all these things, you understand, when it is completed. Anyway, in your case, hearing my compositions without understanding the language in which they are written, would be about the same as knowing a play only by reading it, without ever having seen it on stage.'

My friend was rambling now, but I listened to him, transfixed by the magical, tumbling words that shimmered like gold. However, I must still have looked doubtful and vaguely incredulous, for the artist then turned round and hurried over to an enormous desk made out of lignum vitae, at the far end of the room. He pulled open a drawer and drew out of it a blue notebook which he brandished before me.

'I'll prove it to you!' he exclaimed. 'I'm going to read you some of my poems in Russian! Then you must give me your honest opinion of the reading.'

He started leafing nervously through the book. I remember feeling surprised that such a refined, eccentric artist should write his works in a vulgar student's notebook with a shiny cover, the sort you can buy for 90 centimes in the shops in the Odéon.

'First, I'll read you one of my simpler compositions, an exercise in rhythm.'

I listened . . .

It was a revelation! I heard gently clashing, capricious dissonances, delicate gasps, flowing forth in a thousand tones over a steady violet background, an evocation of smooth, satiny perfumes . . .

It is, of course, pointless to try to describe in words the magic of that miniature masterpiece.

I told him of my amazement, my unabashed admiration . . .

With growing enthusiasm, Petrus Ivanowitch began declaiming poem after poem. I found all of them beautiful, some more than others, of course. And the Russian told me afterwards that the poems I favoured were, in fact, the more complex ones.

I remember, above all, how astounded I was by a certain piece in which multiple wheels turned in vortices of colour, in a tangle of convulsive movement, and where, to my great surprise, I gradually discovered the most elegant curves – helixes, spirals, hyperboles – set loose, freely expanded, in a firework display of sounds, like catherine wheels. It was, in truth, a very precise mechanism, propelled by magic – secretly, in sudden glassy audacities . . . in a clamour of crystals.

Zagoriansky hesitated. He was about to close the notebook, then he stopped, announcing in a frenzied voice:

'*Poème brillant.*'

I was swept away! My admiration for the other poems paled in comparison. I can easily describe, though, the amazement I felt if I tell you, quite lucidly, just this:

The moment he started reading I had to close my eyes.

It's true, my eyes could not bear the coruscating light, the magnetic scintillation induced by the mysterious words that I was hearing with my ears. I am not just raving now. I know what I am saying. Mere suggestion – possibly – but it wasn't like that: my eyes refused to stay open. And I would challenge anyone to listen to the Miracle without closing his eyes.

It was a whole new Art – diademed and ultimate, excessive and secret, intoxicating, inconvertible – whose divine creator was there before me!

When the reading was over, I stood up, half-crazed. I kissed the artist . . . and Petrus, overwhelmed, surrounded by an aureole of light, cried out to me:

'Do you see, do you see . . . didn't I tell you? A gaseous Art . . . flexible poems that stand alone, that can go off in any direction. A seamless Art! *An Art that corresponds to the aerial forms that realities try to pin down!* Intersecting sounds, divided planes, multiple planes, inflected ideas, sudden divergences. Everything swoons, steals away, endlessly variable, undulating, while always remaining part of the same whole. That is what I want to achieve in several of my poems, and, above all, in the whole group of poems, something like a sum of arbitrary factors, but an exact sum made up of different factors!'

To exemplify this, he then translated for me a small excerpt which I print below, in which, according to him, he intended merely to create an impression of vagueness, using only the most tenuous supports from reality, something impossible to encompass, that slips away like quicksilver: shifting water, a shattered golden amphora, mournful aftertastes of the Beyond, and framed there always – certainty.

The simple literal translation that he made of this extract, inspired such feelings in me that, before I left, I made him promise to allow me to translate or, rather, interpret, his poem into Portuguese.

Indeed, some days later, with enormous difficulty and with

224

his help, I completed the version I give below. Hardly a word of the original remains, but even so, it reproduces the quality of the Russian text, insofar as that is possible in a foreign language, using the same sounds and movements, the same chromatic timbres, the same consonances . . .

Later, when I insisted on translating other works of his, even though the artist seemed perfectly happy with my first attempt, he always refused. He would only allow me to translate 'Ballet', which did not form part of his current volume; he had written it when he was eighteen years old and was studying law and living alone in Paris, in a hotel in the rue des Écoles. That, by the way, explains the poem's odd but admirable closing line.

After that night, I often asked about his book, protesting that he should not torment himself so. I urged him to publish this marvel, which I believed would inevitably cause a revolution in all the Arts.

In moments of both discouragement and enthusiasm, he almost always retorted:

'It's still too soon . . . too soon. I have not yet triumphed. Gravity still bears down upon my work, although I believe it will not be long now. Many of my poems, possibly all of them, may, taken on their own, be perfect already. But the whole work is still not quite right. It still contains some dross.'

One evening, however, when I had not seen him for three days, I noticed a new expression on his face, a feverish air about him. He seemed to have grown visibly thinner in those few hours.

I questioned him. He confessed to me:

'Ah, my friend, my friend. I have made huge advances since last we saw each other. Today, yes, I *believe* in my presentiments! I am certain that I am about to reach perfection, that impossibly elusive thing! But it's odd, in my moment of glory, I feel gripped by a vague sense of remorse.'

'It's just your nerves.'

'Let's hope so.'

There followed a week of relative calm in which he

225

avoided referring to his work. One night during that week, in talking about his ambitions as an Artist, he merely spoke of the fear he had always had of seeing his genius debilitated by its very intensity. And he told me that he often averted his eyes in order not to provoke it, that he stroked it, kissed his own mirror image, addressed it out loud, called it 'my love', lavishing on it the tender care of mothers who get up in the middle of the night, in winter, to tuck their children in . . .

He described to me too the wasted agony of recording all the riches that passed through his spirit, the exhausting, simultaneous jealousy he felt at not being able to concentrate on just one idea:

'My dear chap, can you imagine how terrible that is! The jealousy of a man who can never simply possess the woman he is holding in his arms, because at the moment of possession, he is besieged by the strident memory of another, of many others. Horrible, horrible . . .'

And for the first time since I had known him, he ordered an absinthe, he who only ever drank fruit juice . . .

Then he stopped coming to the café where we had been in the habit of meeting almost every night.

I hurried to his house, to see if he was ill.

His mother and his sister received me in tears: 'He isn't actually ill, but he shuts himself up in his study for hours on end, refusing to eat . . . he's restless all the time, pacing up and down, like a wild beast.'

Marpha's pleas, to which he normally always responded, were now useless. He shouted to her through the door:

'Work, I must work! One final effort!'

Only once did I manage to break his isolation. He greeted me joyfully, when I had been prepared to be confronted by his rudeness, perhaps even by one of his sudden, gloomy rages which I had already witnessed in the past.

He exclaimed:

'Yes, yes! It's really true! I am making enormous strides. I was not mistaken . . . I will know when it happens: positively, materially, visibly. I can already glimpse, quite how I don't know, some very slight modification, a molecular change, I presume. A few days more and then . . . Perfection!'

Then he chatted to me for a few moments quite normally. I begged him not to neglect his health, but I left him sitting in front of a large cup of extremely strong coffee into which he had poured half a bottle of a strange, aromatic, purple liquid . . .

I warned his sister. She merely sighed and seemed not to give much importance to the fact. At the same time, though, I noticed in her face a momentary pallor, an odd constraint in her whole manner . . .

I confess that when I said goodbye, I was feeling very worried. Soon, however, in my eternal egotism, those feelings of disquiet disappeared. Indeed, during the eight days I spent out of Paris, I did not give a moment's thought to my last visit to my friend, to his dangerous situation.

The morning after my return, I was woken by the sound of someone pounding loudly on the door of my room.

I went to open it, ready to box the ears of the intruder, but to my amazement, I found Zagoriansky – a horribly changed Zagoriansky, his hair all dishevelled, his eyes bloodshot, his tie undone; he was brandishing in his hand the blue notebook that contained his poem.

The moment I let him in, he launched into a hoarse tirade, half-crying, half-screaming:

'Madness, madness! Perfection! That most elusive of goals! But it's true, it's true. I have achieved it! *Gravity no longer holds sway over my poems!* Why should I complain? Crazy, absolutely crazy! This, at any rate, is the infinite moment! Did I not tell you? I always knew it, *but you should have seen it!* It was exactly as I said, my poor friend, exactly! I was just putting the final touches to the final word, when there was a crack, a dull click, the sound of subdued panting . . . I looked at the pages. *Every single one of my poems had slipped out of my notebook and magically flown away, free at last!*'

He leafed through the book.

I went rigid, an icy shiver ran through me. The pages were blank. All that was left was the frontispiece where I could see the name of the poet and the date. On each sheet, there was only the number of the page and the occasional red smudge which, as I had noticed before, inexplicably obscured the text written in very pale violet ink.

'My friend, my friend. They're out there in space! My poems are out in space . . . ah . . . amongst the planets!'

The rest was lost beneath a rippling peel of foaming, confusing, hallucinatory laughter . . .

. . . .
. . . .
. . . .

Five days later, mad with passion, Petrus Ivanowitch, to the great grief of his family, was interned in a mental hospital, close to Meudon, where the staff had been extremely reluctant to receive him, given the mysterious violence of his attacks – strange, convulsive, spasmodic crises that none of the psychiatrists could explain. They were like the product of some medieval spell, a black magic curse.

We looked everywhere for the notebook in which the artist had written his work, in the house, in the garden . . . with no success. That was the only one we found, its pages blank.

For hours on end, Marpha and myself bent over it, studying it, trying to convince ourselves that it was a different notebook, one that the madman had bought, having first destroyed the identical notebook containing his work. We tried to convince ourselves . . . as if the evidence were not there before us . . .

For the damp stains that were present in the first notebook were in this one too, as were the red smudges, the largest being on page 22 on which was written the excerpt which I had translated with the title 'Beyond'. And that was all that survived of a work of genius.

Ah, the troubling, confused nights that Marpha and I sat staring into that blank notebook – lying vainly open – having to believe and yet *unable to believe...*

. . . .
. . . .
A dream almost . . . an obsession . . .

Camarate-Quinta da Vitória
October 1914

'Beyond' and 'Ballet'
by
Petrus Ivanowitch Zagoriansky
(Fragments)

These versions are lovingly dedicated to Mlle
Marpha Ivanovna Zagoriansky, the Poet's
sister.

I

BEYOND

1.

There drifted through the air, on that pale golden evening, purple emanations from the Soul and longings to not-
be.

The holy hands of a queen, mad with emeralds, bestowed
perfume and dew on the twilight breeze.

The air that evening was all Nostalgia and Beyond.

. . . .

. . . .

And the wings of a chimaera, beating far off, anointed it
with unreality.

. . . .

Gusts of dead leaves, redolent of shadow.

. . . .

An air that tasted of light and that cracked like crystal.

. . . .

And far, far off the white houses . . .

2.

In the great bedroom of victory, all naked and red-gold, I
finally had her stretched out on the fantastic bed of Colour.

A lovely spiral of wild flesh – the beautiful one filled my eyes with mystery, knowing that I loved the waves of strangeness . . .

And her slender, vigorous arms were roe deer . . .

And her ruby lips were pain . . .

. . . .

In the garden the sunflowers were ignoring the Sun . . .

. . . .

I bent over her . . .

The hour swooned . . .

The air grew more unreal . . .

There was a cortège of stars . . .

. . . .

Confronted by that glory, stirring tumultuously so near, the glory that would at last consecrate me, my eyes were pure effort – and my soul a disc of gold! . . .

. . . .

. . . .

The mad woman was sharpening her nipples, to make them more bitter, the better to wound me.

And my yearning lips already longed for the kisses she was about to give me . . .

. . . .

In the distance, the white houses were still there . . .

3.

. . . And it was then, when I already felt entwined with Gold, consecrated by something beyond Colour, when everything was enchantment touched by the infinite, that the moment fell and I fell with it . . .

Above her perfectly balanced body – howls of horror! – the terrifying theory of acute angles soared and cavorted, stridently mocking whirlpools and curves . . .

Brutal blades, whistling maelstroms, destructive broken lines – they cut through everything, they sucked everything dry! Ah, clarity, clarity! . . .

Terror without name!

And a picaresque birdcage built out of lozenges made a

guttural descent and stripped her bare flesh of all colour, all sound, all perfume, enclosing her, spinning about her in a monstrous vortex of overlapping, impossible circles! . . .

Every fragment of her shattered beauty cried out to me to save her . . .

And all my looking – what longing! – was of no use to her.

. . . .

The white houses are unforgiving! The white houses are unforgiving! . . .

4.

Poor wretch, bereft of pain, trembling, still tremulous . . . I wanted to lie to myself, I wanted to go back, but everything was slipping away from me . . .

By dint of an illusion, I became a great lie: I was a Prince with no king, lit by a false light, a light that had no sound, that was hollow, desolate, mediocre . . .

Why? Why?

Soon my body was toppling on to terra firma, night had fallen in my Soul, and everything was crumbling round about me: insomniac wings, golden galleons, silver towers, gilded domes . . . Everything was crumbling, but everything was crumbling as if under a spell, on to other ruins: the gold of lost breasts, the silver of abandoned glory . . .

. . . .

Only the ruins of the white houses were the ruins of white houses!

Paris, January 1913

BALLET

1.

Everything is horizon, only horizon . . .

. . . .

The brusque sound of silence.
The horizon is a Shape that scatters dew . . .
They placed dawn compresses on my fevered brow . . .
Cold water! Cold water!

———————

How the silence creaks . . . and jingles . . . and jingles . . . in
serpentine stripes of stinging Gold . . .
Ephemeral Gold that becomes a flame on the point of
corruption . . .
Apotheosis!
Swans of fire in a sea of Sound breathe out the sea, white on
black . . .
The sea is a tremulous breast . . .
(And the breast, maddened, vomits).
The Orient, the Orient!
Far off there are helmets . . .
Mirages of castles sail away . . .
Spirals rise up . . . dizzy volutes spin . . .
Emblems of glass curl . . .
And the sea capsizes in sentient light . . .
(Singular light!
Light is my ecstasy!)
I am transformed, multicoloured, into a lyre . . .

2.

The great platinum sphinx makes a shadow-Statue out of
the sunlight.
My Soul sets . . .
Now it is night lost in blue fear and intense distances . . .
In some far-off country perfumes jangle . . .

Around the sphinx all is inconstancy . . .
Talons stoop and plunge . . .
Blades grow sombre . . .
Swords break . . .

. . . .

Suddenly, a meteor whistles past and vanishes . . .

. . . .

See the chariot of Triumph ascending the Capitol . . .
See the leonine trail . . .
See the royal brigantine . . .

. . . .

See the lancet window, see the portico . . .
See the cathedral cross! . . .

. . . .

('Where does the great Beast still amaze?'
'The Beast no longer ensnares.')

———————

In streams of growing wings the holy cathedral organ rises
up . . .
    The high altar vibrates with beauty . . .
    The censer floods the Sound . . .
    'Our Lady of Colour!'
    The nave is consecrated with desire . . .
    The Dawn–chalice is raised . . .
    And the communion host partakes of golden breasts . . .

. . . .

The Emperor was sanctified!
(Coronation festivities.)

3.

Shrieks of light . . .
Painted light . . .
Wings lost amidst the setting sun . . .
    . . . Then everything is peace and the blond branches of the
palmtree sway to the music and the air . . .
Oasis . . .
Fleeting freckles . . .
Insidious tresses . . .

234

4.

Here comes the battering light, tiger-striped with Pride.
The flame rarefies me and the twilight is a mirror . . .
(Victory!
– The Ice does not condense me.)

. . . .

In tones of distant scarlet, I sense an aftertaste of Combat . . .
Mist . . . mist . . .
Baptism of Astral-pain . . .

. . . .

And the mist begins to curl into flakes . . .
The mist whirls . . .
The mist is a torrent . . .
The mist no longer conceals
– it unmasks!

5.

Vestiges of Soul, far off, above the battering Gold . . .
Hands folded . . . Resurrection . . .

. . . .

And now I go down the stairs, whilst everything else rises
up in something beyond Shadow . . .
But the descent only exalts me:
I am I, Alone – I am diffusion!

. . . .

Beneath a canopy of nostalgias,
I am filled by Peking yearnings,
Reminiscences – Brocade . . .
I sense the great Mystery . . .
I blanch myself in colour and sound . . .
Harnesses, lances, Rogério! . . .

. . . .

But alas, the dream is real: it finds expression in clarity!
And since it exists . . . it passes! . . .

. . . .

. . . .

Come, transmigratory longings, and fix the moment for
me!

My soul is rich with sound!

. . . .

(Rue des Écoles, cinquante.)

Paris, March 1913

THE FIXER OF MOMENTS

For Guilherme de Santa-Rita

The Fixer of Moments

The moment, ah, the moment!

How others who do not share my secret, my art, can live on life alone, I simply do not know.

I was dying of desire and longing when, one extraordinary night, I won through, I won through by sheer force of desire and I rediscovered the most beautiful of the lost arts. For I do not believe that I discovered my art, I merely reconstructed it. It was a distant memory – from where I do not know – from far, far off, from a world beyond dreams perhaps, that taught me the secret. I was not the secret, I merely awoke it. And I have, it is true – I can shout it out now – I have in my hands the life which, in the hands of the happiest, the richest of men, slips away, inevitably crumbles, grief after grief.

To experience radiant moments, to possess golden bodies, imperial mouths, and to be anointed with glory in a crescendo of light, is that true happiness? It is not. For everything passes, it vanishes as swiftly as time. And we burn with nostalgia, with a longing for what was, the least painful of nostalgias, because it is over, a longing for the future, which we do not yet know, and a longing for the present, which we know all too well, and which, for that very reason, becomes our most painful source of anxiety.

Even the happiest of men is, in fact, a wretched debt collector through whose hands millions slip every day and who, meanwhile, watches his children dying of hunger. Beauty strolls through the fingers of the fortunate man, it is true, but it does not stay; minute by minute it steals away in a breathtaking whirl. And even if beauty returns, if that man has a soul, if he is an artist, his shadowy eyes will fill with tears, longing for what is past and will never return, *simply because it is over*.

Life, yes, life is an enchanted, multicoloured star from the magic lantern show of my childhood. On the sheet that we stretched out and on which the fantastic meteor was flickeringly projected, flooding it with new shapes, new colours, I, unable to believe in its lies, would try to grasp it with my fascinated hands, trying in vain to fix the rapidly fading marvel on the sheet, to touch it and grapple with it, but there was only shifting light staining my fingers, an illusion undone.

It is just like life. You cannot touch life, it is all glitter, a fleeting image. What was cannot be reproduced, there can never be the same kisses, the same sun, the same struggles. And no secret can be repeated.

The man who could *realise* life would be a great man indeed, able to give form and continuity to every beautiful moment that ever existed, tawny with anxiety, but nonetheless magnificent, subtle! For such a person life would take on new dimensions; life, which is pure surface, would have height and dizzying depths!

To reconstruct life, yes, to raise up about it battlements of gold and bronze, to garland it with myrtle if we chose to, and then, at last, to touch it . . . giving consistency to the fantastic bubbles of gas, to the golden foam of champagne — to have had something and yet still to have it! The ultimate glory! Apotheosis!

Well — winged triumph! — therein lies my secret, that is my art, the lost art which, astonishingly enough, I have reconquered.

Yes, I build life out of eternalised longings. I build out of it whatever I have felt, whether beautiful or painful, real or false.

And if, one afternoon, I was pierced by the languid sense of having forgotten a great love that I had never felt, I was able to fix that bizarre, mistaken, disquieting moment: I sculpted it, I have it. I can see it, re-feel it, like someone leafing through a book that they have already read, *but which they can easily re-read*.

Thanks to my secret, I can actually leaf through existence; weary with vague longings, I do not merely evoke its torn pages, for that is what the days of a life are for other people, pages that are torn up the moment they have been read.

And how can you rebuild the moment, make it endure?

In a thousand ways, just as the artist of genius can perform his art in a thousand different ways: the artist of genius – I did not say God. Only God creates. And thus, sadly, I must stress that while my art can build a life, it cannot live it: I can touch the golden moment, see it and passionately kiss it once more, but I cannot, alas, give it new wings of fire. Everyone else has lost everything, the soul and body of the hours. I may have lost the souls, but I have the bodies so that I can remember more intensely. I have embalmed the moment.

That is all.

I do not resuscitate, I set in stone.

One of my most successful works, though I would not say the best, was the fixing for ever inside myself of one year spent in a large capital city.

I felt such a lucid love for that place of ultra-civilisation.

Whenever I became conscious of the inevitable and definitive loss of my existence and was gripped by feelings of great bitterness or mortal tedium, I would go out into the streets, and the moment I saw that Latin river slipping past beneath the bridges, in a tumult of lights, or the tall, slender streetlamps liturgically lighting all that abundant life, or heard the distant city roar that provided the music to that movement, a wave of pride would rush through me, along with a sense of infinite joy at being able to live in that amazing city. It was more than that, because by enlarging my soul, I really was experiencing it – I felt such a nostalgic love for that place – a very childish emotion perhaps.

And since it was inevitable that one night I would lose it, I diligently rebuilt it for myself, inalterable and eternal.

That is how, emotion by emotion, little by little – it was a vast undertaking – I began fixing it, like someone slowly, carefully, pinning together a great sheet of linen.

I set it in stone in my heart, that capital of all desires. I filled up my senses with points of reference, golden trails through all the marvels. I have it now, I have it!

And this is how I did it:

A friend of mine lived in one of the old parts of town, and I would often arrange to visit him there.

In the same lodging house there lived some girls from the north – members of one of those blond Nordic races that I am so drawn to – amongst them there was one for whom I felt a particular fondness. She was blonde like the others, a Slav from Russia, a country for which, oddly enough, I have a special affection.

We used to talk – cool, banal conversations made easy and pleasant thanks to the names of certain beloved artists, certain admired works of art, which moment by moment, drew us closer together.

That sweet creature – so attuned to my sensibilities – was precious to me because she was one of the many vertices on which I would found the deified city. Then, one night, I asked her to read some poems of mine. For a few moments, her enchanting voice thrilled to what, for her, was a mysterious language, a language from the south which, in that company, only I could understand.

She had spoken only for me, and never again, never again would she repeat the words that she had murmured only for me.

And my poetry was golden. And her mouth too was golden.

But that was not all . . .

One day, my friend came to visit me bearing a rose, telling me that he had just come from saying goodbye to her, that she had gone and I would never see her again. When he left, he left with me the flower that his friend had given him as she leapt, slim and agile, on to the great express train. I put the forgotten rose in a vase of water.

The following afternoon, since my friend did not come back to reclaim it, I carefully cut off the stem of the flower, which her Slav fingers had doubtless clutched, along with a few faded petals. I placed these poor remnants in a large envelope which I sealed; then I wrote her fluid, sonorous, blonde name on the front.

Anyone seeing me do that would have said: ah, a romantic souvenir, and anyone hearing me talk about it would explain it away saying: 'Your behaviour, my friend, has its roots in unconfessed feelings of love. I think you were a little enamoured of that distant girl who so fleetingly touched your life. Tenderness, a slight sadness, nostalgia, that's all it is, believe me.'

How wrong they would be! For me, that girl was no more than a character – a delightful one it's true – but spiritually anonymous amongst the whirling crowd, a stranger amongst other strangers. She was valuable to me only as a gentle figure in a particular scene, from a time in my life which I wanted to fix because it was beautiful. Later on, tenderly reliving that sad story of the rose, reciting the poem that her harmonious mouth had spoken, going to my drawer to find the envelope where something of her still existed, something I can touch, *something that I can destroy,* I would use all that in order to rebuild the magnificent city. And one night, if I choose, I will tear up the envelope, I will demolish one moment of that city. That is the greatest proof that I experienced it, that I had it, you can only destroy something that you possess.

The enduring construction of an epoch or of a landscape inside ourselves is made up of the sum of a great number of such fixed moments and it was out of other similar details and moments that I managed to construct that marvellous urban sculpture: reading and memorising notices in the streets, kissing the trees in gardens, touching the ground in the boulevards, studying little-known nooks and crannies, climbing to the top of the highest columns.

But I had to struggle with burdensome reality and the excessive number of things learned.

Having lived for a long time in that wonderful city, I had learned some places in such detail that the next day, once far from them, I would be unable to feel them, so clearly could I re-see them! Being unable to feel them precisely because I could see them, I would be unable to experience them. That is why, just as a painter uses shading on a canvas to make it more evocative, more subtle, I needed to do the same with my city. So I would wander about its more unfamiliar quarters only when I was at my most sensitive, and those hours, along with the accompanying scene, stopped, remained frozen inside me, for I experienced extraordinarily intense feelings during those walks and lost myself in marvellous dreams, all of which, later on, I would use in my work.

Once the moment is fixed, the scene also stops. The scene, however, remains very vague because I have never been back there, and it is just one part of the great city. Tomorrow, I will be able to recall it by *feeling* it, not merely by *seeing* it.

That is how I gave to that whole city the misty vagueness which a work like that requires if it is to be eternal.

At last, at last! I pluck the petals from roses, I scatter perfumes, I sprinkle gold on every exquisite hour that I live, and thus I embrace them.

My friends laughed when I gave a necklace of sapphires and kisses to a certain hesitant young girl who was never mine, and all because she had once squeezed my fingers during an afternoon of love. I needed to hold on to the light of that afternoon, to the shadow of those golden, mordant eyes, the coolness of her fingers, the whole glittering perfume of the fleeting hour . . .

They were people with no soul, no soul at all!

There are so many, many things in my life that no one understands, they are merely tools for my art. For example, the sad letters from the naked dancer.

Ah, how proud I am, what joy my statues bring me! How rich I feel when I wander the endless galleries. For I have a past, yes, I have *the* past!

I fixed the hour, I kept it, and I can see it again whenever I wish.

Can there be any greater triumph?

Sometimes, when I think about the future, I am filled by a wild desire to fix that too, before it even happens, in order to ease my yearning heart. That, of course, is impossible and it causes me great suffering, a suffering which is gradually growing worse.

I love her so much, so very much . . .

When she appeared in my life, slipping by, a distant, tawny figure, I felt as if I were not a true inhabitant of life. For would I, like other living beings, be capable one day of kissing and understanding that flesh, that voice, that light, which were, in fact, part of life, on stage, at night, in the great cosmopolitan theatre?

Then, along with the subsequent nostalgia I felt for her, the strange feeling faded and I realised that we both existed in the same world . . .

. . . .

She was all mystery and enchantment. As she walked, she was touched by golden shadows, transparent-souled shadows that she herself wove from her flesh-made-light into a veiled mirage. Her voice was a torrent of gold shot through with sensuality, gold burnished by an unknown, distant, diffuse sun . . .

Her flesh was daubed with the heady perfumes of mysterious islands, steeping her in vague, twilight longings, tempering desire, perhaps, but twisting her too into the perverse image of a sphinx nostalgic for moonlight and death. Everything about her was sculpted out of flame, she was all oscillation, sonority and amazement, writhing like the mad woman in some fearful poem, dense as the dark hangover that follows a night of love and suffocations . . .

The light surrounding her was a further seduction, and it still span nakedly about her. Spasm by spasm, insidiously, the veils were torn. Her pernicious legs gave off a slender, cool, damp breeze; her belly gave forth fruit. Only her nipples retained their mystery . . .

Her ebony tresses had come unpinned, and when, as she bent over the glittering pool, swooning in ecstasy, she, the libertine, became pure perversity and madness; her naked breasts burst forth, dark, spectral, emblematic of sin.

When the final chords of the score fell at last upon her, crushing her, and the drums closed about the poor, wild creature, I was afraid, yes, afraid that she would never rise again, once the poem was over, dead with love, dead with the desire that she had provoked in me or dead, at least, of self-love.

But no, she stood there glowing and calm, dishevelled, banal and pretty, bowing on stage in response to the base applause.

Later, I met her. And the dream continued . . . Now my life depends on her . . . and we have still not even kissed . . . and I tremble so to kiss her.

. . . .

Her soul is like her body vibrating within that bizarre poem. Her soul is naked too and is all oscillation, vibrant mysticism, shuddering perfumes.

. . . .

How I want her . . . how I would like to experience with her an endless orgasm . . .

. . . .

The most painful part is that she wants me too. One night, inevitably, our bodies will entwine. But then, then . . .

. . . .

My God, once I have possessed her in brilliant ecstasies and harmonious longings – such longings! – I would have experienced the one truly golden moment, the greatest moment of past or future!

. . . .

In vain. How could I then enclose it, freeze it, that divine moment, if that moment is also my pride? Up until now, I have been able to build the beautiful things that I have experienced. Sad things . . . But tomorrow? Tomorrow . . .

A miracle!

. . . .

I am filled with fear, with a subtle magic, in the face of the work of genius that I must undertake – *if undertake it I must*.

At dawn today, a poet shot himself, terrified of his own genius, afraid that he would be unable to embody it in his poetry, weak with weariness. And, like him, I have thought of dying, of deserting my work, blind with it . . .

But no!

I must be strong. I can. I must feel, I must bleed, I must dream and, finally, I will savour the victory of sculpting even the incomparable moment of possession.

. . . .

Possession!

I will possess her cold, naked flesh on many nights, but I will never again know the mystery of that first time . . .

. . . .

Yesterday, we went walking and we were so close . . . She hung about my neck, as if bewitched, trembling, mournful. I feared she might even die of me. And then we parted, wounding each other with our kisses . . .

She too desires me, she too trembles to have me . . .

The great beast!

. . . .

Were I able to construct the future, I would feel calmer now. I would walk the dazzling night, confident that I could fix it in time, even though I have already done so. I am filled by a particular fear: what if after experiencing the moment I see that it is much more than I can undertake?

All will be lost, all will be lost!

It does not matter.

I have to do it.

For one moment, at least, I will have been pure light!

Victory! Before me, on the splendid bed, the great snake lay coiled, like a votive offering. It was only then, in fact, that I could comprehend the awesome nature of the moment, assess the infinite heights my dream-work had scaled.

For how could I fix something so excessive . . . Following her naked body, I grew confused, her limitless beauty was a labyrinth. It never ended, it turned in upon itself. Fearful, I glanced away.

Confronted by the marvel, the sumptuousness surrounding me was seeping away and I needed to hold on to it: the colour of the air, the tumultuous perfumes, the leonine timbres . . . and the silks, the furs, the laces . . . the crystal glasses, the golden candelabra . . . the amaranth leaves . . . the blades of daggers . . .

. . . .

Lost, I hurled myself upon her body as if I were hurling myself into the ocean.

Indeed, I did hear the murmur of waves . . .

.   .   .   .

.   .   .   .

The glory came and went. The moment I had fantasised about was not only the greatest moment, it was something else. Faced by that moment, all other moments I had lived faded like foam. Yes, every hour I had lived lay in ruins on the ground and I was about to be crushed beneath the ruins, never again to arise, unless I managed, by sheer force of spirit, to fix the sublime moment that had so stirred me, *the* moment of my life, now and for ever . . . there was no alternative . . .

I felt the last bitterness dissolve inside me. My wings were broken. But I rebelled, I put all my strength into one final effort . . . When she had fallen asleep, I had a brilliant idea and I grasped it!

At first, I was afraid. Everyone feels afraid when face to face with a marvel. Then I grew bold.

Ritually, with utter lucidity, I approached those fallen rose petals. If she had known what I was about to do, she would have blessed me. Tenderly, I pulled back the covers. I felt dizzy . . . Her holy, iridescent body gleamed like dull silver on the fantastic bed . . . A long shudder ran through me, provoked by that beauty. I pulled back her hair and gently – I did not wish to destroy her – I plunged a golden dagger in her breast.

Her hair seemed to ring out, then an autumnal silence fell, her flesh shimmered, arced with light. Then all was still.

I kissed the nipples of her dead breasts and fled.

.   .   .   .

Now, eternal glory is mine!

Ah, how I suffer, how I suffer . . . No one has ever suffered as I do. I feel only horror, a pointless tenderness and compassion for myself.

What does it matter if, guided by my remorse for what I did, I can triumphantly trace, ecstasy by ecstasy, everything that preceded my crime on that incomparable night?

I had the marvel and I shattered it!

But in doing so, I sculpted it for ever into longing and desire. That is how I now possess it, that is how I have made it malleable. If I had not broken it into pieces, I would have destroyed it anyway, so bright was it, so lofty . . .

And to lose it would have been the greatest sacrilege. Only a wretch would be capable of having such a marvellous dream and then just letting it fade.

I killed her in order not to awaken her inside me.

Some marvels should only be dreamed of.

And I will dream you always, my love!

. . . .

Victory! Victory!

I will never again forget your kisses, though I lost them on the instant; I will never again forget your breasts, though I barely knew them. I fused universal longing with my longing for your body, a longing that I alone constructed, because I alone fixed it in time.

Forgive me, forgive me! It was only in order to pray to you that I gilded you with death.

Oh, statue of the hour, oh colour, sound, perfume, I will feel you always, and tremble and wonder . . .

You see, our victory has no end. For I did not fix only that luminous moment, I did more than that, I stepped free from life – now I am that nimbus of light. *I am the moment.*

I fixed myself in time. I stopped.

As for the rest, who cares?

. . . .

The great shadow! The great shadow!

Lisbon, July 1913